Viper Moon

"Lee Roland is one to watch. She's got scads of talent as a writer, plotter, and character developer, and *Viper Moon* is easily one of the best urban fantasies I've read so far this year. . . . Be careful that you don't start this too late at night or when you have an important paper or job at work to accomplish as you'll get sucked in immediately and won't want to put it down. . . . Fans of Patricia Briggs, Suzanne McLeod, and Faith Hunter will gobble this one up."
—Fresh Fiction

"Roland hits the ground running with an impressive debut that contains an edgy, dark energy. The atmosphere is suitably eerie, which will keep readers on the edge of their seats as things definitely go bump in the night! If *Viper Moon* is any indication . . . [the] series holds great promise!"
—*Romantic Times* (4 stars)

"A fascinating new kick-butt heroine is on the scene of urban fantasy. A disconcerting mélange of potential allies who each have very different assets provide spice and variety to the story. . . . Plenty of action combined with intriguing characters (particularly enjoyed the delivery service provided by Horus) make this an excellent introduction to the series."   —Night Owl Reviews (top pick)

"A creepy world of night creatures and other nasties that will make you shudder. *Viper Moon* is fast-paced and fun, with twists and turns that you may not see coming. I'm looking forward to more books in this brand-new series!"
—My Bookish Ways

"Complete with snakes, bronze bullets, and super strength, *Viper Moon* is a ride like few others. . . . definitely a hit and a book that I am thrilled to have indulged in. You don't want to miss out on it!"   —Café of Dreams

continued . . .

Vengeance Moon

A NOVEL OF THE EARTH WITCHES

LEE ROLAND

A SIGNET ECLIPSE BOOK

SIGNET ECLIPSE
Published by New American Library, a division of
Penguin Group (USA) Inc., 375 Hudson Street,
New York, New York 10014, USA
Penguin Group (Canada), 90 Eglinton Avenue East, Suite 700, Toronto,
Ontario M4P 2Y3, Canada (a division of Pearson Penguin Canada Inc.)
Penguin Books Ltd., 80 Strand, London WC2R 0RL, England
Penguin Ireland, 25 St. Stephen's Green, Dublin 2,
Ireland (a division of Penguin Books Ltd.)
Penguin Group (Australia), 250 Camberwell Road, Camberwell, Victoria 3124,
Australia (a division of Pearson Australia Group Pty. Ltd.)
Penguin Books India Pvt. Ltd., 11 Community Centre, Panchsheel Park,
New Delhi - 110 017, India
Penguin Group (NZ), 67 Apollo Drive, Rosedale, Auckland 0632,
New Zealand (a division of Pearson New Zealand Ltd.)
Penguin Books (South Africa) (Pty.) Ltd., 24 Sturdee Avenue,
Rosebank, Johannesburg 2196, South Africa

Penguin Books Ltd., Registered Offices:
80 Strand, London WC2R 0RL, England

First published by Signet Eclipse, an imprint of New American Library,
a division of Penguin Group (USA) Inc.

First Printing, June 2012
10 9 8 7 6 5 4 3 2 1

Printed in the United States of America

PUBLISHER'S NOTE
This is a work of fiction. Names, characters, places, and incidents either are the product of the author's imagination or are used fictitiously, and any resemblance to actual persons, living or dead, business establishments, events, or locales is entirely coincidental.

The publisher does not have any control over and does not assume any responsibility for author or third-party Web sites or their content.

ALWAYS LEARNING   PEARSON

For My Husband
You will live forever in the hearts of those who love you.

ACKNOWLEDGMENTS

This book would not be possible without professional and personal aid from many individuals. A few, but certainly not all, are listed below. There is no particular order of listing. Each was the "most important" at certain times.

My family, whose love and support kept me going through tragedy.

My editor, Jhanteigh Kupihea, who so patiently and graciously guided me through the editing and publishing process.

My extraordinary agent, Caren Johnson Estesen.

My friends, fellow writers, and critique partners—present and past—whose critical feedback and encouragement was, and will continue to be, invaluable.

We are the Sisters of Justice. For millennia we have served the ancient Mother Goddess. Ashera, Inaras, and Ishtar are but a few of a thousand names they have called the ancient Earth Mother, the Mother of Men. Most of her servants see her as a nurturer, a giver of life. The Sisters of Justice see her darker image.

She hides that darker face and we, the Sisters of Justice, are abandoned—save when she needs us. We are the last she calls when all of her earth witches' gentle methods fail. We worship her. We despise her. We are her dark angels, her servants. Our blades are sharp and we strike upon her command.

—From the journal of Mother Superior Evelyn of the Sisters of Justice Correctional College, January 25, 1951

chapter 1

Sister Eunice tossed me over her head, slammed me on my back, and planted her size-twelve, highly polished combat boot on my stomach.

I gasped for breath. She pushed harder. Acute agony spread while she mashed my guts around my spine. An evil grin split her rugged face as she stood there in her camouflage fatigues. "Oh, poor, poor little Madeline." She laughed at me. "Got you now, you nasty little scar-faced whore."

Sister Eunice is five-eleven and weighs two hundred and forty pounds. She has the body of a weight lifter and the attitude of a pit bull. I'm five-eight and barely make one thirty. I'm strong, exceptionally strong, but it would take serious steroids to make me her physical equal.

While she flattened my intestines with one foot, she had the other firmly planted on the foam-padded floor mat. Grab her ankle and snatch her off her feet? I knew better. That was action-movie special effects. I needed more leverage. I made a tight fist and slammed it into the knee of her supporting leg.

She grunted. The knee gave only a fraction of an inch, but she shifted her weight to compensate. I caught the foot jammed on my stomach with both hands and jerked. At the same time, I twisted my body toward her. She went down.

The vinyl mat hissed as she rolled to her feet.

I'm faster. Blade-sharp pains shot through abused muscles. I ignored them. I leaped up, made a fist, and punched her in the kidneys just as she got up. My fist hit with a solid thump. She crashed facedown on the mat. Her breath whooshed out, and before she could draw it in I caught her right arm at the wrist. I twisted the arm across her back, then stomped my foot on her left hand.

I had her. Sort of. She wore boots and camouflage fatigues. I wore a tank top, sweatpants, and thick socks. Her fingers clawed at my sock; in minutes her nails would tear through fabric. Then she'd rake the skin and flesh off my bare foot.

I couldn't knock her unconscious despite the fact that she punched me out on such a regular basis I marked time by it. The Sisters of Justice Correctional College frowned upon lowly students—aka prisoners—beating the crap out of the faculty, even if upon incredibly rare occasions they could. Secure in authority, Sister Eunice, alpha female and consummate she-devil, lived to teach and torture her unfortunate pupils.

I'd beaten her twice. I surprised her six years ago

when I first came here. Only nineteen, but I'd been in jail long enough to learn a few tricks—and I'd taken martial arts lessons from Daddy since I was six years old. The second time I beat her, last year, I used the skills she herself had taught me. She would never forgive or forget.

Laughter sounded in her ragged breathing. I hadn't beaten her this time either. Unwilling to tear her arm out of its socket and incapacitate her, I was unable to let her go because she would pound the holy shit out of me. Shit-pounding me is Sister Eunice's favorite hobby. Shit-pounding hurts a lot more than a boot in the guts.

"Good morning, Madeline," said a sweet voice from behind me. "What are you going to do now, dear?" Sister Lillian. Dark-skinned, petite, and graceful, Sister Lillian taught knife fighting. She'd immediately assessed my dilemma.

"Good morning, Sister Lillian," I said. "I'm giving serious consideration to freeing Sister Eunice and running away."

"You won't," Sister Eunice said. The mat muffled her words, but she was right. I'd stopped running years ago—and I had nowhere to go that she couldn't find me.

Lillian nodded. "Please release her, Madeline."

I let go and jumped away.

Sister Eunice rolled, leaped to her feet, and hurtled toward me. I kicked out and planted my foot in her chest. Flesh on flesh, bone against bone. She went down, smack on her ass. She rolled to come at me again. I drew a deep breath, planted my feet, and prepared to meet her. She stopped. She remained on the mat, panting like a winded dog after a futile chase.

Amazing. I'd taken her down. Taken her out.

"Oh, my," Sister Lillian said. "That was well done."

Sister Lillian's praise delighted me. "Thank you, Sister."

"Come with me, Madeline." She turned and I followed her, but I walked sideways to watch behind and in front of me. Sister Eunice staggered to her feet. She glared at me until I left the room. Pride filled me at the win, even though she'd make my life hell next week— and the week after. A small price to pay for such a rare and precious victory.

I changed into shoes and pulled on a jacket before I followed Sister Lillian. They kept our hair cut brutally short, so I didn't need a brush. My hair is white as mid-January snow. That hair, my pale blue eyes, and the scar on my face isolated me long before I arrived here. Sister Eunice wasn't the only one who called me a freak.

I didn't ask where we were going. The Sisters had taught me the futility of questions and defiance. I'd stopped asking questions. The defiance issue remained a work in progress.

We walked the brick path through the sculptured flower gardens to the administration office. Summer approached upstate New York and brought a multitude of blooms, red, yellow, and white, offering their pretty faces to the afternoon sun. Sometimes, in my few free hours, I'd come here to lose myself in the sweet fragrance of the growing season.

The two buildings of the Sisters of Justice Correctional College could pass for weathered stone medieval castles with incredible English gardens growing between them. Ivy covered the walls in some places and green algae grew at the foundation on others. I was intimately acquainted with the algae. I spent many hours with a bucket and brushes scrubbing at the damn stuff, only to have it grow back within days, sometimes hours. The smaller building housed the Sisters' apartments and offices and the larger building held dorms, classes, and training rooms.

"The Mother has given us a lovely spring this year," Lillian said. She drew a deep breath of the delightful scents.

The Earth Mother—the ancient goddess of men and superior of all witches and the Sisters of Justice—ruled their lives and directed their actions. I don't know why, but she made her presence known to only those few she'd chosen, her special servants, and let the rest of humanity rule over and destroy everything—including my life. The earth witches, the ones she dealt with most, were keepers of the world's magic: earth magic. My mother, a skilled earth witch, loved the Earth Mother, worshipped her even—and received a brutal death as her reward.

When I first came to Justice I thought the Sisters were nuns. Maybe they are, in a bizarre way. I don't know what they wear outside this place, but in Justice they all wear black robes—except Sister Eunice, who dresses in fatigues like a soldier. They rarely speak without imparting some factual information. Some are kind but stern teachers. A few are ill-tempered hags.

The key word, *correctional*, went by me the first week. No wall or fence surrounded the grounds, and no bars covered the windows. No one had ever escaped, though. I tried twice. Each time, two Sisters met me and hauled me back before I made it to the property line. I'd never seen more than thirty young girls here at one time. Now there were only ten. I'd been here longer than most. The Sisters came and went, too. It seemed as if Justice were a sanctuary for them, but a prison for those like me.

Sister Lillian slowed to walk beside me. I straightened, uneasy at her action. She'd broken a firm rule. Students are supposed to walk behind the Sisters. The hem of her black robe brushed the stone path, giving the illusion that she floated rather than walked like a mere mortal.

"Do you remember when you first came here, Madeline?" Her voice usually carried soft laughter, but this time a more serious note crept in.

"I remember." How could I forget? I'd expected state prison when they put me on the transport bus, not to be dropped off at a massive country estate.

"A powerful rage burned in you." She spoke in a softer voice.

"I'm still angry." I always told Sister Lillian the truth. She never judged me.

"And you learned . . . ?"

"I have a right to be angry." I knew the mantra, the lessons they had pounded into me with complete indifference to my pain. "Bad things may happen. But I can, and will, control my emotions."

"And why do you control them?"

"Control makes me stronger." Again, I recited the mantra. "Control permits intelligent action rather than reckless disaster."

She gave me a wonderful smile, angelic and genuine. I had to smile back. I loved this woman. Sister Lillian laid a hand on my arm and squeezed hard. The intensity surprised me. She then brushed her hand against my cheek. "Madeline, if we could have the scar removed, we would."

"I know, Sister."

Her compassion warmed me, but the scar, the smooth, flat, silver streak across my cheek, was created by magic, and far beyond the skill of the finest dermatological surgeon to remove. Other than Sister Eunice's occasional taunting, the Sisters ignored it. In the world outside of Justice, however, it had caused problems.

I hated it because it bound me to a terrible duty. In other ways, though, it was my armor, my shield. My solitary nature and the scar kept my fellow inmates at a distance. I neither wanted nor needed friends. Whatever I endured here, I endured with only occasional comfort or counsel.

In my time there, the Sisters had never broken me, but they'd come close. For the last six years they'd beaten me down and raised me up again as a deadly weapon. Even now, I don't know why. I was twenty-six years old and the State of New York criminal justice system had given me twenty-five-to-life.

chapter 2

On my seventeenth birthday, my mother's last gift to me was a vision of death—and a curse. I should have known better than to touch a witch's corpse. I grasped her cold hand and laid it against my cheek. As I stood by her side in the morgue, the latent spell she'd left for me in her body gave me images of my father tortured to death and her raped and strangled. It played like a vile horror movie in my mind. A very long horror movie.

Before I collapsed unconscious to the floor, I saw their killers. Three men whose faces will be forever chiseled into my memory like an obscene fresco carved in hell. As I lay on the floor, my mother's strident voice demanded vengeance. Her curse? A compulsion within me to kill their murderers, one I could not deny.

My once dark hair, the legacy of my Chinese and Hawaiian-born father, turned pure white that day. My eyes, also dark, faded to the strange pale blue they are now. My mother the witch had marked me with the scar on my cheek where I'd held her hand against my face. She'd given me a constant reminder of my duty.

Only seventeen, I had never killed anyone, nor had I ever wanted to kill. I was not by nature a vengeful person, and if it had been up to me, I probably would have allowed the police to pursue justice. But my mother's will, amplified by the power of her magic, forced me to accept the burden. For two years I diligently pursued those three men.

I'd caught two. It was simple enough to take them. Got them drunk and promised sex. The first one died quietly, bleeding out in a dark alley in Seattle, my knife in his heart. An easy kill with no witnesses. The act itself, quick and cold, left me crying and washing nonexistent blood from my hands for days, sick at what I'd done. Then the need for revenge rose again and I had to continue the pursuit of the second killer.

I was a young girl, though, deep in mourning, and at the time unskilled and reckless. The second killer died the same way in New York, this time in a parking garage under the lens of a security camera I hadn't noticed.

Had there been proof that he was my parents' killer, the court might have been lenient. Visions of murder from your dead mother don't count as evidence. Driven by the compulsion to kill and the knowledge that I would never fulfill my duty from jail, I fought. I injured two of the police officers who captured me. I was lucky they didn't kill me, though maybe I wanted them to. Death would free me from the nightmare my life had become.

Two things kept me going during my first years at Justice: my absolute rage and the hope that I might one day escape and fulfill my need to kill the final murderer of my parents. After I learned to control that rage, each day was filled with the desire for knowledge of how to kill silently and competently, should I one day be free.

Sister Lillian and I went through the massive double doors and—bad news—down the grim, silent, stone hallway to the Judgment Room. A sudden chill slid over my body as if a winter wind glided down the hushed corridor. The building darkened and became more medieval, with its arched ceilings and stained-glass windows. Brown and beige rugs stretched across the floor to mute the echo of footsteps. Our feet gave only soft brushes of sound, barely more than a whisper. Paintings hung along the walls, weapons and artifacts, the thousand-year history of the Sisters of Justice. I had no details on that history, only stories of the valor of Sisters long dead. The place reeked of secrets.

I drew a deep breath and exhaled. My brain would need oxygen to deal with this. I'd been here before, though I usually knew why. My mind raced through scenarios of possible infractions. I could think of none that I believed they had discovered.

I walked into the room, and Sister Lillian directed me to stand by a chair facing a long table where Mother Superior Evelyn sat on a dais. Three Sisters sat on one side of her and a Sister and two empty chairs were on the other. Sister Lillian went to sit with them.

Prisoners were required to stand for an inquisition. I'd been here before. The chair surprised me, but I hadn't been given permission to sit.

The aptly named Judgment Room had the requisite stone floor, high windows, and bare stone walls that were known to weep at times. An ill omen, that weeping. A skeptical person would call it condensation. I didn't check the walls. I focused my attention on the judges.

I stood before them, supposedly filled with remorse and contrition. As I waited, Sister Eunice stalked in and filled the last chair. Seven judges dressed in black and one ill-tempered enforcer in fatigues. I was in deep trouble.

Sister Vera, seated next to Mother Evelyn, gave the formal speech that one of them gave before every gathering, including meals.

"We are the Sisters of Justice. We serve the Earth Mother, the Mother of Men. Our blades are sharp and we strike upon her command."

"By life and death, we serve." The others spoke simultaneously.

A moment of silence followed; then they turned their attention to me.

"Be seated, Madeline," the formidable Mother Evelyn said. Her blind, milk-white eyes stared at me. Eyes aren't the only means of vision, and it frightened me to think what she knew about me.

I held steady for long seconds—resistant to authority, as always—before I sat.

Sister Eunice scowled.

I refused to show weakness or apprehension. That lesson had been pounded into me over the years.

Mother Evelyn smiled. Unlike some of the Sisters,

she seemed to perceive my defiance as an asset. She leaned forward. "Tell me what you want, Madeline."

I frowned. No one had asked me that in years. "I don't understand, Mother."

"Do you have no goal beyond these walls? This prison. If you were free . . . ?"

I'd long since learned the futility of lying to them in such a tense situation. The occasional casual lie might pass, but here they would sense falseness and gouge out the truth—or incite such fury that I would give them far more than they wanted. In spite of my control over my anger, they still had the power to do that. Over the years, these women had stripped all the deep secrets from my soul, save one.

But I could speak the truth this time without giving that secret away. They knew what had brought me to Justice. My mother's deadly vision, her desire, remained vivid. I would remain true to her.

"I want the man. The third killer. The man who strangled her. I want him to die."

Mother Evelyn laid her hands on the table in front of her. Odd, since, like the others, she usually kept them hidden in her robe, probably close to a weapon of some sort. "Madeline, the Earth Mother created the Sisters of Justice a thousand years ago to fight evil. Evil most men do not know exists."

I knew the dogma. To kill the creatures they called the Drows. Invaders who slipped through places scattered across the earth where the boundaries between parallel worlds are weak. Creatures that can be killed only by bronze. Though they were named after the ancient dark elves of myth, I was taught that while they came here through magic, they were not magic themselves, only evil monsters who pollute our earth. When asked, the Sisters who had seen them refused to offer any description.

"The one I want is a man, Mother, not a Drow."

Mother Evelyn didn't move. Finally, she relaxed. "Very well, Madeline. We've trained you, and your services are required. You may refuse and stay here with us for the remainder of your very long sentence, or you may accept your assignment. This offer concerns a parole, not a pardon. If you fail, you will go straight to prison, not return to Justice."

I fought an inappropriate smile. "Mother, given my training and desire to kill, if I fail I will most likely be dead."

"Yes. It is good that you understand that, too."

The Sisters glanced at one another, faces wide with surprise—or maybe alarm.

I thought it would be years before they let me go. I had questions, though.

"Mother, may I know the assignment before I choose?"

Sister Lillian opened her mouth as if to speak.

Mother Evelyn abruptly raised her hand.

Sister Lillian drew a sharp breath, but said nothing.

Mother Evelyn slowly lowered the hand. She cleared her throat. "Do you know why those three men came to your parents' home that night?"

"The police said robbery. They wrecked the place. Broke open a safe." Suddenly uncomfortable, I caught myself before I betrayed that emotion.

"The Earth Mother gave your mother, one of her blessed witches, a precious stone to guard," Mother Evelyn said. "Your mother, rather than keeping it hidden and safe, wore it around her neck like an ornament."

I heard her contempt at my mother's vanity. The word *vanity* personified my mother, but with her extraordinary beauty, her loving nature, and her kindness, I didn't condemn her for it. She'd laid an agonizing curse upon me, but I did not believe she'd done it maliciously, only out of fear and pain. I loved her and my father, and desperately missed them. I kept my face rigid, but I'm sure Mother Evelyn saw my anger at her words.

The stone Mother Evelyn spoke of was jet-black and laced with threads of gold, as if tiny creatures with feet dipped in precious metals had trekked across its surface.

"The Portal," I said. "She called it the Portal."

"Do you know its use?" Mother Evelyn asked.

"As a focus for her magic, she once told me. Mother Evelyn, don't look to me for magic. I can feel it, recognize it, and sometimes see it. But I am not a witch. I *cannot* use it. You know that."

The Sisters of Justice acknowledged magic and its uses. But to the best of my knowledge, while they served the Earth Mother, too, they did not have the power to work with it as earth witches did. The Sisters' weapons involved bronze and blade, not the ritual of potion and spell.

My mother was an earth witch, and like all the witches I knew, she had served the Earth Mother all her life. The holy bitch had deserted my mother, her faithful servant, the night she died. My mother should have been able to use her earth magic to defend herself against the three men who killed her and my father.

I shut down my thoughts. Control. I would control my emotions.

The Sisters whispered among themselves, then slowly fell silent.

Mother Evelyn stared straight at me with her milk-white eyes. "The third man, the one you seek, has the Portal in his possession. He took it from her that night. We, and others, have searched for it all these years. It was located last month. You, Madeline, must retrieve it for us. If you kill the man in the process, so be it. But the Portal comes first. If you retrieve the Portal, you must return it to us without delay. After that, you may exact your revenge against your parents' killer."

The Sisters gazed at Mother Evelyn as if she'd uttered heresy. Sister Eunice glared at her with pure fury in her eyes. She'd taunted and sneered at me over the years, but she'd never burned me with the wrath she now focused on her superior.

In five minutes, I'd seen more expression on these warrior women's faces than in the last six years. I had to know more.

"Mother, you and the Sisters have taught me many things—not just how to fight. If the decision is mine, then I respectfully request additional information."

Sister Lillian gave me a happy grin. Her own lesson. *Know your enemy and the situation around him as much as possible.* Much as I wanted to leave, I would not jump blindly into even limited freedom. To my surprise, Sister Eunice smiled, too.

Mother Evelyn nodded. "You will have a guide. But for the most part, you must find your own way in this matter. Consider it a final examination, a test of your power and ability to survive. If you are successful, you may return and receive full Sisterhood." She laughed softly. "Though I doubt it would suit you."

I'd already made a decision. I didn't want Sisterhood. I wanted to live again. I wanted to be free of my mother's vision and free of the Sisters and their patroness, their goddess, whom I would never forgive for abandoning my mother. I understood perfectly well that the task was dangerous. Those trained by the Sisters of Justice were never given easy missions.

I stood. "I accept the assignment."

Acceptance, yes, but I required something else. They would bear some of the burden of responsibility in this mission, too.

"Mother Evelyn, I suggest you and the Sisters consider it your test, too. The measure of my success may be judged by the lessons that Justice has imparted to me."

Mother Evelyn nodded. "You are quite right, Madeline. This test, this burden falls upon us, too. We pray we have taught you well."

I lost my hard-fought battle with my temper. "Pray? To whom, Mother? Your Earth Mother? The demon whore of magic? I place more faith in the Sisters and their fists and blades. Their lessons will serve me far better than your prayers."

Silence fell on the room. I'd just uttered a mortal insult to their goddess.

They all stared at me. Their faces had reverted to the same blank neutrality with which I was familiar. Had I totally blown my one chance at freedom?

Mother Evelyn cleared her throat. "Know this, Madeline." Her voice was hard and cold. "By placing your faith in your teachers, you have made a choice. By your own words, you are one of us."

By my own words, I had a feeling I had totally and royally screwed myself.

chapter 3

I had only one personal item when I arrived at Justice: a picture of my mother and father. By the time I returned to my room, someone had cleaned out the meager possessions I'd acquired since that first day. Gone were the drab brown uniforms, the few necessary toiletries permitted, library books, and all my underwear except the pair I wore. In their place were a small cloth tote bag, socks, sneakers, jeans, a light nylon jacket, and a white T-shirt. The Sisters didn't provide a bra, but I didn't have a lot to fill one out anyway. I would be permitted to take very little from Justice except memories and the skills they'd taught me.

Inside the tote was my parents' photo and a small drawing of the third killer, made years ago by an artist as I painstakingly described him from my vision. The police had taken it from me when they'd thrown me in jail. How and when they obtained the drawing was a mystery, but mystery personified the Sisters.

There was a wallet with two hundred dollars in twenties. I'd need the money. After my arrest, my paternal uncle, may he rot in hell, petitioned the State of

New York to give him my parents' considerable estate. The state obliged—after it confiscated a good percentage.

The obviously wealthy Sisterhood could have provided more funding, but that wasn't their way. Nothing would be easy for me. Ease of accomplishment breeds complacency—one of the first lessons they had taught me. I could be on a desperate mission to save the world, but I'd have to be a heroine on a budget.

The wallet also had a social security card and a Missouri driver's license with my name, Madeline Carlotta Corso. The driver's license also said I lived in Duivel, Missouri. Duivel? I had never heard of it.

I'd just changed into the jeans and T-shirt when Sister Eunice stalked in. She always stalked or marched. Simply walking wouldn't suit her. My body assumed a defensive position, as it always did when I spotted her. She liked to ambush me. She'd do it anywhere. She'd drag me out of bed or hit me in the shower, anywhere she thought I'd feel complacent or secure.

Sister Eunice's posture indicated she didn't want to fight. I relaxed. A little.

She came to me, closer than she'd ever been except for when we fought hand-to-hand, as we had only an hour ago. Her dark eyes held a shine I'd never seen before. Surely not tears. Her thick, rough fingers brushed my cheek, lingering for a moment on the scar. "I'll miss you, bitch. You're so beautiful. Beautiful and brave."

While I stood speechless at the first gentle words she'd ever spoken to me, she removed the amulet she always wore around her neck and slipped the gold chain over my head.

"Don't take it off," she said, her voice husky and low. "Wear it in the shower; wear it when you sleep." She laid her hands on my shoulders and kissed me softly on the mouth. A lovely kiss, but it aroused no desire in me. I'm sure she knew that. I was leaving, though, and for all her cruelty, she'd taught me well. I kissed her back. After a moment, she broke away. This time, I'd surprised her.

"Thank you, Sister Eunice." For the first time in all my years at Justice, I smiled at her. "I'll remember you every time someone kicks my ass."

"You damned well better remember me when *you're* the one kicking ass." She whirled and marched out of the room.

The pendant was round, an inch and a half across, and incised with tiny runes in a spiral on both sides of the flat surface. Ancient and indecipherable, they meant nothing to me. I turned it over in my hand. I'd never seen her without it. Sister Eunice, my teacher, my tormentor, had given me a precious gift—and she'd called me beautiful. How amazing. I tucked it under my shirt.

Sister Lillian followed her. Sister Lillian always carried a knife strapped to her forearm, a slender six-inch blade in a leather sheath. She handed them to me. "This blade is bronze, forged in the shadow of Mount Ararat before Christ's birth. It has a power of its own. Use it wisely and honorably."

I accepted the weapon and she walked away, tears in her eyes.

These women, strange and dangerous women, had taught me the art of killing. Not necessarily killing for revenge as I had done, but the cold skill of an assassin. They'd also fostered my education. I could read Latin and ancient Greek writings and understand some of the runes, the symbols created at the beginning of recorded time. The Sisters required me to constantly observe the outside world via computers. I read the news, books . . . and researched prison breaks—until they caught me and made me stop.

But with the exception of Lillian, it never occurred to me that anyone might actually care for me, especially not Eunice.

Something more shocking and painful came next. Van Gogh arrived. Van Gogh got her nickname because she looks a lot like the painter, beard and all. She isn't a Sister; she's a sadistic tattoo artist. She grinned at me.

"Drop 'em, baby. I got something for you."

The Sisters of Justice have tattoos, a two-inch knife blade in a place of their choosing, usually on an arm or a leg. One blade for a novice; a full Sister has five. I'd been here for three years when I got my first. I didn't want it. To my knowledge, prisoners were never marked as Sisters, no matter how competent they might be. Though I quickly figured out that I was being treated in a different manner than the others, I never knew why. My questions, as usual, went unanswered.

When they had asked me where to put the tattoo, I'd said, "Kiss my ass." It had required three of them to hold me down while they decorated my butt. Their idea of entertainment. Ha. Ha.

I had fought each time Van Gogh arrived, but I'd always lost the battle. I had three blades on my right butt cheek. Apparently I was to have a fourth, although it made me one step below something I did not want to be. Since my declaration of faith in the Sisters in the Judgment Room, it seemed useless to fight. Van Gogh left me hours later rubbing what every traveler doesn't need—a sore butt.

I stopped at the door of my austere room and looked back on the narrow cot, bare wood floor, and single window overlooking the sweetly scented garden. I had suffered and fought hopeless battles, but for six years I'd been safe. This place had given me back something I'd lost: the security of a family. Bad things might happen, but a family can maintain you and the integrity of your soul. A damned dysfunctional bunch of violent siblings lived at Justice, but they were family nonetheless. Perhaps that was the source of my impromptu vow, a show of faith in my only family. More likely it was just stupidity, my juvenile reaction to their goading.

A finger of fear, perhaps dread, traced a fine line down my spine. They'd prepared me for that, too. I'd recited the mantra so many times, I'd come to believe it. *Fear is a gift, a precious thing that keeps me alive. Fear is a weapon to manipulate and control. Fear is the enemy. I will not be conquered by fear.*

I had to return to the administration building before I left. Mother Evelyn stood alone in the silent entry hall, waiting for me.

"Madeline." She sounded uncertain, as if she didn't know what to say.

"Yes, Mother."

"Most of the other young women who leave here are not like you. I think you know that. A tiny fraction will become Sisters; the rest will go on to live safe, benign lives. Not aggressors, but no longer victims. It was evil of your mother to curse you and make you a killer. I am no less evil in sending you to fulfill that curse."

I wanted to object to the epithet applied to my mother, but as I was this close to even limited freedom, I kept my mouth shut.

She'd surprised the Sisters back in the Judgment Hall when she'd given me permission to fulfill my desire to kill. Did she now regret it?

I thought I knew what Mother Evelyn wanted from me. "You are sending me to retrieve an object. If I kill a man, it will be my decision. There is no guilt for you in that."

Mother Evelyn bowed her head. Tears leaked from the blind eyes of the powerful matriarch of the Sisters of Justice. The spectacle of a conscience-stricken Mother Superior of fierce warrior women unnerved me. "Mother Evelyn, you're carving my tombstone before I get out the door."

She straightened. "We're sending you to a person in Duivel. She will be your guide. I strongly urge you to listen to her." She wiped her eyes with the sleeve of her robe before she spoke again. "Before you go, you must know the true calling of the Sisters of Justice."

Something in the tone, the power of her voice, shimmered over me and demanded my absolute attention.

"The Sisters of Justice are trained to fight Drows,

those who slip through places where the walls between worlds are thin. You know that. What you do not know is that we have a greater calling." She bit her lower lip. Was this the powerful Mother Evelyn? Where was her iron resolve? "Madeline, we are the enforcers of the Earth Mother's greatest law. At maturity, an earth witch takes a powerful life-binding vow to do no harm. Malicious magic, black magic, magic that injures, is forbidden. Since the power to use magic is a birthright of the witch, the only thing that stops malicious magic is the death of the witch. At the Earth Mother's decree, the Sisters of Justice are called upon as executioners. We kill those witches."

Silence stretched through the hall, silence as dead and unfeeling as the stone walls around us. It held me tight. I could do nothing but wait for her next words.

"Madeline, your mother was an earth witch, one of great power. That she was able to curse you from beyond the veil of death is proof of her strength." She paused. She stared straight at me with those blind white eyes.

"The Mother could forgive a witch's foolish vanity and the loss of the Portal. It is your mother's curse, her demand that her innocent young daughter wreak vengeance on her behalf . . ." Tears leaked from her eyes again. "It's evil. Appalling evil. Had she done this in life, the Mother would've sent the Sisters to execute her."

I knew magic. I knew the Sisters of Justice and their skill. I knew my mother and her power. I also knew she loved me and would not have hurt me intentionally.

Unintentional injury is hurtful, but not evil. Pride, probably misguided pride, filled me. I drew a deep breath and fought rising anger. "Mother Evelyn, I think it would have required more than one."

"Indeed."

The impact of the last hour's events had not yet settled in my mind. The pronouncement of the Sisters as law enforcement for earth witches would probably stun me when I had time to think about it. For now, it was only words.

"I have to warn you," Mother Evelyn said. "You now look and act like a Sister of Justice. For obvious reasons, there is no friendship between the Sisters and witches. I know you loved your mother and will not think ill of her. If you meet a witch outside, she will not likely harm you. But neither will she provide you with aid, should you need it. You must depend only upon yourself."

"I've done that for a long time, Mother Evelyn."

I had one question that had deeply concerned me. Maybe she, in her sudden openness and emotional distress, would answer it. "Mother Evelyn, why didn't my mother defend herself when the killers came? She had the power and magic, and self-defense is allowed. Why didn't she use it?"

"I don't know, Madeline. I don't know." She grabbed me in a sudden, ferocious embrace. Just as quickly, she released me and hurried away.

Over the years I had hated her and the Sisters with a passion that burned my soul. They had offered few acts of kindness. Now I was deeply curious about why the Sisters were upset that Evelyn was sending me out into the world.

There would be nothing for me that a woman my age might expect: courtship, love, marriage or family. The scar and my hair set me apart. And even after these last few years, I still felt no guilt for my actions. As each murderer died, a bit of my burden was lifted. I had no doubt, though, that eventually I would bear other, less visible scars from those deeds.

chapter 4

June 20—Duivel, Missouri

The man who drove me west from New York had the personality of a fifteen-year-old basset hound with arthritis. His depressed nature didn't stop him from powering the SUV straight through, eyes on the road, stopping only for gas. Since I'd learned the value of silence at Justice, his inability or possible unwillingness to communicate with more than a few single-syllable words did not trouble me—sitting for long hours on a fresh tattoo did. I finally disregarded my dignity, filled a plastic bag with ice at one of the fuel stops, and wedged it under my new artwork.

We arrived in Missouri at six a.m. and rolled into Duivel at eight. The morning sun, barely above the horizon, promised a lovely day. The compact downtown area raised a few tall buildings to the sky, twenty to thirty stories, but no major skyscrapers. I let the window down to check for significant odors. I excelled at the Stink, the blindfolded smell test given by Sister

Lois. Nothing here spoke of anything but the usual hydrocarbons and vegetation.

We went by a mall, a school, and some churches. The SUV crossed a river with the unusual name of the Sullen. The water spread slow and calm, indicating a deep channel. Patches of ghostly morning fog skimmed and swirled low on the surface between the tree-lined shores.

My driver slowed the vehicle and stared at the road signs. He pulled over to the curb, stopped, and continued to stare. Unlike the persona he'd been projecting earlier, he made no effort to hide his emotions now. The man was afraid of something ahead of us. The sign said River Street. He visibly swallowed, gripped the wheel tight, and drove on.

Traffic was light on River Street. Small businesses lined the four-lane roadway. An occasional shopping center, restaurant, or gas station appeared, but all were placid as we rolled by—until we hit a wall. Not a literal wall, but one built of powerful magic. While I can work no magic, my mother's blood makes me sensitive to it. For a brief moment, it covered me like thickened air, then faded away. We had passed through a ward, a ban, a prison wall of psychic energy—incredible, powerful energy. Was it designed to keep someone or something in—or out? Curious about this new situation, I leaned forward, studying my new home.

The ward we passed through was, in itself, benign. I did not feel threatened, though it was clear my driver did. I realized what the ward guarded, or kept out, might not be neutral. I expected I'd discover the truth of that eventually.

The image of prosperous commerce faded to a struggle against blight. A valiant struggle, though. We passed one brick building, possibly a warehouse, with a sign that proclaimed it to be the Archangel. No other description, but the parking lot held Porsches, Mercedeses, and other high-end cars, even in the early morning.

Five blocks farther, my driver pulled to the curb and handed me a piece of paper. His heartwarming farewell consisted of two words. "Get out."

As soon as I stepped onto the sidewalk and closed the door behind me, the basset hound punched the gas, made a tight U-turn, and roared away. "Thanks for the ride, sunshine!" I shouted after him.

I drew a deep breath of morning air. I was free. Not free of duty, of responsibility, but free of the walls of Justice.

Some tangible but faint power in this place nagged me, suggesting but not demanding that I recognize it. I closed my eyes and let my mind search. I did not usually sense magic this way, but I often found other things of interest. Immediately, I found a shadow. It hung heavy over the streets and buildings. It was low-key magic, inactive, but there nevertheless. I went no further. Though it seemed benign, I would not prod a sleeping tiger with a stick to see if it jumped.

I unfolded the piece of paper that had been included with my few things. *Armory Pawn*, scribbled in a barely legible script. The address was the same as the one on my new driver's license. As I searched for a street sign, I realized it was right behind me. The wide storefront had generous but grimy windows filled with battered furniture and appliances. A decrepit couch, minus cushions, was tipped on its end and looked like it might crash through the glass at any moment, crushing some unlucky passerby on the sidewalk.

A sign on the door, tilted at an odd angle, read OPEN, but the hinges squealed in a high-pitched complaint when I entered. Air thick with stale cigarette smoke as gray as if it were from a bonfire of green wood greeted me. I forced myself to take shallow breaths.

Pawn? More like extreme junk: shabby furniture, bicycles, tools, dusty glass cases with old film, cameras, and watches. I stepped around a vacuum cleaner lying on its side like an obstacle course for the rare and brave customer. The window decorations appeared more pitiful from the inside, and they blocked most of the natural light.

A woman with bushy brown hair and a horribly crumpled brown shirt stood behind the counter. I'd caught her in the act of lighting up. She stopped the lighter in midair. She was tall and rawboned, and her gaunt face was lined with a road map of wrinkles. She had a strong jaw and shrewd, intelligent eyes.

"Who are you?" She stabbed the lighter at me.

"Madeline Corso."

She grunted and muttered something about Evelyn, and I caught the word *bitch*. "So, you're on some noble mission for them and I get to play fucking fairy godmother." Her voice was as rough as the stone walls of Justice.

I didn't know what to say.

She lit and puffed on her cigarette and blew a stream of smoke out of the side of her mouth. She cocked her head and studied me with eyes neither friendly nor unfriendly.

"You got any money?"

"Not much."

"Figures."

"Who are you?" I asked. The whole scenario was becoming bizarre.

"I'm Hildy. You gonna listen to me?"

"I've been strongly urged to take your advice."

"Huh. Strongly urged. That was Evelyn, I bet." Hildy gave a deep, liquid cough. "Okay, honey. Here's your advice. The Barrows is a place where you can—and will—die tonight if you don't pay attention. You think you're a warrior, but you don't know shit. You'll learn. If you survive."

Hildy grunted, and then wheezed a few breaths before she continued. "Most people talk about the Barrows, they talk about those disgusting businesses here along River Street. Porn shops, titty bars."

I refrained from staring at the disgusting junk around me. At this point, anyone providing me with information was not to be insulted.

She tapped the lighter against the glass counter. *Clink, clink, clink*—any harder and she'd break through. She laid the lighter down. "There's a spell over the Barrows. A spell and a ward. You know what that is? You know what the difference is?"

I did. "A spell is magic that affects something. A ward is a barrier. I felt a ward as we drove here." Hildy studied me now, as if my words caught her attention.

"You . . . felt?"

"I'm sensitive to magic. And no, I'm not a witch."

She stared, the wheels of her mind obviously in motion. What did it mean to her, that I was sensitive to magic? The Sisters had ignored it. Finally, she spoke.

"The spell over this area keeps things from being seen. Unless you know it's there. But we're just on the outskirts. Behind the businesses that line River Street to the east"—she nodded again toward the street—"past the first block, that's the heart of the Barrows. Massive ruins, square miles of ruins. Don't go there."

Hildy picked up and fiddled with the lighter, turning it over and over. She seemed desperate to finish her story and fire up—regardless of the still-burning stick of tobacco she held in her other hand. "The Earth Mother cast the spell over this area to protect outsiders. It's a world of its own now. People might see things here, but as soon as they look away, they forget everything. Doesn't mean they don't got a sense about the place, though. They know enough to avoid it. The decent ones, anyway. The spell works real good on strangers, people who come here once in a while," Hildy said. "They don't see nothing. People living in uptown Duivel don't know it's here. Us living on River Street can't ignore it, but we don't talk about it. We don't go into those damned ruins, either."

She pointed toward the window. "Go across the street and rent a room from Harry. Harry's a nasty old bastard. If he touches you, tell him you'll cut his balls off. If he touches you again, do it."

"No. Then I'd have to touch him."

Hildy laughed, choked, and stubbed out her smoke. "Smart-ass. But I suppose you got muscle to back up your mouth, coming from Justice. Violence first works for the bitches there." She looked up and stared hard at me. "You're gonna need a job. I bet they gave you hardly anything to live on. Damn cheap bitches. You could die, but that's okay. As long as you live in poverty and . . . Fuck it." She picked up the phone on the counter and dialed. She listened a moment before she spoke. "Hell yes, I know what fucking time it is."

The person she spoke to was obviously not a morning person. She snarled a string of vicious words into the phone, then ruined their venomous effect with a massive coughing spasm. Her voice wheezed when she finally finished. "You still need a bartender?"

The person on the line apparently thought her important enough to wait out her cough.

Hildy growled—literally. "I don't care what the fuck you want. I'm sending her over. Hire her." She hung up the phone. The fact that she'd just pissed off my possible future employer didn't seem to bother her.

She snagged another cigarette from a pack on the counter. "After you get your room, go down the street." She flipped a hand in a general southerly direction. "Ten blocks. Bar called the Goblin Den. Man named Riggs will hire you. Place still got that nasty name, but it's a little higher class than it used to be."

I nodded. This wasn't bad. If, as they said, my man

was in Duivel or this place she called the Barrows, I'd be more likely to find him in a bar than anywhere else. I'd lured one of my killers out of a dirty tavern near the shipyards and the other out of a cocktail lounge.

Hildy lit up and sucked in the poison, and a look of ecstasy passed over her worn face. She sighed and savored the moment, then went on. "You look out for the Bastinados. Gangs. Nasty, mean-looking bastards. Always run in packs. Avoid them. Don't walk around at night. Period. If you have to be out, stay in the light. There's a bus runs up and down River Street every hour, twenty-four seven. It's cheap. Use it."

Some fleeting emotion passed over her face but too quickly for me to read it. She stubbed out her cigarette. "Two more things. The ward around the Barrows. It keeps something in. The Barrows is a prison. Down in the heart of the ruins, in a place called the Zombie Zone, there's a demon. A big, badass demon. He's not just a Drow—he's king of the Drows. He's intelligent, and he's deadly. Do not mess with him.

"Second thing. The Mother . . . she don't come into the Barrows. If she crosses her own ward, she'll break its effectiveness and let that demon out. That don't mean she can't see, though. And . . ." She hesitated as if deciding what to say. "The demon. They say the Mother is . . . fond of him. She won't let him out, but she treats him like a pet of some sort. If that makes any fucking sense. Now get out of here."

She abruptly walked away and through a door, out of the room.

Hildy was a tough bird. Nothing warm and fuzzy

about her. A former Sister? Maybe. I did like her. I liked her strength and the fact that she didn't seem to worship the Mother like so many others I'd met in my life. But she raised an unusual question. If I were a true Sister and they sent me out to kill a witch, not just retrieve an object, would I have to do it on a budget?

chapter 5

I dodged light traffic as I crossed the street. The air outside Hildy's shop, filled with exhaust fumes, wasn't perfect, but I breathed deeply anyway. My first hours in Duivel and the Barrows were already proving interesting. For some reason, the place appealed to me. I had yet to see the ruins—or the king of Drows—but after the years of discipline and pain, it was good to have some freedom. My life did not have to be focused on the next lesson, the next battle. A battle might come in an instant, but right now, this moment, warmed me.

A small sign on the plain, two-story redbrick building across from Hildy's proclaimed it to be Harry's Rooms and Apartments. The structure looked steady and solid, even if the brick was covered with years of vehicle exhaust. Harry himself greeted me when I walked into the tiny lobby. He didn't look nasty. He was short and round with chubby red cheeks and hair as white as mine. A miniature Santa Claus—only he never raised his eyes above my breasts. At least he didn't stare at the scar.

"Hildy called." He spoke directly to my chest.

If Harry had any perversions other than a mammary fixation, he hid them from me. He offered me an efficiency apartment, but it cost twice as much as a single room. With my meager funds I could stay in the single room a week and a half—if I didn't eat. Given the address on the driver's license, I suspected the Sisters had meant for me to stay with Hildy. I doubted either of us could stand that.

After the minimal comforts of jail and Justice, I liked my new room just fine. The shower was down the hall, but I had a half bath connected to the room itself. It was clean and painted a neutral beige. There was a double bed, a chest of drawers, and a single chair. I ran my fingers across the pretty blue chenille bedspread. Soft from multiple washings, it was the first comfortable bed cover I'd seen in years. The rules said no food in the room. I could work around that.

There was a thrift shop next door to Hildy's pawnshop where I could get some new-used clothes. I went down the stairs and had started out the door when I saw them.

I noticed the woman first. She had glorious red hair and was pregnant, so pregnant she should've carried a basket around in case she suddenly popped out a baby. She laughed with a man, but her body language said he wasn't her lover. He opened the car door for her and hovered, holding her arm while she climbed in. His touch was caring but not a caress. His hand lingered a few seconds too long, though, as if he wanted to touch her more but didn't dare.

As he closed her door, he turned, carefully scanning

the area around them. An odd gesture; what danger did he watch for? I stepped backward through Harry's doorway. I could peer through a small pane of glass by the door and see him.

This was the man of a lifetime. Tall, over six feet, his white-blond hair spread over broad shoulders like a sleek silk curtain. The hair framed a perfect face, an angel's face.

I drew a sharp breath in surprise. I could feel the man's presence as if he were standing beside me. Close beside me, in my personal space, in my head. He could have been whispering in my ear. I can feel magic, but this was something different. This had never happened to me before. I forced my body not to run. My hands clenched into fists and I jammed my back against the wall near the glass panel to keep my legs from buckling.

He stared straight at where I was hiding. I didn't think he could see me, but he knew someone watched him. Had he the same awareness of me that I had of him? Impossible. His expression grew tight. He walked toward Harry's. The woman spoke. He stopped and turned back to her. Whatever he thought, whatever he wanted, she was more important. He hurried around to the driver's side. His eyes never left my hiding place. I laid my hand against the scar. The skin felt hot and tight. The connection to him remained in my mind like a banked fire, glowing embers, burning deep and slow.

I ruthlessly shoved the feeling down. I recited the control mantra over and over. *I can and will control my emotions. Control makes me stronger. Control permits rational action.*

The angel climbed in the car and drove away.

I'd never felt this kind of deep emotion. It didn't seem like desire, but what did I know of such things? My mother and father died just as I was beginning to blossom, and my ordinary and happy life ended. Compelled to vengeance, I had not wanted sex; nor did I want it now. I'd been a virgin at seventeen and remained one to this day, but I was not an innocent. For three years I'd walked streets where all manner of perversions were bartered and sold.

I did not particularly want to dwell on my sudden connection with the man I'd just seen. It was some freak emotion that did not belong in my life.

I left the building and walked toward my potential new job. The shops I passed seemed prosperous enough. I stopped two buildings down at Tony's Grocery Store and bought a ready-made sandwich and a small carton of milk. And a candy bar. Chocolate. Cheap chocolate that I let slowly dissolve in my mouth. Meals at Justice were nutritious and edible, but we weren't encouraged to fixate on food. Food equaled fuel, not gratification.

As I walked south toward the Goblin Den, the businesses grew more sordid. I walked past strip bars, liquor stores, and bail bondsmen who offered twenty-four-hour service. Pink Pussy, Boobs and Butts Galore, and Fire-Water Spirits had their front doors open for morning cleaning, letting stale beer and stinking cigarette smoke drift out into the world. Lockout Pawn had a multitude of weapons laid out and chained down behind barred windows.

At night the signs would flash in a kaleidoscope of neon, but this morning the sidewalk was a concrete desert—except for the remains of dissolute living. Used condoms and needles competed with the usual filth of crushed cans and broken bottles near the buildings and in the alleys.

Farther south, occupied shops became progressively scarce and windows boarded with weathered plywood became prevalent. Heavy traffic, mostly trucks, rumbled down the road, spewing carbon monoxide into the atmosphere. Six blocks south of Harry's, the trucks tended to veer to my right, toward the river.

As I crossed one side street, I stared down it to the east . . . and stopped. There were no cars. A block away I could see a building facade crumbled into the sidewalk. Curiosity tugged at me. I wanted to see more. Hildy had warned me, though, and until I knew the place better I would, as Mother Evelyn strongly urged, take her advice. I passed more side streets on my journey south to the Goblin Den and saw some businesses running for a block east. But beyond that was a barren landscape of ruins. Ruins that, according to Hildy, were ignored by a large number of people in Duivel. Just looking at them told me a wise person would stay away. I'm not wise, but I remained cautious. Someday, I would explore. Someday, I would probably be forced to explore.

I continued to walk south to where the street ended and the river began. The deepwater Sullen River overflowed onto acres of open green and brown marshland that stretched to the horizon. Small islands covered with trees rose above the marsh occasionally. A cool, fresh wind came across the water. I caught the scent of flowers somewhere out beyond the limits of my vision.

The Goblin Den was on my left, to the east. The tall box of a building had a fresh coat of cream-colored paint, a newly paved parking lot, and workers toiling diligently on the roof. The stink of tar filled the air as if the hot black stuff spewed up from hell. The owner was putting a lot of time and money into the place. *Better than it used to be.* Hildy's words. What did it used to be?

I entered through double glass doors propped open with concrete blocks. The aroma of hot tar followed, but whispering fans set strategically around the room made a valiant effort to force it back outside. Construction was evident here, too, where men were refurbishing a stage. Everything in the place seemed new. Classy tables and chairs made of oak and upholstered in a shiny copper fabric filled the room. A well-stocked modern glass bar stretched along one wall. It seemed as if the owner had engaged in a courageous but misguided attempt to create an upscale ambience—and instead created the equivalent of the cliché about a sow's ear and silk purse.

A man sat on a stool at the bar. He wasn't tall, about my height, with clothes that hung on him like he'd lost fifty pounds and couldn't afford anything new. His head had a short skimming of brownish gray hair and his eyelids drooped so low, I wondered how he could see. If ever a man could be described as mousy, he fit the picture.

I went closer. "I'm looking for Riggs."

"That'd be me." He cocked his head and stared at

me so long I expected him to laugh and order me out. Instead: "You know how to mix drinks?"

I shook my head. "Do you have a recipe book? I learn fast."

He sighed, but he'd do what Hildy wanted. Did she know some secret of his? She had influence over Harry, too.

"Come on. I'll get you a uniform."

Riggs led me to a close and uncomfortable storage room filled with drink mixers and bottles of liquor. He dug around in a box and, along with a battered recipe book, drew out two plastic-wrapped articles of clothing and offered them to me. According to the picture printed on the package, my uniform consisted of shiny black stretch leggings and a top made of silver metallic fabric that draped from neck to waist like a glittery handkerchief. The back was left open except for two thin straps that crossed to hold it in place. My breasts would be covered, but I hadn't shown this much skin in public since I was ten years old.

"Four nights, seven to three," Riggs said as we left the room. "Wednesday, Thursday, Friday, Saturday. You get minimum wage." He lifted his chin and appeared almost hopeful that I'd refuse. When I didn't say anything, he sighed. "And you keep your tips."

That sounded like he thought I wouldn't be getting many.

Riggs showed me to the back door that opened to a parking lot and alley. The surrounding buildings appeared abandoned like the ruins I'd seen up the hill. He told me to enter through the back door.

"Get here before dark, though. You come after dark, you use the front door. You have a ride home tonight?" he asked.

"The bus."

"Okay. Stay in the light." Mousy Riggs spoke the words more firmly than I expected. He stood back. "Don't talk much, do you?"

"No."

Riggs cocked his head and surprised me by looking like a man rating a woman on a scale of desirability. "Are you for sale? Or do you give it away?"

"Neither."

Riggs grunted. "Good. You don't sell or give in the Den. You do and you're out. Damn Hildy anyway." He turned and walked away.

I'd been in enough bars to know that waitresses and bartenders sometimes moonlighted as prostitutes, occasionally with the knowledge of the bar owner, who demanded a percentage. I thought it was bizarre; then realized I'd applied that word to a number of things I'd seen since I arrived early that morning.

I rode the bus back to Harry's. With my near photographic memory, I had Riggs's cocktail recipes memorized before I climbed off. I went to the thrift shop and purchased a pair of black shoes. They weren't designed to be sexy like my uniform, but my feet wouldn't hurt. Since I hadn't slept much on my journey from New York, I stretched out on the bed to rest. I'd be up most of the night.

I'd had constant nightmares about the murders during the years between my parents' deaths and my time in jail. They dominated my life and drove me on. Then Justice taught me control. Even the need to kill the third killer eased. Memory of it lingered, ready to explode. It probably would, but I could handle it better now. I hesitated to sleep, but it had to come eventually.

As I slept, I dreamed. I dreamed of my mother, angry, as she'd been so many times when she attempted to give me magic lessons. I heard myself crying, telling her that I'd tried to do the magic, but I couldn't. I dreamed of Daddy soothing me. Papa loved me as I was.

I dreamed of the angelic face of the man I'd seen earlier in the day. He smiled, and I saw desire in his eyes. A fantasy, yes, but desire rose in me to meet his, desire that had never plagued me before. More important was what I didn't dream. The final killer's face did not leer at me, taunting me, telling me that I would never find him. To my surprise, when I woke I found that I'd rested well.

I dressed in my so-called uniform. There was a full-length mirror on the back of the bathroom door. My body looks good, thanks to daily exercise—and scrubbing algae. Long, lean, and mean, I had shapely legs and a tight butt. The white hair and brutally short haircut added to the effect. I donned the jacket and stuffed the wallet and knife in the pocket. No way would I walk these streets without a weapon of some kind. I started to take the drawing of my mother's murderer to ask if anyone had seen him along the way, but it was my only one and I needed to have copies made. Better to leave it in the room until I knew my way around.

Now I'd enter my new world. A world filled with miles of deserted ruins I'd seen down the side streets stretching eastward. There would be Drows, vicious gang members, magic—and one big, badass demon. For the briefest of moments, my mind turned to the relative safety of Justice. I rejected it. Safety was not for me. I was young, trained, and experienced. Freedom beckoned. I ignored the nagging, whiny voice in the back of my mind that told me I was a novice in many things.

chapter 6

When I left the boardinghouse, I wanted to go to Hildy's and ask questions about the ruins behind the facade of River Street. She'd told me about the spell, why no one noticed them, why no one talked about them. But what had caused the devastation? I'd slept too long and a CLOSED sign hung on her door. I wanted to be, as Riggs ominously warned me, at the Goblin Den before dark.

I wished the Sisters had been more specific about the things they called Drows and their appearance and weapons. I wished Hildy had been more specific about the badass demon. Of course, asking the Sisters to be specific was like asking a statue to talk. I'd spent a lot of time scrubbing algae off of the stone walls of Justice for asking questions. But the reasons for Hildy's vague answers remained unknown. She was supposed to be my mentor.

The morning had been cool, almost chilly, but the sun had warmed the asphalt and concrete and the coming evening promised to be pleasant. A soft breeze off the river brushed away the stink of exhaust fumes. I walked south again as the day rolled on toward twilight.

The legitimate shops had closed and the others began to stir. As I walked through more disreputable areas, I passed a few early-rising prostitutes, male and female—some so young it amazed me that they walked openly and obviously on a well-traveled street. The young had an air of quiet desperation that time had not yet hardened into aggression. I'd walked among their kind once at seventeen, not to solicit sex, but to lure the first killer to my knife.

I passed the Lockout Pawn as a weary-looking man checked the locks that held the guns on display in the shop window. If I had money later, I'd consider one. I could shoot. Twice a month, two of the Sisters escorted me to a gun range and watched as I learned. They also led me into the woods around Justice and had me practice firing in various situations and positions. I was the only student trained that way. As usual, there was no point in asking why.

The next shop was called Took's Serpent City. A sudden spike of extrasensory power jolted me. It hit hard and I stumbled. I looked in the large window that formed one wall of a long glass cage. On one side of the cage was a snake. A boa from the markings, gray and black, long and thick, it had coiled into a tight ball. On the other side was a . . . lizard? It appeared to be a gray-green miscegenation of a gecko and an iguana. Maybe two feet long, but much of that was tail. It had two hard curved ridges down its back that ended at the tail. And teeth it flashed in the direction of the boa. It looked a bit like a miniature dragon.

A man stood between them, brandishing a stick. He poked at the lizard. The lizard jumped out of the way. The snake didn't move. I do love animals, but I didn't have time to stare. Until . . . the lizard turned and stared at me. It actually saw me. It made contact on a level much like another human being. It had to be a familiar, one of those semi-sentient creatures that the Earth Mother occasionally sends to aid witches. My mother had a raven. It was her constant companion. It hated me. It would shit on my head and peck me hard enough to draw blood. I found it dead in the laundry basket a few days after she was murdered. It had wrapped itself in a garment she had worn and died, probably of a broken heart. Not being a witch, I didn't need a familiar. But for my mother's love of her raven, I would attempt a rescue. I entered the store.

"What are you doing?" I asked. I tried to sound curious, not angry.

The man glanced up at me. His brow furrowed in a frown. He was a thick, solid man and appeared a bit brutish. He sneered at the cage.

"Trying to feed my fucking snake." His voice was higher pitched than I'd expected.

I glanced around the room. The glass cages holding the reptiles were lit, and some near the floor had heat lamps in them. The place was ripe with the fecund smell of reptiles, but there was nothing to indicate abuse. The man obviously cared for his snakes, if not this lizard.

"What are you feeding him?"

"Something I caught in the live trap last night. Rats been scarce lately." He glared at the lizard. "Couldn't sell it so I decided to make it Vickie's dinner. She don't want it, though." He suddenly grinned. He looked me up and down and studied the scar as if fascinated. "You wanna buy a snake? I got plenty." The last words came out as an obscene suggestion.

"No, I want the lizard."

His eyes narrowed. Now a bit of greed peeked through. "He's pretty rare."

"Then why didn't you sell him?" I reached for the lizard. It didn't wait. It leaped onto my arm, then onto my shoulder. I forced myself to stand steady as it wrapped itself around my neck and stuck its head under my collar.

The snake man grinned. "I'm selling him now. Five hundred." The lizard burrowed even further under my collar. The snake man's grin widened. He knew he had a sale.

I stared at him and realized I was prepared to take the lizard by any means. And I could. This brute was out of shape and had a gut bigger than Harry's. I could take him. But in spite of my imprisonment and training, I was not a thief. I pulled out my wallet, opened it, and grabbed my four remaining bills. I showed him the empty wallet. "Eighty. It's all I have."

"Okay. Eighty. And you stay and keep me company for a while."

I tossed the bills in the snake cage. "Eighty and I don't tell anyone about the illegals in the back room." I didn't specify what I meant by illegals, but I gambled that this man had something he wanted to keep hidden. I'd gamble that every place along River Street had illegals of some sort in the back room.

"You don't know about . . ." He stopped. I'd won the bet. He leaned forward. To attack? He sneered. "Get out of here."

I left.

As soon as we were outside, the lizard's head came out from under the collar of my jacket and he started chattering. Talking. His mouth formed sounds, repeated hisses and clicks that could only be a language. My mother's raven couldn't form words, but he did communicate with her.

"Hey, I know it was rough." I spoke when it fell silent. "But you better stay out of traps."

The lizard crawled down my arm headfirst. It stopped at my elbow and stared up at me. The greenish skin had small white spots on it like a collar, and the odd hard ridges down its spine were like nothing I'd seen before. I'd never studied lizards except in biology and couldn't call myself an expert, though. But again, this was the Barrows, the essence of weird.

"Okay, Spot. I'll try to take care of you until we find out where you belong."

Spot chirped once. He climbed back up to my shoulder.

"Don't shit on me, buddy. Or I'll take you back to the snake."

A few people stared at me as I walked along, but I couldn't tell what interested them—the scar or the odd-looking lizard hanging around my neck like a scarf. I didn't care. My father taught me that there were more strange things in the world than I knew, so I shouldn't be surprised when something presented itself. I accepted the lizard—the miniature dragon—as part of the natural world.

Per Riggs's instruction, I went to the back door of the Den. There were fading painted white stripes on the wide alley street where cars once parked. The ruins began not far from the Den. I could tell some of those crumbling buildings had once been storefronts. How many people had once called this area home before it disintegrated?

Spot chirped. He jumped off my shoulder. I thought he'd splat on the pavement, but he didn't. To my amazement, the bony protrusions on his back suddenly flipped out to reveal wings. He glided to a place twenty feet away. He let loose with another barrage of sounds I assumed to be his way of talking. He ran toward the ruins, stopped, and stared back at me. He chirped again. He wanted me to follow him.

"Sorry, Spot. I have to go to work. You go on, and don't get caught again."

Spot watched me for a moment. Then the investment of my last eighty dollars rushed off into the ruins. Spot might be a familiar, but he was certainly an unusual one. Oh, well. Maybe I'd get enough tips to make up for the spent money so I could eat tomorrow. I hadn't seen a soup kitchen, but one probably existed somewhere and would tide me over in the meantime.

Riggs met me inside the bar and introduced me to Kelly, the other bartender. Kelly pointed out my section of the bar. It even had a tape to divide our customers.

Kelly wore a silver top like mine. It draped differently over her much larger breasts. She had red hair, but unlike the redhead I'd seen earlier in the day, Kelly's obviously came from a bottle. The three floor waitresses who came in exposed more skin. Their stretchy pants were cut below the navel, but then they had to work the crowd. When someone came to sit at the bar, I already had a sale.

Riggs gave me instructions on handling the money and my tips. The Goblin Den's patrons drifted in around us and I was dismayed to realize that my killer would not likely be among them. They appeared to be upper-middle-class professionals. Not what you'd expect for a warehouse at the end of the road with a trashy name. They must've really liked the bar to come so far south from uptown. Thus far, I'd seen nothing spectacular to draw them here. Kelly informed me that the Den was once "smoking" hot. She ecstatically praised some bands I'd never heard of.

"Now we got this." She flung her hand at the growing crowd. "They're even going to change the name of the place to something soft and stupid." Her contempt was such that she glanced over her shoulder to be sure I was the only one hearing her traitorous remarks.

While a few customers stared at my scar, none asked how I got it. Kelly warmed to me, especially when some of my customers made a point of going to her side. One glance said she felt sorry for me. I mixed my drinks correctly, smiled pleasantly, and collected my tips graciously. A couple of men with kind eyes tipped more than necessary. I didn't need sympathy, but I could use the money.

At ten o'clock, Riggs told me to take a twenty-minute break. I grabbed my jacket with the knife and wallet tucked inside and went out the back door. Brilliant lamps illuminated the small parking lot like sunlight at noon. Cool night air drifted from the Sullen Bog, bringing the scent of growing vegetation. I walked to a more shadowed area, within the light but less glaring, and sat on a wooden box by the back wall of the Den. I let my body grow still and went into a state Sister Lillian called calm awareness. She said it was the closest thing she knew to true psychic ability for a non-witch.

My heart rate slowed and my breath deepened. I observed. And I sensed I wasn't alone. Something moved toward me in the darkness fifty feet away. A slow, stealthy creep of a shadow within a shadow. Then it came no closer. A faint scratching sound made me look up.

An abandoned building stood behind the small parking lot. Two stories with its roofline shadowed, but not completely dark. Something squatted there. Easily the size of a man, it had a head like a gargoyle and the body of a chimpanzee. Wings. It had wings. Its mouth gaped open as it bared its fangs. It was nothing of this world. It had to be a Drow.

I drew my knife. I had to get back inside.

Lights flashed in the alley as a car drove in, a fine midnight-colored vehicle with sleek lines. It parked on the edge of the light—directly under the thing on the roof.

The Drow unfurled its wings.

It leaned forward and focused on the man who exited the car—the blond man who had profoundly affected me that morning. My stomach tightened. The connection I felt to him earlier in the day soared through my mind. This could not happen. I could not let him be attacked. The connection grew so strong it was almost as if whatever happened to him would happen to me. I rose and drew my knife. Not much of a weapon against such horror.

I had no time to shout a warning. The creature plunged down.

I raced toward the angel.

He glanced up as I approached. I ignored him. Focus, focus on the enemy.

I leaped on the hood of his car and threw myself up, colliding with the Drow midair, knife first.

The bronze blade sank deep, and the Drow's own momentum gutted it. Intractable gravity caught both of us and dragged us down. My body landed first. I managed to keep my head up, keep it from shattering, but the rest of me received a massive, breath-stealing hit.

The abhorrent thing landed beside me, its organs spewing from the gaping wound where my blade had eviscerated it. Dying, it had one last defense. It opened its mouth, hissed a breath of foul air, and sank those terrifying fangs into my shoulder.

I shrieked in mindless anguish as molten fire poured through me and gnawed its way into flesh and bone, boiling my blood. My body jerked with a spasm as a massive jolt of electricity, like a bolt of lightning, tore through it.

The creature's body was dragged off me and I was in the angel's arms.

My blood burned. The thing had a venomous bite. I struggled to move. The angel held me closer. I maintained my grip on my knife. A death grip. I'd laugh at the cliché if it didn't fit so well.

"I'll get help for you," the angel said. His voice was soft.

I released the knife. Despite my misery, I wanted to touch him. With supreme effort, I raised a bloody, trembling hand. My fingers left a scarlet trail down his cheek, across that perfect face.

I don't remember much after that, only bits and pieces. I rode in a car, lights flashed, and agony throbbed with every beat of my heart. My lungs kept sucking in air, but that air gave no relief. I suffocated.

We crossed that line again, the one separating the Barrows from the rest of the world. That, I could feel. Everything grew cold and numb. I passed beyond pain, closer to the realm of death.

"Can you help her?" the angel asked someone. Had we stopped? Had they taken me to a hospital? There would be no healing for me there. How could they treat venom from a creature that shouldn't exist?

"I don't know." A woman's voice. "Put her on the bed. I need to see how bad it is."

I forced my eyes to focus. The woman stood over me. My senses barely functioned, but I recognized an earth witch. Her magic was as clear as my mother's. It gave her a soft gold aura. I remembered Mother Evelyn's words. *You now look and act like a Sister. A witch will not likely harm you, but neither will one provide you with aid, should you need it. You must depend only upon yourself.*

But this witch could not help me, even if she desired to do so. The one secret I kept from the Sisters at Justice was the one that threatened my life now: While I can feel it, I am completely immune to the effects of earth magic. I couldn't be harmed by it, but I couldn't be healed by it either.

I could feel her undressing me with less-than-gentle hands.

"Let me help," the angel said.

I didn't want him to see me like that. I tried to speak, to say no, but it came out as a moan.

The witch hissed. They'd stripped off my pants. She'd turned my body and seen the tattoos, the art that marked me as a Sister of Justice and possible enemy of any witch. "What is it?" the angel asked.

"Nothing. Take that thing from around her neck," the witch demanded. She referred to Sister Eunice's amulet, her last gift to me.

They'd covered me with a blanket and I tried to draw it closer. Lying on my side now, I could see my fingers. I couldn't feel them.

The angel came close, kneeling beside the bed. I realized that I was probably in shock.

The witch touched me, murmuring softly. I grew colder. I knew her efforts were hopeless.

"I can't help her," the witch said. "For some reason, I can't reach her."

"No!" My angel sounded like he cared.

I would have smiled, but the paralysis from the Drow's venom was almost complete.

A voice filled my mind, filled the room, filled the whole world. I could feel magic and power in its words.

"Use the scar."

The witch rolled me over and slapped her hand against my cheek. My body convulsed.

"Hold her," she said.

The angel had me in his arms again. As he turned me on my side, I saw . . . her. She stood to the side of the room—a specter with an incredible aura of power. The Earth Mother had come to witness my passing back into her realm, into the cauldron of death and rebirth. I couldn't speak, couldn't scream in rage at her. I couldn't express every filthy name I'd called her over the years. While I understood she would not intervene with most of humanity, I'd never understood why she wouldn't save my mother, one of hers, a witch who loved her. She let my mother die a horrifying death and did not help her. Now she had come to torment me in my last minutes.

I could hate. I poured every bit of my remaining life into that hatred.

"Peace, daughter."

Gentle words came into my mind, drifting like a thin cloud of smoke.

I refused to let the hatred waver.

"I understand. I watch you. Know that I am proud of your courage."

As her ghostly figure faded, so did my consciousness.

chapter 7

June 21

I woke in a room, warm and comfortable, something I hadn't done since the morning before my parents' murder. I lay quiet, unmoving, a bit bewildered, allowing sound to seep in. Birdsong came and street traffic hissed and hummed at a distance. For now, little would disturb this place of peace. I opened my eyes and saw the half-open window, a window covered with white lace curtains. Memory of the night before spun through my mind and gradually subsided.

I slowly sat up. The covers fell away from my naked body. My shoulder? I rubbed my fingers across it. Sore, but not bad. Scars? Nothing disfiguring, like on my face. The thing's teeth had poked four-inch-deep holes in my shoulder. Whitish marks remained, but those would probably fade. The witch had done a good job of healing me, but only with the intervention of the Earth Mother. A surprise, really, given the vile, hateful thoughts I'd sent her way. I couldn't figure out why she was proud of me either.

The chair beside the bed held folded clothes—jeans and a T-shirt. Sister Eunice's amulet lay there, too. No sign of my knife, wallet, or jacket. I slid my legs over the side of the bed and pulled the pants on as far as they would go. I tried to stand—and plopped back down. I had seriously miscalculated my strength. My legs tingled. The bed had a cast-iron headboard. I drew a deep breath, grabbed it, and hoisted myself up. And sat back down again. I put on the shirt while I rested. The tingling in my legs lessened, but they began to itch. They were not ready for serious action.

Last night I'd saved the angel from one of the Drows. I'd been a hero. And then he'd helped the witch undress me. Humiliation, ugh. Yes, I knew he wasn't really an angel—and he kept close company with an earth witch who obviously disliked the Sisters.

I tried to stand again. Better. I seemed to be standing on tiny needles, but the room stayed right-side up. I didn't know what had happened to my shoes, but I slid the amulet over my neck and tucked it under my shirt.

I could hear the faint sound of voices through the open bedroom door. Holding on to the wall, I headed in that direction. As I came closer . . .

"What does Mom say?" A woman's voice.

"We are not to interfere." Ah, the witch. Dismay filled her voice.

I entered the kitchen, clinging to the wall as I did.

The fragrance that filled the air smelled of lavender and citrus, and strangely enough, home. Like my mother's kitchen.

The pregnant redhead I'd seen with the angel yesterday sat at a round table covered with a homey red-checkered cloth. The witch sat by her. The redhead was still pregnant, still smiling. She turned that smile on me. She had tiny freckles across her nose and happiness in her eyes.

The witch did not smile. She watched me with relentless and unfriendly eyes. She was a woman with silver hair and the ageless face some powerful witches attain after many years of service. I'd met a couple of those as a child. As I started to mature, Mother kept me away, not wanting them to ask about me and magic. She didn't like to admit her daughter had no power at all.

"Good morning," the witch said. Her voice carried a note of caution. "Sit and let me make you some tea and food. They'll help you regain strength." She rose. "My name is Abigail."

The healing this witch had performed on me required that she give me a part of herself, her own life. My mother had taught me the polite—and cautious—greeting. "Honor to you, Abigail. Innana's Daughter, I thank you for your gift."

Abigail smiled, but it carried irony, not warmth. "Well, at least you have manners. This is Cassandra." She nodded at the redhead.

I wobbled to the chair and slowly lowered myself.

Cassandra chuckled. "Oh, Abby, she reminds me of the good old days. Burns, broken bones, monster bites. I don't know how I live without it." And to me, "What's your name?"

"Madeline."

"Well, Madeline, are you my replacement? The new Huntress?"

"No!" Abigail spit the word out. "She cannot be." She shook her head and turned back to the stove.

Cassandra frowned. "Oh, shit. The Mother is at it again. She's got some secret scheme, manipulating and— Fuck it. I hate it when she does this."

"Don't curse, Cassandra. Your babies can hear it." Abigail came back to the table with a steaming cup she placed in front of me. It smelled awful, but I knew it would help.

Cassandra sighed. "Take your medicine, Madeline, and she'll let you have some coffee."

Abigail stared at the tablecloth, then lifted her eyes to me. She was obviously distressed. "Will you tell us why you are here?"

Did she think I was a Sister, sent to kill a witch? "I need to find someone."

"Very well." Her voice tightened. "I did not refuse to help you last night, Madeline. But once you leave here, I'll ask that you not return."

"Abby?" Cassandra sounded shocked. "What's going on?"

Abigail's face turned bleak as winter in upstate New York. "She belongs to the Sisters of Justice. Assassins. Killers."

"Executioners." I stupidly allowed the word to pop out of my mouth before I thought.

Cassandra's eyes narrowed. "Now is the time you explain, Abby."

Cassandra's curls moved and a small red and black

snake appeared. It slid down her arm to the table and coiled in her hand. I heard a growl. I glanced down. A brown and black ferret sat by my foot. Its lips drew back to reveal teeth that might belong to a badger.

Cassandra wasn't a witch. But she had familiars. *Huntress*, she had called herself. I'd have to figure out what that meant later.

Abigail told Cassandra essentially the same story Mother Evelyn had told me. Cassandra listened without interrupting. Then she said, "So, what's your problem, Abby? You don't think witches who work black magic should be taken out? Or does it upset you that your precious Earth Mother has a dark side? That she employs killers as well as witches?"

I smiled and sipped the foul tea. Cassandra cut through things with razor-sharp words. I liked it. Abigail stood and walked out the back door.

"Damn," Cassandra said. "Now I've upset her." Far less affable now, she narrowed her eyes. "But I still consider the Barrows mine. I suggest you tell me who you're here to kill."

I set the teacup on the saucer. I formulated what I hoped would be a believable scenario. Her deadly familiars would probably strike at her command. "I've been sent to retrieve an object from a thief. I will do what is necessary to obtain it, but I'm not here as an assassin."

The snake crawled onto my hand. I sat very still. Cassandra nodded. She relaxed, apparently accepting my statement, at least. "From the sound of it, the Earth Mother is definitely playing chess with us again. Abby's gang of witches and your Sisters are her game pieces." She sighed with what seemed begrudging acceptance. She shifted her body awkwardly. "There's nothing we can do about it. But thank you for saving Michael's life last night. The Archangel is very dear to me."

"Archangel?"

"Michael. That's what people call him. He runs the Archangel Studio down on River Street. Tall, blond, perfect body, perfect face. He owns the Goblin Den, too. I talked to him this morning. He told me what happened." She grinned. "You really impressed him. He told me how beautiful, wonderful, and courageous you are. You hadn't met him before you saved him?" She leaned forward, obviously intrigued.

I shook my head. Now I could put a name to the angel's face. Michael. I tried not to think how he saw me last night, bloody and convulsing—dying. But he had called me beautiful, wonderful, and courageous? Surely he exaggerated for her.

Another thought struck me. If he owned the Goblin Den, he was my employer. I didn't know how that would affect me yet, but it made my own feelings complicated.

The snake apparently decided I was okay and left me and returned to her. I managed to hold tight while the ferret licked my toes. I'd been accepted but was neither friend nor enemy yet.

"You don't talk much, do you?" Cassandra echoed Riggs's words.

"No." I smiled at her. I felt a kinship with this

woman. That kinship had no place in my life right now, any more than the man she called the Archangel, but I appreciated her warmth as I had appreciated Lillian's in the cold halls of Justice.

Cassandra laughed. "Maybe we can have a spirited conversation after I squeeze out this litter. I'm told there are only two, but I have my doubts."

I wanted to know who she was and her relationship to the Earth Mother, whom she had called *Mom.* For my own mother to speak of the Mother Goddess in such a manner would have been blasphemy. And yet the witch, Abigail, took no offense.

Abigail came through the back door. Her demeanor had changed. She was polite, but not warm. She insisted on feeding me. Cassandra gave me a pair of sneakers and more clothes. Apparently, she had lived at Abigail's house at one time. Jeans and shirts, but I was grateful. Abigail returned my knife, wrapped in a soft cloth. "I cleaned it for you. If the bites were poisonous, the blood might be, as well. I burned your jacket, too."

Cassandra insisted on driving me to the room I called home, though I wondered how she could reach the gas pedal and brake in her condition.

"Madeline." Abigail stopped me as I started to follow Cassandra out. She laid a hand on my shoulder. "The Mother has a plan. She trusts you to carry it out."

"Maybe. But I don't trust her. I despise her."

"Oh, I do understand. She has her schemes, and as Cassandra often says, we are merely puppets made of blood, muscle, and bone." She sighed. "I believe she does care about us in her own way, though. Nevertheless, please forgive my earlier words. If you are hurt, or become ill, come to me. I'm a healer. I should be above such angry personal feelings. I respond to need, not politics."

"Thank you." I admired her control, that she could put aside a witch's natural concerns to aid me.

"I do not understand why I couldn't heal you using my regular methods. Why I had to go through the scar. The Mother is absolutely silent on that one matter."

She frowned and shook her head. "Will you tell me why they sent someone inexperienced to this dangerous place? You're more than a novice, but not a full Sister. Are you a rogue? Will they show up on my doorstep looking for you?"

"No. I have an assignment. As I told Cassandra, it involves retrieval rather than assassination, though assassination might be the result." I stayed with the simple truth; a powerful witch could easily pick out a lie.

Mother Evelyn had warned me. A complex and justifiably uncomfortable relationship apparently existed between the Sisters of Justice and the earth witches. I'd seen it in my own home growing up. My mother had definitely played politics, constantly on the phone with other witches, chattering. As a young girl, I had thought them cool, that confab of the keepers of the world's magic. I wasn't sure what to think of them now.

chapter 8

Cassandra drove. I didn't know much about Duivel, but it seemed we were north of the Barrows. When we reached River Street, she turned the car toward Duivel. "I spent ten years working in the Barrows," she said. "I wish I could help you, but I don't know what's going on around here anymore. Things have changed since I went into Mommy mode. I can do one thing, though. Nirah and Tau say I can trust you. Abby and Mom are going to be totally pissed, but I'm going to do this anyway."

"Nirah and Tau?"

"Snake with venom and rodent with big teeth." The snake remained in her hair, but the ferret had crawled under my seat.

She drove north through the suburbs and into the outskirts of Duivel. After a few minutes, she pulled into the parking lot of the Down Wind Gun Range. The parking lot looked like pickup truck central. The range itself was blocked by twelve-foot-high earthen walls. When we climbed out, Cassandra opened the trunk and handed me a satchel. "This is my gun. Shoulder holster, too. Now they're yours. I'll put you in touch with my bronze bullet guy. I have a couple of hundred rounds I'll give you, too. In the meantime, I'll get you some regulars to practice with." She grinned. "If I know Mom, she's sent you here with no money and an impossible task to fulfill."

I had absolutely no money at all after my evening had been interrupted with violence. Kelly had probably absconded with my few tips.

"Bronze bullets?" I accepted the satchel. I'd spent hours learning to shoot. Sister Eunice and the others had me crawl through the woods and creep silently through an abandoned warehouse, miles from Justice. I was no stranger to a gun.

"When I came here, there were all kinds of monsters in the Barrows' ruins. The only thing that would kill them were weapons of bronze or massive trauma. The Earth Mother sent me into the Barrows at eighteen, carrying only a bronze knife. My job was to rescue kids in danger who'd been kidnapped, lured into, or ran away to the Barrows. My husband, Flynn—his sister was one of those kids. That's how I met him. There are things in the Barrows that would've visited unspeakable things on those kids. Still, Abby and Mom frowned on guns. 'Bullets are not bronze' was always Abby's excuse." She laughed, a joyous sound for such a deadly subject. "Well, I found someone to make bronze bullets and I used them. Jump one of those things in the Barrows with just a knife and the probability of you surviving is virtually zero."

I had to smile. "Yes, I know that now."

She drew the gun from the satchel. "If you'd had this last night, you could have saved yourself a lot of pain."

I accepted the satchel and we headed into the range. Everyone, mostly men, stared when we walked in, but for once not at me. The very pregnant woman waddling in front of me received all the attention. Two hailed Cassandra by name; another called her Huntress. Others carefully stepped out of her way. The manager followed us, nervous but unobtrusive. Huntress. The finder of lost children.

Cassandra paid for me to practice on stationary targets and run a course where cardboard figures popped up out of nowhere. To my delight and the gun range manager's dismay, she followed me and cheered me on. I tried to match her enthusiasm but wound up sore, dirty, and aching.

I was amazed at the power of Abigail the witch. Last night, I had lain paralyzed and dying, seemingly beyond saving. And yet, at the Mother's command, Abigail had drawn from the purest magic of the earth and channeled it through herself—enough power to not only save me but return me to good physical shape. The Mother had also told her how to heal me using the scar. A strong spell like that weakened a witch for a while. Abigail would pay a price for what she freely gave me.

When we finished, Cassandra grabbed me and gave me an awkward hug. She wanted to be friends. I wasn't sure it was something I could deal with. I'd spent all those years at Justice as a loner, living only to fight and learn my lessons.

"Will you tell me about Michael?" I asked once we were back in the car. We were headed toward the Barrows and stalled in traffic. "Or is it too personal?"

"No, not that personal. I heard him talking about what you did last night. You made a powerful impression on him. But there are things you need to know about Michael. He's not exactly like everyone else. He's—" She stopped, as if she'd heard something. Then silence filled the car as the clamor of the street disappeared. Cassandra froze, her hands gripping the steering wheel with great intensity. Alarmed, I started to touch her arm when her breath hissed through her teeth. In a moment, everything returned to normal.

"I'm sorry, but I can't tell you anything. I've been told that you have to learn about Michael on your own."

I stared at her. "You receive instructions from the Earth Mother? Did she just talk to you?" I tried not to sound incredulous. I'd heard—even seen—the Mother myself last night, but that was the first time, and the situation had been critical. On rare occasions, she spoke to my mother, who described it as a profoundly religious experience. Cassandra, who was not a witch, was on speaking terms with what my mother considered a goddess.

Cassandra nodded. "Yes, she talks in my head from time to time. At least she wasn't mad about the gun." I was intrigued, but I decided not to press her.

I looked out the window. "The Earth Mother abandoned me and my family years ago. I've made my own way since then. I'll do it now, too." She had come to Abigail last night to save my life, but it was not enough to make up for the destruction she allowed to happen. "I despise her."

Cassandra winced at my words. "She gave me strength, the ability to see well in dark places, a killer sense of direction. Madeline, she must've given you something, too, if she sent you here."

"Not that I'm aware of. I'm not a Huntress. Just the daughter of a witch."

Cassandra laughed. "Trust me, the Mother didn't give me much more than that to work with. Everything I learned about fighting, I did on my own or with the help of some special friends. You, at least, had lessons. Maybe that's the Mother's gift to you. That you are trained to fight."

"I would not call my years in prison or at Justice a gift from anyone."

Cassandra sighed. "Mom works in mysterious ways. Like the gun thing. For five years, I rescued children and dodged Bastinados with fists and knives. Thank goodness that I had Abby to love me, heal me, and provide sanctuary when things got rough. When I took the gun off a Bastinado, Mom wasn't happy."

"Why?" I asked. It seemed like a logical thing to do.

"Mom lives in the past. Knives, not guns; that's her way."

Cassandra's casual use of *Mom* for the sacred Earth Mother still amazed me. I rubbed the blister on my finger and flexed my sore wrist.

"I think that's the idea," Cassandra said. "She didn't

want me to do callous killing at a distance. For me to become a cold-blooded killer."

"Cold-blooded killer? Like the Sisters of Justice? How hypocritical—and typical."

"The Earth Mother doesn't live by our ideas of justice. She's ancient. In the past, she was worshipped, or at the very least respected."

"That was thousands of years ago," I reminded her. "Time to evolve."

Cassandra sighed. "I know. You'd think things would get better. But she's been even worse lately. A lot of it has to do with what happened a couple of years ago. There was a dark moon conjunction—stars lining up and all that shit—and some stuff went down in the Barrows that I don't even totally understand. It changed the Barrows. It changed her. I know it changed me a lot."

I was confused by her vague words. "Is this conjunction something you're allowed to talk about?"

"No. This, and Michael, are off-limits." She saw my look of annoyance.

"One thing to remember, Madeline: She's not human. She plots, plans, and schemes, never consistently. She sees possibilities of things to come and dumps one of us into the fray in hopes that things will turn out okay. There's not much you can do about it. She considers you hers, even if you never took a vow to serve her. She thinks meddling in your life is her right. The bad thing is, she once told me she has rules she has to follow, just like us." She shivered and laid an arm across her stomach, across her babies. "Someone, something, is more powerful than she is. I don't like to think about who—or what—that is."

Cassandra had given me many things to think about. That the Earth Mother had to answer to some higher power was beyond what my small mind could conceive.

We drove south on River Street and Cassandra dropped me off at Harry's. Before she left me there, she said, "When I made my vow, Mom promised me compensation. It happened, but I had to earn it. The gifts she gave me, strength and speed, were simply tools to help me do my job. I got my reward, though. I got my husband, Flynn, and this." She rubbed a loving hand over her bulging belly.

"A reward?" I shook my head. Her halfhearted attempt to convince me of the fairness of the Earth Mother and the burdens she had to bear didn't move me. The Sisters fought, but at least they were trained. The Earth Mother had thrown Cass into the shit without a thought. "Cassandra, from what you say, it seems to me like its payment for a job. A dangerous job that almost killed you several times. She owes you more."

She gave a faint smile. After I waved good-bye to her, I had to get another key from Harry since mine was in my jacket, which Abigail said she burned. He wasn't happy about it. I went upstairs and sorted the clothes Cassandra had given me. Jeans, knit shirts, and best of all, a light, comfortable jacket that would cover my knife, and—if I wore it—the gun. I shoved the satchel to the back of a shelf in my tiny closet. It was actually a problem for me at the moment. Eunice had taught me that if you have a weapon and go around flashing it where everyone can see it, some hothead would challenge you to use it. Eunice, however, loved a good battle and would occasionally go out of her way to pick a fight, especially with me. I had no inclination to do so myself.

A knock came at the door. I drew my knife and held it ready.

When I opened the door, Riggs stood there.

He glanced at the knife. "Who are you expecting?"

"Not you." I let him in.

He handed me a bag. "Here's a new uniform. Last night's tips and a week's advance on salary. In case you need anything."

A week seemed generous, but maybe he was feeling guilty. His only warning to me had been "Stay in the light." I accepted the money.

He stared around at my room; then his attention came back to me. "When I came out the back door last night . . . I've never seen anything like that."

"Do you know what it was?"

"The thing you killed? No. They started coming into the Barrows about eight months ago. But that's not what I mean. You . . . across the lot . . . You almost flew up to meet the thing. I didn't think anyone could move that fast. Who are you?"

"Your bartender." If I wouldn't answer questions for an earth witch, I certainly wouldn't answer his.

Riggs picked up on my reticence. "Michael said he'd see you later. Would you take tonight off? Maybe rest?"

The workout at the gun range had left me exhausted. I could probably recover, but . . . "Rest would be good."

Riggs had taken both the Drow attack and my miraculous healing in stride. What had he seen that inured him to such things?

"Is it okay if I wear my knife tomorrow night?"

"You do whatever makes you comfortable."

I thanked him. After he left, I counted my money. The week's advance was more than minimum wage. I'd be okay for at least a month. I realized the whole incident with Michael and the Drow had set me on a different path. When I hunted the first two men, I completely shut out any unnecessary interaction with others around me. That way wouldn't work here. My mission to return the Portal to the Sisters and kill the third murderer had taken a more complex turn.

Michael owned the Goblin Den. He would probably come in and thank me. Not something I would relish, but it was inevitable. He'd have questions I might not be able to answer, but he might answer some of mine. Sometimes people answered my questions just to get rid of me. The scar and my hair made them anxious to get away. I realized things were different here, though. Riggs wasn't like that; nor was Hildy. Even Abigail and Cassandra saw past my odd appearance. The people I truly connected with took no note of it.

What would Michael think? My connection with him was something so odd and new to me, I had no clue.

Of course, I had a mission that came with the scar. I couldn't forget that.

I took out the picture of the third killer and headed out. I had a copy made at the small grocery store so I'd have an extra. I walked the street heading south, going into every business that was open. I gave each a story as to why I wanted the man. I told the pawnshop owner he owed me money. The owner could relate to that. So did the waitress at a small café that was closing for the day. I helped an elderly woman carry her packages up the stairs to her apartment and said he was my long-lost brother. Then I crossed River Street and made my way back up to Harry's. I'd learned nothing.

When I got back to the apartment, I lay across the bed. I didn't wake until after dark. Well after dark. I showered at midnight and crawled back into bed. I had one nightmare, one I'd never had before.

I heard the sound of my knife as I killed the first murderer. It hit a rib and scraped along the bone before it punched into his heart. The sense of satisfaction I felt at that moment filled me again—followed by the sick sound of his dying breath.

I jerked awake. Only silence filled the room. Remembering the dream, I also remembered the intense shame and guilt that had plagued me after that first kill. Shame that I had killed the man, shame that I had enjoyed it—shame that quickly dissolved as I locked into the hunt for the next one. I quickly fell back to sleep. I opened my eyes a little before dawn, cold in spite of the warm room.

chapter 9

June 22

The same cloud of noxious fumes greeted me as I walked into the pawnshop a little after ten that morning. Hildy stood behind the counter, cigarette in hand, just as she had when I walked in for the first time yesterday morning. She wore the same horribly wrinkled clothes.

She frowned at me. "Didn't take you long to get in trouble."

I shrugged. "Someone needed my help."

"The Sisters of Justice aren't about helping."

"I'm not about the Sisters of Justice." I couldn't tell if she was bitter or angry.

"And, of course, you saved that man." Sarcasm filled her words.

"How do you know about that?" I presumed Michael was that man.

"I know everything in the Barrows. Riggs called me."

"An accident, Hildy. I happened to be there when the thing attacked. I'm trained to fight, and I reacted."

She grunted. "Okay. You get one warning. That man, that Michael, is demon spawn. Do not get sucked in by his beauty."

Annoyance flared in my gut. "Of all the hypocritical . . . If he's so bad, why did you send me to work in a business he owns?" I shoved my hands in my pockets and glared at her.

It was too late not to get sucked into anything with Michael. I was already there. Hildy stared out the window, and I could almost feel the turmoil in her mind over my apparently stunning revelation. I felt a little smug. Apparently there was something about the Barrows Hildy didn't know—that Michael owned the Goblin's Den.

"Hildy?" She jerked when I spoke. "Do you happen to have a knife sheath? Mine went missing last night."

Hildy grabbed her cigarettes and squeezed them, probably crushing them beyond use. Seemed like she was still absorbed by the news. She spoke softly, with only a little wheeze. "In the back. First door on the right."

Through the door, into a dark hallway, I discovered why she called the place the Armory. Like the barrier around the Barrows, the first door on the right was protected by a ward. No doorknob, only a wall of power. I ran my hand down it, feeling its weight. It whispered with welcome and the door opened. I walked into a bright, spotlessly clean, long, high-ceilinged room filled with instruments of bloody death, lovingly collected and cherished. Nothing here would be for sale.

Racks on the walls held swords and spears, fine

edged, pointed, and barbed, and barbaric axes a Viking berserker would love. Some were tied with brightly colored ribbons, crimson and sapphire, marking the owner's tribe or clan. Even the decorated halls of Justice did not have such a murderous display. Long, glass, table-type display cases around the room offered a glimpse at a multitude of different knives. Some of the weapons seemed new, but others carried the patina of age. Some called to me. Like phantoms, they spoke in my mind. *Choose me*, they whispered. *I'll kill for you. I hunger; give me blood.*

Only my own breathing broke the silence of that room.

A single knife lay on top of a glass display case, as if someone had placed it there for me. Who had forged such a beautiful thing? Was it . . . ? It was. Bronze. Harder than iron, softer than steel, the metal that evil not of this world feared.

Longer than Sister Lillian's blade, this knife would fit nicely on my hip. I moved closer. An ache filled me, a longing to touch it. Runes etched in the metal seemed to crawl across the surface. The smooth bone hilt appeared small, made for a woman's hand. *I'm yours*, it murmured. *My edges are honed; my point is sharp. Take me.*

"You may choose one, if you like." I whirled to find Hildy standing behind me.

I drew a deep breath. "I learned my lessons at Justice, Hildy, and these blades have to be earned. I can't just pick one up."

All were imbued with magic. If I did choose one,

would it then own me? My mother's lessons were clear on that. Objects that carried supernatural power could also have power over their possessors.

"Are none of them speaking to you?" Hildy asked.

"Yes. Some of them call. I can feel magic. I told you that."

"This is the Barrows. Sometimes bronze weapons carry as much weight as magic."

"That's . . . interesting." So many new ideas had bombarded me in the last two days.

"Don't you think you've earned one of these?" She waved her hand around the room.

My gaze went back to the rune-carved knife. I held my hand over it and it sang in my mind. *Death. I am death. Choose me.* The perfect weapon for a killer. An assassin. I lowered my hand. A sense of power filled me. Life, death—all mine to control.

I stood divided. A part of me mourned my beloved parents but wished to walk away from the pain and loss forever and live my life. The other part of me was a killer, a killer driven by my mother's dying curse to avenge hers and my father's deaths.

"I am not a Sister, Hildy. I want to kill a man who harmed people I love. I do not wish to kill for any other reason."

Hildy came to stand beside me. "A blade is just that, Madeline, as easily used for defense as offense. You will need to defend yourself here." Her voice softened, sounding both sad and resigned.

I remembered Sister Lillian's words when she gave me her knife. *Use it wisely and honorably.* I laid my hand on the hilt, the beautiful thing, and picked it up. It no longer spoke in my mind. It hummed and became a part of me, like an extension of my arm.

I lifted it to the light. The runes along the blade shimmered. "I was told yesterday that the Earth Mother is playing chess with the lives she considers under her power. That she has some great secret plan, and we're all just pawns."

Hildy laughed loudly and broke into a coughing spasm. "Why do you think I live here, out of her reach?" She nodded toward a cabinet on the wall. "Sheaths are there."

Did Hildy really believe she was out of reach of the Earth Mother? Even though she was protected by the ward from the Earth Mother herself, the Sisters of Justice wouldn't hesitate to come here. They served the Mother with deadly purpose. If Hildy crossed any lines or seriously broke any rules, they would kill her in this place as easily as any other. The idea that a person could live out of the reach of the Earth Mother seemed implausible and impossible.

Had something happened to Hildy, something she could not bear, something that drove her from the Sisters? How and why did she come to be the mistress of this Armory of very special deadly weapons? I doubted I'd ever find the answers to those questions.

After we exited the weapons room, Hildy opened a fresh pack and lit up. She sucked the smoke into her lungs with great enthusiasm. My hint to leave. I made my way to the door with a new forearm sheath of thin leather for Sister Lillian's shorter knife and the new bronze blade in a sheath on my hip. I had an extra sheath that allowed me to carry Sister Lillian's knife hooked to the back of my jeans at the waist, just in case I needed my arms bare. Hildy had also given me a cleaning kit and cloths.

Cassandra's gift jacket was long enough to cover the knife on my forearm, the one at my waist, and the gun, if I chose to carry it. I wore the comfortable shoes she had given me.

Okay, supernatural evil, Drows, whatever. Bring it on. At least that's what I told myself. After a while, I realized my anticipation revolved not around a battle, or even my search for the Portal, but when I would see Michael again. I chastised myself even as I smiled at the thought. The smile faded as I walked out of the Armory and found him waiting for me.

chapter 10

Michael leaned against his Jaguar, which he'd parked directly in front of the store. It was long and sleek, with a small stylized version of an angel painted on the side of the front fender. His dress was casual—khaki slacks and a pure white shirt—but they made my T-shirt, jeans, and sneakers—perfectly acceptable on most occasions—look shabby. His white-gold hair shimmered like a halo in the morning sun. He cocked his head and smiled.

I forced myself to breathe. The connection, that thing that drew me to him that first day, jumped to life. How had this happened? How should I deal with it?

"Good morning," he said. "I wanted to thank you for saving my life." His voice was deep and low, but sweet as golden honey and smooth as fine oil. "Maybe get to know you under better circumstances."

I remembered he'd seen me naked and dying. Appalled, my face burned. I wanted to leave. "I have to get ready to go to work." How pathetic was that?

Soft laughter rippled through him. "You work for me, Madeline."

"Yes." Suddenly drowning in more unbidden and confusing emotion than I'd felt in years, I didn't really know how to react. I focused on the street and refused to look into his eyes.

He held out a hand. "Yes, you work for me? Or yes, I may get to know you?"

I could smell him. My mind marked his scent, clean and bright with a hint of precious sandalwood.

I turned away. "I need to go."

He caught my arm as I turned. His hand had a loose grip, but it might have been a chain. I couldn't move. "Please, Madeline, come ride with me. Talk to me. You . . ." His voice trailed off, as if he was uncertain what to say. Why should such a man hesitate?

Something was happening with me and this undeniably attractive man. That much was obvious. I had no clue what it might be. What did he want? I had faced a Drow for the man. Surely I could face *him*.

I held up the bag with the knife-cleaning supplies Hildy had given me. "Okay. Let me go and put this away."

"I'll be right here." He released my arm.

I dodged traffic and crossed the street without looking back. When I reached Harry's doorway, I stopped and drew a deep breath. I turned to see Hildy come out of the pawnshop and speak to Michael. *Demon spawn*, she'd called him. I bet that conversation was interesting.

Michael should be moderately grateful to me for saving his life, but there were lots of ways he could be grateful that didn't involve such personal contact.

I watched as he spoke with Hildy. She stood firm, feet planted and arms crossed. He remained loose and graceful. She whirled and stalked back into the pawnshop.

Eunice stalked like that. Eunice stalked everywhere. Amazing, but I thought I missed Eunice a tiny bit.

I carried my bag upstairs, then went to the bathroom and splashed my face with cold water. Getting through the next few hours would be difficult. I stared in the mirror and studied my appearance, something I'd avoided for years. I laid my hand over the scar. Would he be embarrassed to be seen with someone like me? I jerked my hand away. I'm Madeline, white-haired, scar-faced Madeline. I lived with it. He could too, or he could leave me alone.

Just as I was about to leave, I realized that I carried two knives. I wondered if I should remove them but decided against it. If danger followed us, I would be ready for it.

When I went back down and across the street, Michael opened the Jag's door and I slid into pure luxury. Smooth cushioned leather, silver gray, tucked, padded, and shaped to perfectly conform to the human body. It smelled new and opulent. He climbed in and shut the door, and the hiss and roar of traffic subsided to a murmur. With a touch of his finger, the engine started. That, too, was barely audible.

Wealth suited the man. An aura of riches clung to him like the aura of poverty clung to a sidewalk beggar. He held the wheel with perfect hands, long fingers, precisely manicured nails. The Jag eased smoothly into a stream of traffic. As if another vehicle would dare strike such a superb machine.

The closeness of the car created, for me, an uncomfortable intimacy.

"Hildy told me you were looking for someone," he said.

Well, damn. Hildy was a broken sewer pipe spewing shit. She had no business spreading word of my mission around.

"She asked if I'd help you find him," he said. "She said he hurt someone you loved."

"Hildy talks too much."

Michael shrugged. "It does seem odd. She's not known for long conversations."

"I thought you were arguing with her."

He gave a good-humored chuckle. "A small running feud she and I have. It amuses us."

I didn't point out that Hildy hadn't looked amused.

Michael slowed the car for a light. "Hildy seems to care for you, though, and thinks you're in danger. That you haven't been given enough information to help you survive here in the Barrows."

I said nothing. I tried to stare straight ahead, but my eyes kept cutting toward him. When they did, I caught him looking back. Whatever possessed me affected him, too, though I doubted it tore at him as savagely as it did me.

He drove down River Street, straight for the Goblin Den, but turned onto the cul-de-sac where the road ended and a large wooden sign proclaimed the marsh beyond to be Sullen Bog.

He turned off the engine. "I want to show you something. Explain something."

I climbed out where the road dropped off and the mucky brown stuff began. A glint of open water lay out there, single ponds near the small islands that dotted the horizon. I'd bet that Sullen Bog was a treacherous place for people. A flimsy wooden rail fence barred the end of the road. The center of the fence looked new, as if more than one car had missed the turn at the cul-de-sac and plowed into the muck.

A smaller sign attached to the fence proclaimed the wet expanse to be Sullen Bog Wildlife Sanctuary. Fast-moving water wouldn't freeze in the winter, but the shallows would. Any wildlife there was safe, even without the dubious protection of the sign.

Michael came close to me. Too close. The gesture bordered on intimate. He turned back to face Duivel, straight up the gentle hill of River Street to the distant buildings of the city. "I was born here in the Barrows, about six blocks from where you live. It's part of the ruins now. You do see the ruins, don't you?"

"I see them. No one's told me what happened."

Michael nodded. "The truth is only partially known. Sometime between 1930 and 1950 there was an earthquake . . . or something like it. Maybe a series of earthquakes. Most of the infrastructure collapsed. The Barrows was so named because so many men died building it in the late 1800s. After the earthquake, people moved out. Then, people seemed to forget it existed. I've heard a number of versions, but this is what oral history tells us. If it was once written, I think it's been removed from any official records. The important thing is, it's been forgotten for a reason. It's not a good place to be, especially the Zombie Zone."

"I've heard of it."

He laughed softly. "Hildy tell you about it? Sounds like you don't need me to guide you."

A pause. "I don't know. I don't know anything about you."

A smile curved his mouth. "Shall I tell you a story about myself, then?"

"A story? That implies fiction. I'm only interested in facts."

"Once upon a time . . . ," he teased, dangling the words. "No, it's not time to talk about me yet. It'll be easier for me to show you than tell you. Until then, will you tell me something about yourself?"

My nature, my years with the brutally honest Sisters, had marked me with a lack of subtlety. "What do you want from me, Michael?"

He looked directly into my eyes. "Whatever you'll give me."

I drew a breath to speak, then couldn't think of anything to say. So, the connection I felt the first time I'd seen him had affected him, too. I suspected that he had no clue what it meant either.

"I'm sorry," Michael said. "That came out wrong. I want to know more about you. You're incredibly . . . interesting. I'd like to be your . . . friend." He crossed his arms over his chest. Guarding something, holding it close. *Interesting* wasn't what he started to say. Neither was *friend*.

Since I had no time for games, I decided to see how he would deal with me. "All right, friend, here's a show of faith. My name is Madeline Corso. I'm twenty-six years old. I've spent the last six years in a combination prison/paramilitary training college, where they taught me how to do a lot of things, most of them not very nice. My mother was an earth witch like Abigail, my father a retired soldier turned restaurateur. One night when I was seventeen, three men came into our home and murdered them. I'm here looking for one of those men."

Michael raised an eyebrow. "And when you find him?"

I shrugged.

He focused on me for a moment, his eyes blue and clear as the sky above. Then he looked back out over the Bog for a long time before he spoke. When someone takes that long to figure out what to say, odds are good he's holding back his opinion—like what he really thought of my need for revenge.

"I need a bouncer," he said. "At the Den."

I laughed. "I'm a bartender."

A smile turned up the corner of his mouth. I could almost read that thought: *A bartender who spent the last six years in a prison/paramilitary training college where they taught you to do many things, most of them not very nice.*

I raised an eyebrow and let my skepticism show.

"Pay is ten times what you'd make as a bartender. And I'll help you find your man. If he's in the Barrows, I will locate him." The smooth confidence returned.

"Right. I'll relax and let you do everything." It

sounded like a bit of a ploy. *I like you, so let me take over your mission, your life.*

"No. No. I mean if you need time off to search, you can have it." He sounded flustered. How could such a magnificent man become so unsettled? Surely it could not be my doing.

I turned away and promptly rationalized. I could use the money. And I could insist on wearing proper clothes.

Damn. I hated that I had to hold down a job while I was here. They shouldn't have sent me from Justice almost broke. Of course, I foolishly spent the last of what they did give me on a flying mini-dragon that had immediately deserted me.

I faced him. "I'll take the job. No promises on how long I'll stay, though."

Michael grinned. "Good. Now, will you let me show you around the Barrows? I think there are things you need to know, things Hildy *hasn't* told you yet."

I nodded. It seemed like a good deal. Too good. Work as a bouncer and see my new world from the comfort of a Jag. But could I trust him? He'd given me a bit of information about the Barrows, but none about himself or the event that Cassandra referred to. No, I wouldn't trust him yet. I'd have to rely on myself for the mission. With a little luck and a little searching, I might come across the third murderer, or even the Portal.

chapter 11

The sun was directly overhead as Michael drove north on River Street, away from the Barrows but still within that magical barrier of the ward. Summer stood poised to bless everything in the city. More prosperous businesses flourished here. Auto parts stores, gas stations, a small discount store—commerce far more benign than the sex and liquor trade farther to the south. I'd traveled, searching for the killers, but I'd never been to a place like Duivel and the Barrows.

Michael turned into the almost full parking lot of a restaurant called the River House Café, into a spot marked RESERVED—TOW AWAY ZONE. He turned off the engine but didn't move to get out.

"I want you to meet Oonagh," he said.

"Who?" It sounded like he was clearing his throat.

"She's the owner of this place." He saw the look of skepticism on my face. "Just trust me."

I didn't, but I'd go along with it for now.

"How good of an actress are you?" he asked.

"Fair. Depends on how observant the audience is."

After six years, I'd managed to occasionally fool a few Sisters. Not a small achievement.

"She's sharp, but I'm going to try to keep her focused on me. Meanwhile, I need you to be the observant one."

I frowned at him. "You need to stop being so cryptic and explain yourself." How irritating. He appeared to think everyone accepted what he said at face value, not to be questioned.

He stared at me and I stared back. Obviously, he wasn't used to being challenged. He smiled, but it quickly faded. His voice became more ominous. "Oonagh will probably have learned what happened the other night. I spent all day yesterday raving about your heroism and fighting ability. She's probably heard that, too."

"So?"

"I need to send a message that you can take care of yourself. Oonagh can be . . . dangerous." He climbed out and I followed him. I hated how he left me hanging, teasing me with his words but never quite explaining himself.

River House Café was an unimposing structure on the outside, a rectangular box with windows, but we walked into a most pleasant place decorated in the Mediterranean style my mother loved. Terra-cotta floors, lots of plants in clay pots, ambience galore. The soft whirr of overhead fans stirred air filled with the scent of delicious things.

"Is Oonagh available?" Michael asked the host at the front podium.

The man nodded at the woman strolling toward us.

Tall and slender, Oonagh was an attractive, sophisticated woman in a beautifully draped gray silk dress.
She looked to be about forty. She had a strong square
jaw and rich dark hair that accentuated green eyes.
And she was a witch. I could feel her presence as I had
Abigail's, though she was most certainly not as powerful as Abigail. Abigail burned with magic like a giant
bonfire. Oonagh burned like a candle—a very small
candle. I felt something else, too. Oonagh desired Michael. She longed for Michael and projected that longing with the ferocity of a swelling tidal wave that
would flatten everything in its path.

Michael grasped the hand she extended, leaned forward, and kissed her cheek.

"This is Madeline." Michael flipped a hand at me
but kept his eyes on her.

Oonagh nodded, haughty, imperious. I bet she hated
me on the spot. I had arrived with him, ridden in the
same car with him, and breathed the same air.

If Michael saw Oonagh's adoration, he didn't ac-
knowledge it. He was kind, spoke softly, smiled and
laughed, graceful and lithe as a swan. I suppressed a
sudden spike of jealousy. Even though I knew it was
probably an act, I wondered if he would ever do that
for me.

Oonagh led us to a table in an alcove. At Michael's
invitation, she sat with us. Michael pulled out a chair
for Oonagh like a gentleman. I was his employee. Playing the role of bouncer, the muscle, I briefly scanned the
room, then seated myself in the chair that kept my back
to the wall.

A waiter quickly came and brought crystal glasses of water with no ice and wedges of lemons on the rims. Michael insisted that I order. "All the food here is wonderful," Michael said to me.

I glanced down at the menu. No prices. I kept a straight face. The Barrows wasn't a place for that kind of exclusivity. My father had run an expensive gourmet restaurant and I had worked there all through my teens. Believing that people should know what they were going to pay for, he always put down the prices, no matter how high.

I ordered a salad, though they did have one of my favorites, crab cakes, on the menu. I needed to observe, not eat. I also didn't need to be spoiled and eat food I couldn't afford on a regular basis.

I started to remove my jacket, then stopped. I would have to show the knives if I did. Michael lifted an eyebrow. I was his bouncer. I removed the jacket.

Oonagh froze.

"There's been some trouble at the Den," Michael said, as if his words totally explained everything. "Madeline is my new bouncer. She's quite good at defending my property." He reached out to grasp Oonagh's hand. She instantly relaxed.

I wondered what she would have done if the Sisters' tattoos were on my arms instead of my ass. A witch's power should never be dismissed. Even the weaker ones were capable of wreaking havoc—especially when they felt threatened.

Michael and Oonagh spoke of things I had no interest in. Business, the weather, the coming summer. I tuned out the words to watch her body language. Oonagh spoke to Michael as if he were the only person in the world. Her eyes focused on him and she cocked her head toward him, absorbing every word, every nuance, desperate for a sign of affection. He did not speak to me. She would try to tear my heart out if Michael offered me one scrap of personal consideration in her presence. I wondered exactly how far her obsession would go. Far enough to destroy him if she couldn't possess him? Maybe.

Observe, he had said. The waiters and waitresses were immaculately dressed, with fresh pressed white shirts and black pants. Not happy though. All their smiles were tight and forced. One suddenly met my eyes. He quickly turned away, but not before I saw the fear. Four men lounged at a table in a back corner, men that would make any Godfather proud. They stared at me as if they perceived a threat. They seemed casual, but their body language, tight mouths, and narrow eyes spoke of menace. I lowered my eyes, but I memorized their faces.

A painting nearby was a magnificent floral still life. I'd never seen colors so rich and vibrant—but it looked off, not quite real. Little prickles ran along my arms, and I shivered. I studied the painting. Something shimmered around it, some slight movement of air. Magic? I forced myself to be still, to relax. I lowered my eyes and drew a slow breath. When I opened them, I could see through the spell surrounding the painting. The underlying painting was nice, but nothing special. The rich colors faded and ran together in places.

Something was different about this magic. Caustic and hollow, it bubbled rather than flowed like my mother's earth magic. Though I had no facts to base the fright upon, I was terrified. The fear closed around me and all else disappeared. I stared at the table, squeezed my hands into fists, and silently recited the words I'd learned from the Sisters. *Fear is a gift. Fear is a weapon. I will accept fear and I will not allow it to cripple me.*

After the third recitation, calm returned. The clink of glasses, gentle conversation, and laughter, sometimes strained, sometimes genuine, flowed over me. Inevitably, curiosity rose. Why would a witch waste magic on a painting? Even my mother wasn't that vain.

I raised my eyes.

Another spell swirled around Oonagh, a powerful glamour made of the alien magic that surrounded the painting. The dress she wore, the graceful, pale gray silk, hung on her like a shroud. She wasn't disfigured like me, but she looked as if she was dying. Some atrocious disease wasted her and left her a pitiful old woman. Hideous mottled skin draped over her thin arms, and her eyes burned with a feverish glow. The rich dark hair was gray, and patches of scalp peeked through in places. It was all I could do to keep my eyes averted from her. I also managed to keep my hand from the knife. Something was dreadfully wrong here, and eventually I'd have to find the source of the problem.

I finished the salad, wishing I had more. Michael barely touched his. They stood and said their goodbyes. The waiter never brought a bill, and when Michael asked for it, Oonagh refused to let him pay. Both ignored me, and I stayed as far from them as possible without making it obvious. I did not want to take a chance on physical contact with her.

As the daughter of a witch, partially trained in the hope that I would actually grow into power, I knew that what Oonagh was doing might technically be black magic. It seemed harmless, but earth magic should never be used for personal reasons, especially vanity. I doubted that anyone would care, but if she was willing to use power for personal reasons, what else would she do? Most important, where did she find such an unfamiliar power?

My mission was greater than the mystery of a strange witch and her strange brand of magic. But right then, I couldn't think of anything else.

chapter 12

"What do you think?" Michael asked as the car rolled out of the parking lot. "Could you see? She's quite ill."

I nodded, a bit surprised at his sight. "You can see through spells?"

He shook his head. "I don't know what a spell looks like. I see her. The real her. It confused me at first. People kept telling me how attractive she is. They believed it. They didn't see what I did. Just as many people don't see the ruins." He started the car. "She's a witch. Like Abigail."

"A witch. But not like Abigail."

"Dying?"

"Probably soon."

Michael turned to face me, his eyes intense. "What else did you see?"

"Her waiters are miserable and frightened. There were four gangster-type thugs sitting in the corner who probably work for her."

"Do you now understand why I wanted you to go there?" He laughed softly.

"To show me that she's powerful, dangerous, and

insanely in love with you. She probably has you followed. If she sees me with you now, she'll see me as an employee, rather than a rival. Might save me some trouble."

"Yes. I don't think she would do anything drastic." He reached over and patted my arm as if to reassure me of my safety. I knew better than that.

"Michael, she'd hire a professional hit man if you adopted a puppy. What does she do that she needs so much muscle?"

"I don't know, but the Barrows is and has always been a dangerous place. She may have dealings outside. I simply don't care enough to investigate. I just don't want her attacking you."

I wanted to ask why, but I let it pass. Whatever was between Michael and me required a bit more diplomacy—and I had a mission to accomplish. I dared not lose sight of that because of a strange attraction to an unusual man.

I could call the Sisters, let them look into Oonagh. Mother Evelyn had told me that was their job. But she'd also said they acted only at the Earth Mother's command. I didn't think they, or the Earth Mother, would care enough about a dying witch to investigate. As long as Oonagh didn't sic her thugs on me—or Michael—I'd let it be.

Michael dropped me off at Harry's. He said he'd meet me at the Den later. I wanted different clothes to fit my new job description. The shiny handkerchief that covered my breasts wouldn't work, but Cassandra had given me some nice black jeans. Since I hadn't received the promised "ten times the money" yet, I headed for the secondhand store again. I bought a pair of black lace-up boots with thick soles. A soft blue conservative knit shirt would go with the jeans, as would the dark gray tailored jacket. Bouncer I might be, but I didn't have to look like one.

Later that afternoon, after a good bit of twisting and adjusting, I had the gun holster fitted across my shoulders and the gun in an easy draw position. The rune knife was at my waist, and I had Lillian's smaller knife hooked to my belt against the small of my back. The jacket had inside pockets for extra magazines. I watched my image in the mirror as I turned. The jacket added some class and covered the weapons. At least I didn't look like a walking armory.

I drew the blade I'd acquired from Hildy and tried to decipher the runes. I recognized them. I dug the amulet Eunice had given me out of my shirt. Instinct told me that the blade and amulet belonged together. The runes, cut with precision like the writing on ancient Babylonian tablets, were like none I'd ever seen before. I ran my fingers over the runes, feeling the slash mark indentations. For an instant, they vibrated under my fingers. The pair had to be objects of power, even though they were in no way spelled. I would have seen a spell right away. Why had they both come to me?

I rode the bus down to the Goblin Den rather than walked. The bus wasn't crowded, only a couple of older women and a woman holding a baby. A little boy sat on the seat beside her. I sat behind them on a worn brown vinyl seat with bits of foam thrusting from the separating seams.

I watched the passing shops as they began the decline into blight and wondered what it would be like to live here. A miserable foul-smelling jail cell in New York and the silent halls of Justice had been forced upon me by my own carelessness. But my original home was suburbia, a bright sunny house behind the shop where my mother practiced her gentle magic and sold handmade soaps, oils, and earth-centered jewelry. Daddy's restaurant was next door. I could picture living nowhere else, at least not by choice.

The little boy turned to watch me. Children often stare at me, at the scar. They are usually guileless little creatures, innocent of the tyranny of good manners. This boy was different. Something troubled him, and his face was as solemn as a mourner at a funeral. His dark eyes held questions. He slipped out of the seat and came toward me. I judged him to be about six. His clothes were clean but worn. He stood in the aisle and leaned toward me like a conspirator.

"Did your daddy hurt you?" he asked softly. "Your face."

"My daddy?" I hid my surprise with a smile. "No. It was an accident."

His eyes darted around. "My daddy hurt me."

He lifted his shirt. My mouth dropped open. Burns. Round cigarette burns, and . . . shit, the monster had heated a knife blade and laid it to this innocent child's tender skin. I touched it gently with my fingers as if I could smooth it away. It felt hot and fevered, as if had occurred only moments ago.

The woman holding the baby realized the boy had left her. She turned to face me. I guess she saw the horror on my face.

"I left the bastard," she said. Desperation filled her voice. I think she felt the need to explain that she was a good mother. "They arrested him," she went on, "but he made bail. I have a restraining order, but I think he has people watching me. I shouldn't be down here where he is, but I want to see my mother. She's been sick."

I nodded. I grasped the boy's shirt and slid it down to cover the scars. I'd seen some of the girls at Justice who had been brutalized like him before they arrived. I kissed him on the forehead. He smiled and went back to his mother.

The bus stopped for another passenger. I didn't pay attention until the little boy rushed by me toward the back of the bus. The high-pitched keening sound coming from him was of purest terror. He tripped and scrabbled along the floor to crawl under one of the seats behind me, still wailing in mindless panic.

The source of that panic stalked down the aisle toward us, grinning like a demon that had found something to kill. He wore a dirty white T-shirt over low-cut jeans. Several chains hung around his neck, and one thick set of links held a devil's head—obviously some gang affiliation.

He stopped and towered over the woman. He snatched at the baby. She tried to turn and hunch over it to protect it.

"What are you doing here?" she screamed. I guessed he'd been following her since she boarded the bus. Probably had his friends keeping tabs on her.

"Gimme that little bastard. It ain't mine, so it belongs in the trash."

Oh, no. This wouldn't happen on my watch. I hadn't spent years training to ignore a bloodthirsty animal like this one. Excitement rose in me. Only two days from Justice and I'd missed my daily exercise in violence. I wanted to do this.

I stood.

"Hey, asshole." I got his attention in my usual delicate way.

He glanced at me. As most did, he fixated on the scar. "Go fuck yourself, bitch."

He stood straight, feet planted wide against the sway of the bus. In a blur of movement, I kicked him in the balls. He squealed and dropped to his hands and knees. I kicked him in the face. My new-used boots worked just fine. I used the bus seats to vault over him. Once behind him, I grabbed the thickest chain, jerked him backward, and dragged him down the aisle toward the front of the bus. He kept making noises, but since I was dragging him by the neck like the overfilled garbage sack he was, he couldn't use words. My boot had made a bloody mess of his face.

His hands clawed at his pocket. A gun? I used the chain to swing his head to the side. It banged against the metal braces holding the seats. Back and forth, a hollow sound, flesh and bone against muscle; my arms strained to get force out of a short but very satisfying arc. After six solid whacks, he went limp. I relieved him of the contents of his front pockets. A pistol and a knife—and a roll of bills held by a rubber band. I laid them on an empty seat.

The downed bastard moaned. I jerked him into a sitting position.

His eyes rolled a bit, but he was awake. My shoe had flattened his nose. A stream of blood leaked across his mouth and chin to stain his shirt. I dragged him onto the loading platform at the front of the bus. I glanced at the bus driver. "Open the door."

He grinned and complied. He'd slowed down when the altercation started, but the bus still moved, creeping along. I rolled the beast who had tortured an innocent child down the steps onto the sidewalk. He flopped a few times.

The two elderly ladies sitting behind the driver smiled and gently applauded. The bus driver closed the door and drove away. He laughed. "Lady, that was great. But you know that was a Bastinado, don't you? One of the Slum Devils."

The little boy had gone back to his mother and sat huddled against her side, crying. I grabbed the roll of bills and the gun and plopped down on the seat across from her. I handed her the money. "He's not going to move fast for a while. You take a cab back home. Stay there. Take your mother with you."

Tears smeared her face. She didn't speak, or maybe she couldn't. The boy jumped into my arms. He cried in great hiccups. By the time we reached their stop, he'd calmed a little. He kissed me good-bye, as did his mother and the two elderly ladies who climbed off at her stop.

"Do I get a kiss?" the bus driver asked when we reached the end of the line and the Goblin Den. He had a blunt, square face and lots of gray in his dark brown hair. Wrinkles wove around his eyes as though he smiled a lot.

"No kiss." I handed him the Bastinado's gun and knife. "See if you can pawn these where they won't be traced. The gun is a nice piece. It might be worth something to you."

He accepted them. His face crumpled. "I'm pretty useless, I guess. I couldn't help you. I lost a lung in Iraq. Had internal injuries, too. The company won't let me carry a gun on the job." He sighed. "You remember what I said. You need to watch out for those Bastinados. That was only one. His gang will be looking for you."

"I'll be careful."

"You don't understand. Bastinados are more than a gang. To get in, you have to earn points. You get them by killing. Everyone in any gang has murdered someone. Men, women. They get extra points for cops."

"And if I had killed him . . . ?"

"No one would care. Cops know. You kill a Basto down here, they look the other way." The bus had stopped in the cul-de-sac overlooking Sullen Bog. "There's other things out there, too. Especially at night. They don't believe me uptown." He chuckled. "See that thing up there?" He pointed over my head.

I saw. A camera. My stomach clenched. Technology

had nailed me. How stupid. Again, I'd allowed the moment to get away from me.

The driver must have seen my dismay. "That little jewel hasn't worked in a year. Cheap bastards uptown don't give a shit about us drivers. I do the four to midnight most of the time. You see me, my bus, you need help, you wave me down. I'll stop for you. Name's Jim, by the way." He held out a hand and I accepted it.

"I'm Madeline. I'll probably see you again, Jim."

He grinned as I climbed off and waved as he drove away.

I'd let myself be sidetracked, dangerously, but I couldn't have let that scene unfold any other way. Would a Sister do that? Compromise a mission for a child? Lillian would. And Eunice. They would have handled the event more efficiently, though. They would have dragged him off, not tossed him. They would've hauled him into an alley and promptly rid the world of such vermin. Do the deed where no one could see, and clean up the mess. No one would ever know it happened. And my mother? Had she been on that bus, she would have smiled and his body would suddenly be covered with bleeding, oozing, and incredibly painful sores. Defense is appropriate, even for a witch. I'd overlooked a camera—again. The very thing that had nailed me when I'd killed my parents' second murderer. I was lucky this time, maybe not so lucky the next.

chapter 13

Since light and color still filled the sky, I walked around the building to the alley. No sign of my battle remained. Perhaps it was the confidence of the new weapons, but I wanted to take a few minutes to explore.

I walked into the alley, away from the Den, past the walls of ruined buildings. Some of brick and block stood strong; others with wooden frames sagged. Once upon a time this had been a vibrant street. No housing, but probably wholesale businesses, from the look of the large bay doors and loading docks that faced the alley.

I heard no out-of-the-ordinary sounds, only the distant traffic of River Street and the occasional soft whistle of a breeze through the buildings. Light faded as I walked back toward the Den.

Riggs met me as I walked in. "Michael called. Says you got a new job."

"Yes. I'm your bouncer. You got someone to bounce, you let me know. I'll take care of it."

"I'll bet you can." He shrugged and walked away. Riggs was a man of few words. I appreciated that.

His departure, of course, left me with nothing to do.

I walked out front and watched the sunset. It turned the watery parts of the Bog into sheets of gold. As it faded, the lights came on in the front parking lot—brilliant lights, not the soft yellow of those in the suburbs. They left only the undersides of cars in darkness.

With my promotion, Kelly had to work the bar by herself. I felt sorry for her so I brought her supplies, clean glasses, bottles of mixers, and booze from the storeroom. I mixed a few orders for the floor waitresses, too.

A little later, I walked back outside to the scene of my earlier disaster. The back parking lot had no additional lights installed, but the roof did, apparently in the belief that it would scare flying things away. I went back to my box, the one where I'd observed my first Drow.

A Dumpster sat about twenty feet from me. Something moved inside. Trash rustled and banged against the side. A large plastic bag flew out and plopped on the pavement. I froze.

A creature vaulted out of the Dumpster. Human shaped with two arms and two legs, it stood at least eight feet tall. It had four-inch claws and brownish gray armor-plated scales covering it from its rounded head to its massive clawed feet. The bulge in the scales between its legs strongly suggested a male. His claws were blunt, but formidable. He straightened when he saw me.

As my little dragon had, he stared at me with odd but intelligent eyes. Somebody was home there. He made no move to attack. I slowly stood and held out my hands, palms up, to show I had no weapon. Something whimpered and I saw a smaller creature, very similar to the large one. A young one, holding back in the alley. The male, apparently deciding I was harmless, tore open the bag and began to sort through things. The Den didn't have much food waste, but he found some old moldy oranges. The young one scrambled forward. He gave it what he found. An herbivore, not carnivore, he fed the child first. How had they come to be here? The young one devoured the oranges in seconds. He was starving.

I went back inside. Pity had overtaken me. No one was around. I grabbed a bag and went to the refrigerator. I raked packages of celery, oranges, and apples into the bag. In the storeroom, I found a whole case of nuts in small packages and dumped them all in.

When I went back out, the large male had finished sorting through the Dumpster's pitiful contents. The young one was holding the remains of someone's fried chicken lunch, a single leg bone. He stared at it, then dropped it. The male stood as I approached. He flexed his claws. He was not a killer, but he would defend himself. I held out the bag, laid it on the ground, and backed away.

He stared at me for a long time, then went to the bag. The not-so-shy little one had full faith in the ability of the big male to keep him from harm. He raced forward to receive the bounty. I stood back and watched. I knew I shouldn't feed strays. That never stopped me when they collected behind Daddy's restaurant. And the day Animal Control stopped by to pick up my friends, I used a butcher knife to poke holes in their tires. Daddy had stood by me and sworn to the juvenile judge that the Animal Control officers were on private property.

I went to sit back on my box, pleased with myself and at the same time thoroughly confused. These creatures were far from the monsters Cassandra had described.

Another creature rushed out of the darkness. Spot, my little rescue dragon.

"Hey, Spot."

Spot chirped and started toward me as the back door of the Den opened.

The male grabbed the bag and the young one and raced away into the darkness. Spot followed him. I stood and faced Riggs. "I'll pay for the food," I said. I lifted my hand toward the dark alley. "These creatures are not evil. They're starving."

He stared into the darkness, his face blank so I couldn't tell his thoughts. Finally, he just turned and went back inside. I followed him.

chapter 14

At seven p.m., the tables and bar filled, though not to capacity. I sat at a corner table and watched the act onstage. The lead singer had a nice, if not spectacular, voice. If the Den were to attract a better clientele, it needed better talent. At first, the mood in the room seemed genial, professionals winding down after work. After eight, those looking for more serious action began drifting in.

Michael came back around ten, and I discovered why men and women came from uptown to this renovation project at the end of the road. He walked into the room and, for a brief moment, all voices ceased. Then the crowd gave a collective sigh and went back to their drinks and conversation, casting an occasional glance his way. While Michael had an instant effect on everyone around him, I didn't believe this was the same as the connection that I had with him. I wondered if his charisma was intentional or simply beyond his control, an unintended effect or a weapon. He was impeccably dressed in slacks, a shirt, and a jacket in brown and cream; everything about him screamed money and class—and sex. He'd drawn that glorious corn-silk hair back and clipped it at the nape of his neck.

Michael's enchantment was not magic as I knew it. He'd created it out of his own hypnotic presence. I doubt that even the most powerful witch could have spun a stronger spell of rapture over this crowd.

He walked the floor, a smile here and a few words there. A nod of his head created futile longing. The blessing of his warm smile enthralled. Control. It was about control, and he was a master. But he had not tried to control me in that manner. Why? He obviously wanted something from me. Did he see me as someone who could provide him with something he wanted and needed me to be free of his spell to accomplish that?

Michael graced me with an occasional smile, but mostly ignored me. I watched him and the individual reactions to him. If someone came across as angry or resentful, he paused and soothed ruffled feelings. He was cool and polite to attractive women and kind to those who were less comely. I concentrated on everything. Details. The women who wanted to touch him but didn't dare. They curled their hands into fists in their laps. The men he spoke to as comrades. They accepted his neutral offer of semi-friendship with smiles—and an occasional glance at their women.

I did notice one thing. No one actually touched him. No one.

At midnight, I gazed out over the crowd. My mouth fell open. I almost dropped the glass of water I'd been sipping. Sitting in the back, watching me, were Sister Lillian and Sister Eunice.

Eunice had traded her fatigues for khakis and a brown shirt, but she wore a vest with many pockets, every one probably stuffed with deadly weapons. Lillian wore navy pants, a crisp white shirt, and a jacket that I'm sure covered her own personal arms. What were they doing here? Had something changed? I went to them, more than a little perturbed at their presence.

"What's going on?" I sat at the table.

Eunice gave a deep, rumbling laugh. "I wanted another one of your kisses, sweet child."

"Oh, be still, Eunice." Lillian spoke without any actual censure. "We are worried about you."

"Thank you, Sisters, for caring." I had to confess—or maybe brag. "I killed something night before last."

"And I hear it almost killed you." Lillian spoke softly, but I heard the concern. "I hear an unusually gracious earth witch drew a mighty spell to keep you in this world. Why did you confront something like that? We couldn't show you the Drows, but did you not believe us when we said they could be deadly?"

"I heard your lessons, but I couldn't let him . . ." I stopped myself. "I couldn't let someone die if I could help it."

Eunice raised an eyebrow. She'd heard the word *him*—and the unintended emphasis.

"We're not Sisters here, Madeline." Lillian reached over and patted my hand.

I grinned at Eunice. "You won't hit me if I call you Eunice?"

Eunice's mouth twisted down in a fake pout at the accusation.

"Did Mother Evelyn send you?" I asked. "I've been here for only three days. She doesn't expect me to find it this soon, does she?"

Eunice scowled. Her voice turned sharp. "No. She did not send us."

Uh-oh. Trouble.

"She doesn't know we're here," Lillian said.

"I don't believe it. Mother Evelyn knows everything. And I'll bet I know you two. You asked. She said no. You came anyway. Why?"

Lillian smiled. "We hadn't seen Sister Hildegard in a number of years. It's time we get reacquainted."

"Did you bring oxygen masks?"

Eunice laughed, deep and low. She lifted her glass to salute me. So, Hildy was a Sister or former Sister, and apparently these two knew her well enough to know about her noxious habit.

I spied Riggs at the door arguing with a man about twice his size. "I have to get back to work."

Lillian's eyes narrowed. "Hildy said you were a bartender."

"I got a promotion."

After I helped Riggs put the colossal drunk in a cab, I went back to observing. I kept an eye on Lillian and Eunice through the evening. Lillian simply sipped a glass of wine, and the floor waitress brought her a new one occasionally. Eunice went to sit with a lovely young woman who'd caught her eye. The woman was obviously fascinated with the rough Sister. Lillian rolled her eyes when she saw me looking. Knowing the cheaper house wine, I bought her a glass of the better stuff and took it to her.

"Don't you have any faith in me at all, Sister?" I couldn't make myself leave off the title. I placed the glass in front of her and sat by her side. "I thought I needed to do this on my own."

"We have faith." She laughed softly. "But a gray curtain of boredom fell over Justice after you left."

I smacked my hand on the table. "I knew it! You and the others sat around at night and plotted evil things to torment me."

"And we rejoiced at your triumphs. Each day, we watched you learn, overcome obstacles. We watched you fall and get right back up again." She sipped the wine. "Oh, this is much better." She lowered the glass. "You're not ready for this, Madeline. You were to be sent out with an experienced Sister for mentoring and more training. I don't know what Mother Evelyn is doing in this matter. I can't challenge her, but I can try to protect you."

"I think the Earth Mother wants me here for some reason. Beyond that, I don't know either. I thought this was my mission. My final exam. You want me to cheat? Okay. I'll let you help me. Give me answers. Give me facts and not platitudes and surreptitious hints."

Lillian nodded. "I can't. I know much, but I know little of this place. The Barrows. Hildy is the expert here. She is supposed to guide you."

"She has." I drew the knife out of the sheath at my hip and handed it to her, hilt first. "She gave me this."

Lillian hesitated, then accepted the blade with careful fingers, as if it would bite her. She turned it over and stared at the runes. "Hildy did not *give* this blade to you, Madeline. This is a Morié. It's one of five in the world. Like the blade I gave you, it was made thousands of years ago. Legend says the Earth Mother herself created it in the heart of the earth and melded the metals with powerful magic. And like many objects of its kind, it chooses its custodian." She frowned. "You have a gun."

She'd seen it when I drew my coat back to draw the knife. "Yes. Filled with bronze-coated bullets."

She made no further comment on the gun. She handed the knife, the Morié, back to me. "That trinket Eunice gave you to wear around your neck is called the Solaire. You should keep the Solaire and Morié together and on you at all times. Each is powerful in its own right, but together they offer great protection, protection from magic. They allow three Sisters to come together and form what we call a Triad of Sisters. And they enable a Triad to take down, to kill, any witch." She sighed. "I'm happy you have the Moiré, but I had no idea Sister Hildegard had one in her keeping. But then, she is one to keep secrets. She has a long history of animosity toward the Sisterhood, much as you do."

"Secrets are the daily bread of the Sisters of Justice. How many of you have died because one of you hoarded secrets?"

Lillian leaned back. "We are far from perfect, Madeline. I'll ask you, do you have no secrets? Eunice and Mother Evelyn believe we've torn them all from you. I disagree. Will you now tell me one thing about you I don't know?"

I bit my lip. Yes, there was that one thing I'd been able to hold back. I didn't need the Moiré or Solaire to protect me from magic. I'd been born without a witch's power, but I was also immune to it. It seemed that I could tell Lillian that, but years of reserve were still ingrained in me. She was still a Sister and I kept my secret from her.

She laughed. "I thought so. I swear, you would make a perfect Sister."

"I doubt it. There's the obedience thing."

"Obedience? Eunice and I aren't here because we obey orders."

chapter 15

Riggs needed help again. A hysterical woman in the bathroom and another escort to a cab took at least half an hour. Having little experience in my life with people who regularly overindulged in alcohol, it seemed a mystery to me. I went back to my observation and watched as a couple of attractive men approached Lillian. She quickly sent them on their way. Michael was in his second round of dispensing charm on the floor when he stopped at her table. Oh, this would be good. What I wouldn't do for super hearing.

He turned the charm on, smiling, acting so delighted to be with her, allowing her to worship him.

Lillian stared, appeared interested, then threw back her head and laughed.

Michael frowned. Like a mother with a misbehaving child, Lillian pointed at the chair next to her. And like a child, he sat. Sister Lillian had her own way of control. I'd faced it many times. She always won with me. And she won with Michael. He quietly listened to whatever lecture she gave him.

Beautiful, charming Michael. How many layers were

there to this man who had so captured my attention? Captured my attention to the point I rarely thought of my mission or revenge when I was with him.

When Lillian finished, he spoke. He wasn't smiling, but he wasn't angry. His face seemed to have a look of sincerity. I saw no hint of artifice. I longed to hear the conversation. Maybe it was my own ego, or maybe paranoia, but gut instinct said they were talking about me. Riggs brought and opened a whole bottle of wine for them. It came from the most expensive one-hundred-dollars-a-bottle stuff in the locked wine cooler behind the bar. It wasn't sold by the glass.

A loud discussion began between two men at the end of the bar and I was suddenly occupied. After one of the would-be combatants left, I went back outside for a break. The arrival of Lillian and Eunice had disturbed me. I wondered if Hildy had called them. Had she told them about Michael, that he was distracting me from my mission? Lillian had paid special attention to him, after all.

After a careful survey of my surroundings, I sat on the box outside the back door, my Barrows' throne. Nothing stirred in the darkness right then. A chill came creeping in with a thin mist of fog. It smelled of rotting vegetation and fish, probably from the Bog. The sweet odor of the day died with the sun. After a few minutes, Michael came out to join me.

He sat beside me. The box wasn't that big, and he was close enough to scramble my senses. His leg was tight against mine. He grasped my hand. "I like your friend. Lillian. She's interesting."

"And immune to your charm. Is she the first to see past it?"

"No. Cassandra was the first. Cassandra was so interesting, so smart and full of fire. I tried very hard with her, but she wouldn't have it. Now there's you."

"You've never tried to charm me."

"I did. This morning. You ignored it. You should have smiled and come to me, eager to work in any capacity. Instead, you challenged me."

"The size of your ego astounds me."

"It's not ego. It's what I've lived with all my life. Now you, you demanded to know what I wanted from you. You asked for honesty, not fantasy. Lillian said I should always be truthful with you. So did Hildy. That's what I'm going to do."

He held out his hand. "Let me hold your small knife."

I slid the small knife out of the sheath at my back and handed it to him. He thumbed the blade. "Sharp. Bronze." Before I could speak, he opened his other hand and abruptly drew the blade across his palm. The blade cut through skin, deep enough to draw a thick line of blood. He held it and let the blood drip to the ground.

"What the hell are you doing?" I was too stunned to move.

He swiped his thumb across the wound and wiped away the blood. The cut had healed. "I'm not invulnerable, Madeline. But not many things in this world can hurt me."

I grabbed his hand and ran my own fingers across

his palm. Smooth. On the surface of his hand, his blood felt thick—and far warmer than it should.

"I need you to know this. My father, like the creature that attacked you, isn't human. He's close to human, close enough to be able to create a child, but . . ."

I released his hand and stared at the blood, his blood, on my fingers. Not human? Could that be? He spoke so honestly, in an almost pleading tone. I wondered how often he volunteered this information. I thought of my own situation. Had I ever said, "My mother is a witch"? Certainly not to a virtual stranger. But then Michael had thrust himself deep into my life from the moment I first saw him. Did revealing secrets mean the same thing for him as it did for me?

My mother had expected genetics to make me a witch, as her own mother's had made her one. Genetics, which were the realm of the Earth Mother, failed her. Was it the same for Michael? If he was telling the truth.

He'd been prepared for what he'd revealed to me because he drew a cloth out of his pocket, grasped my hand, and wiped the blood away. He wiped his own, cleaned my knife, and handed it back to me, hilt first.

I couldn't think of anything to say. What do you say to something like that? *Prove it? You're a liar?*

I had just sheathed the knife when Riggs rushed out the back door. "Madeline, one of your friends—"

"Can't you take care of it?" Michael scowled at him.

"Not if it's Eunice, he can't." The interruption was fine with me. I needed time to process what he'd told me. "She'll use him or anyone who gets in her way like a rag to wipe the bar."

I could feel Michael's reluctance to let me go. I had a feeling there was more to tell, but it would have to wait. I stood and hurried in. Michael followed.

I expected chaos, but everything was over by the time I arrived. Tables were shoved aside and chairs tossed; the smell of spilled drinks filled the air like some barroom perfume. The patrons had stepped back to watch the brawl. Eunice stood in the middle of the floor and four men lay sprawled around her like dolls discarded by a child. One didn't move. The others moaned. Eunice grinned like a kid with a new toy. Her face had a light I'd never seen. She didn't look like that when she beat the shit out of me. She'd looked at me with a kind of grim satisfaction. Could it be that she really didn't enjoy making me suffer? No way.

One of the men on the floor rolled and drew a pistol from under his coat. Eunice grabbed it and twisted it out of his hands. He screamed when she deliberately broke a couple of fingers.

"Oh, shit," Riggs said. "He's a cop."

Lillian stepped up beside me. She smiled happily. "Look at her, Madeline. She's having such fun. We stayed at Justice too long."

"Why did you stay?" I suspected I knew the answer.

"To train you, of course." She chuckled.

Of course. Matter-of-fact. But why? Two premiere Sisters of Justice had made me the prominent focus of their lives. Damn it, why?

"Eunice?" Lillian asked. "Are you finished? I'm tired. We really should go."

Eunice grunted. The girl she'd sat with earlier sidled up to her. Eunice wrapped an arm around her. "You gonna be okay, honey?"

"Yes. You'll call me?" The girl had a soft, breathy voice. Eunice hugged her tighter.

"You bet, baby. I'll take you somewhere with more class. Come on. I'll see you to your car." They walked out smiling.

That I had been specially trained was not news. That Lillian and Eunice were specially chosen to do it seemed incomprehensible.

I helped clean up the spilled drinks and the crowd sat back down to talk about the fight. Apparently it was quite spectacular and I was really sorry I missed it. Eunice's only violence at Justice had been directed at me.

Michael and Riggs got the wounded men into the back storeroom and patched them up. I went in later. Apparently the blame game had ended, and they had agreed that maybe it wasn't all Eunice's fault. The girl was one man's date and he had objected to her responding to Eunice's advances. He had slapped her and snatched her away and Eunice had taken her back. Out of obvious prejudice, the cop had objected a bit more strenuously.

"They started it, Becker," Riggs told him. "So you decided to jump in and help the assholes?"

"I'm a police officer. I was trying to break up the fight."

"You were trying to hold her so they could beat on her." Riggs jabbed a finger at him.

"Her kind don't belong here." Becker sneered.

"I say who belongs here, Becker." Michael stepped forward. "And you won't, if you cause trouble."

Eunice had returned to the barroom when we came out, and Becker glared at her as Riggs escorted him across the floor. Riggs had called him a cab and sent him to the emergency room. I think some cash changed hands, too.

"Will he say anything?" I asked Michael.

"No. He's been warned to stay out of bars. I could file a complaint, but I'm willing to let it go if he is." His fingers brushed mine. I glanced at that wonderful face. I could read nothing in his brilliant blue eyes.

Eunice suddenly had an arm around me. She dragged me away from him and kissed my ear. "You can do better than him, love. He's too pretty to be real." She didn't bother to lower her voice when she spoke of Michael.

"She could do better," Michael agreed, more solemn sounding that the occasion required. "But I swear, I'll do my best to be worthy of her."

I squirmed inside at Michael's pronouncement. His words felt too honest—and premature. I wasn't about to admit that I liked hearing them. He'd just finished telling me he wasn't all human. I still had to deal with that.

I relaxed and let Eunice hold me. It was easier than fighting. "Eunice, where are you and Lillian going to stay?"

"With Hildegard." Lillian approached. "After we fumigate. Tonight we'll be at a hotel uptown."

"Be careful," Eunice whispered in my ear as she released me. "That pretty one is not what he seems." Great Mother, what an understatement.

"No, he's not." I looked straight into her eyes. Something I didn't dare do often at Justice. "You be careful, too, Sister. Nothing is what it seems in the Barrows."

She stared at me for a moment, then gave me a quick kiss and walked away. As they did, I realized I was glad to see them. A complication, but I knew they would stand with me should I need them—or interfere when I didn't.

"Are you tired?" Michael came to me and asked as we closed. He'd kept his distance since Lillian and Eunice left.

"I'm okay." I was tired and hungry, but I would, as I had at Justice, deny it. To admit fatigue would be to admit weakness. My traitor stomach betrayed me with a loud growl.

"Would you come with me tonight? Please. I want to show you more of the Barrows." There was no deliberate charm when he asked, which was, in itself, quite charming. His smile was simple and warm, not blinding.

I nodded.

We went out the back with the others and Riggs locked up behind us. Michael led me to his Jag. When he climbed in, he said, "Madeline, I meant what I said. About being worthy of you."

"Worthy of me?" I did not like where the conversation was going. "You assume too much. I'm your bouncer. Your muscle. Not your girlfriend."

It wasn't a nice thing to say, but I didn't feel nice at that particular moment. He had disturbed me. Worthy, my ass. I realized my fingers were rubbing my scar. When had I picked up that habit? It told the world that I was uneasy and confused.

Michael didn't speak as he turned the car out onto River Street and headed north. He drove to an all-night diner and I ate a wonderful burger, dripping with grease, while he sipped coffee and smiled at me. Apparently my appetite amused him.

Back in the car he asked, "What do you think of me, Madeline? Will you tell me the truth?"

Oh, no, I would not do that. I did have an opinion, though. "You're eye candy. And a master manipulator of men and women. I don't know what to think about the half-human thing. Other than that, I don't know you, except . . ."

"Except what?"

I couldn't say that he confused me and messed up my mind. I grasped for something. "You were fair to Eunice. I think Lillian likes you. That says something. Eunice didn't try to squash you. That's good."

"I'm grateful for Eunice's restraint. Lillian is very perceptive. Will you tell me who they are?"

"Not now." I could not and would not talk about the Sisters of Justice. I knew them, but at the same time there was still a mystery to them I couldn't explain.

He didn't argue. Just before Harry's, he turned left and into the ruins.

The streets were clear here, but the buildings loomed over us like a claustrophobic black fortress. The night closed in. Where there should have been some ambient glow from the city lights, only a few dim stars appeared above. Was that the see-but-don't-see spell? Or could it be the function of the ward around the Barrows blocking out the light?

Piles of blocks and the rubble of building materials were neatly stacked on the sidewalks. Recently repaired potholes smoothed the road under the tires. Having been raised in suburbia with abundant parks and green space, I would never find the appeal in living among the rows of look-alike buildings crowded close to the sidewalk, even in pristine condition.

Michael drove into a wide plaza and parked.

Other vehicles were parked there, a few trucks, too. Lights illuminated the area, but not like the high-powered ones at the Den. There were plenty of dark holes for things to hide. It still had the feel of incredible emptiness. He switched off the engine.

Michael grabbed my hand and squeezed lightly. He instantly released me, as if afraid to touch me. I did appreciate his hesitation. He'd been sending me so many mixed signals since the first time he spoke to me that morning.

"Riggs said you robbed the kitchen to feed the monsters."

"They're not monsters. And the ones I fed were herbivores. I told him I'd pay for it."

"You were kind to them, those beings from another world." He smiled. "I hope you feel the same kindness an hour from now. I'm taking you to meet my father."

chapter 16

I remained silent while I processed the idea. Then . . .
"Why are you taking me to meet your father? I'm your employee."

He sighed and shook his head. "You're not just an employee. I don't . . . Okay, I'll try to explain. That night I held you in my arms, after that thing had bitten you, I thought you were . . . Damn. I usually have all the words I need, but . . ." He ran a hand through that corn-silk hair. His former charming demeanor was gone and he looked thoroughly unsettled. "You fascinated me, with your hair and that incredible face and—"

"Incredible face!" What was he talking about?

"Madeline, that scar does not disfigure you. Never believe that. I wanted to hold you, know you. I hated to strip you down at Abigail's, to invade your privacy . . . but it had to be done."

I was intrigued. "I know it had to be done. Keep talking."

"Okay . . . the honest truth is that from that moment on, I've just wanted you by my side. I don't know what

I'd have done if you hadn't agreed to work for me. You have to understand—I think you do understand—that I am different. And that means I don't connect with most people. You'll understand when you meet my father."

Something moved in me. I sensed his isolation despite his beauty and charm. I knew what it took for him to declare that he wanted me by his side. Did I want to be with him? Yes. Did I want him to desire me? That too. All that beauty, all that physical perfection drew me as it would almost any woman. And as he had begun to show himself to me, I realized that it was his difference that drew me, too. But I simply could not give my feelings back to him, at least not yet. I had a mission to fulfill, and until it was done, I had no time for that sort of thing.

I lifted a hand in mock surrender. "Okay, Michael. Let's go meet Daddy."

He laughed. "Daddy. That's not a word I usually apply to him."

A whisper of caution slid through me when I stepped out of the car. The buildings were the same ruins, but they lacked that foreboding sense of emptiness that characterized the ones we passed on the way there. The streets met at odd angles, forming a wide plaza. A few dim lights made irregular rectangles and squares on the buildings. None higher than a second floor, but inhabited nonetheless. Who lived in such a place?

Michael parked the car. "This is the Zombie. The dark heart of the Barrows."

The same place that everyone had been telling me to avoid. Great.

"Your not-human father lives here?" My voice broke the silence.

"Yes. Not by choice, though. He's a prisoner. The Earth Mother won't let him out. Apparently they have a history. Not that I blame her. He's dangerous. When you meet him, you'll understand."

Michael led me toward one of the buildings and into an empty, well-lit, high-ceilinged room. It might have been a bank at one time. A commerce center in what had to have been a vibrant part of the city. What had devastated this place? What happened to leave it so desolate that the patroness of this world shielded it from humanity? Was it really an earthquake, as Michael had told me? No, there had to be more to the story.

We walked across polished white marble floors toward stairs that led to a balcony. Our footsteps, though light, sounded loud, and a slight echo danced around us.

Michael seemed calm, too perfectly calm to be genuine. The calm turned to pure tension as a man came toward us from the side of the room.

Michael stopped. He muttered under his breath and stepped away from me. All his body language said he was prepared to fight. He spoke to the man. "Get out of here, Clark."

I barely knew Michael, but had he spoken to me in such a voice, I would have run. Apparently, that marvelous charm he exuded at times had an equal and terrifying opposite.

Clark sneered at him. He wore rumpled fatigues like

a soldier who had been in the field for months. A pregnant gut hung over his belt. Even at a distance I could smell him—unclean; not just unwashed, but filled with some deeper rottenness.

Clark carried a serious gun. Not that he'd ever be able to draw it in time to do any damage to me. He had it in one of the holsters that strapped to the thigh, a holster a little too big for the weapon, so it slid down too far. I'd put a knife in his heart before his hand could close on it.

I glanced at Michael. "Who is he?"

"Clark is a pedophile and murderer who has long escaped the justice he deserves. He's the poster child for the FBI's Most Wanted List. For reasons I don't understand, my father thinks he needs a security force with absolutely no morals. Clark's résumé qualified him."

Clark leered, running his gaze up and down my body. "Now, where did Daddy's boy find the little freak?" He had a voice well abused by alcohol and other unsavory things. He chuckled. "You want to come play with a real man, bitch? We can put a bag over your head."

I glanced at Michael, then back at Clark. "A pedophile?"

Clark grinned. "Nope. I just like to fuck little bitty pussy. The littler, the better. I like it when they squeal."

He liked to hear them squeal. I'd seen some like him during my time on the streets, looking for the killers. Always hunting the youngest, offering to pay for even younger. *You got a little sister, honey? I'll give you money for her. More than you'll make here.* At the time, I'd lacked the skill to seriously injure the assholes. Things were different now. As with the Drow that had attacked Michael, this was something I could do. Something I should do. Like the Bastinado on the bus. My years at Justice demanded it.

"Michael, I don't want to be a poor guest in your father's house, but may I express my loathing for this man with violence. Please?"

"My father has no objection to violence. He considers worms like Clark beneath notice."

Clark gave a deep, grunting laugh. "I got a job, and you know it. What I do on my own time is my business."

Michael chuckled. His genuine mirth was far more appealing to me than the magic charm for a crowd he sometimes displayed, as was his faith in my ability to handle Clark.

"As you wish, Madeline." He graciously nodded his head.

The game changed. Six men came out of the darkness and surrounded us. None of them appeared to be armed like Clark. If Clark was their leader, he would be understandably reluctant to let them carry guns.

"You go talk to Daddy, pretty boy." Clark moved in closer. He chuckled. "Leave the bitch with us."

"Madeline?" Michael said, his voice growing steely.

"Yes, Michael," I responded coolly.

"Do it."

Clark stepped forward as I pulled back and drew the small knife from the back of my belt. I wouldn't honor him with the big blade.

Clark grinned. "Come on, bitch. Let me make both sides of your ugly face match." He pulled a knife, too. He stood with his arms open, hands flung out. "Do it, you ugly whore. Cut me!"

How stupid was the man?

I jumped in and slashed his face—not deep, but a good clean cut. For the first time, I actually paid attention to my speed. I'd always been fast. Never that fast, though. A gift from the Earth Mother? Maybe.

Clark screamed. My cut ran a diagonal across his face and had taken out one of his eyes. He dropped his knife and slapped his hands over his wound. He staggered back and choked on the blood pouring between his fingers. I kicked him in the knee, dislocating it, and grabbed the gun from his holster as he went down. He made mewling sounds for a second, then passed out.

I whirled to help Michael. Except for the unconscious Clark, we were alone.

"Where . . . ?"

Laughter danced in those beautiful blue eyes. "They were smarter than Clark. They left."

Another man approached. Tall, over six feet, dressed in jeans and a T-shirt, he had tan skin, dark hair, and tattoos on every inch of his forearms. Nice muscular arms for such a slender and graceful man. Not gorgeous like Michael, but compelling anyway. This one would not be taken as easily as the ill-fated Clark.

"Étienne." Michael nodded his head, recognizing the man.

Étienne returned the nod, but his attention was on me. He had really nice dark eyes and his mouth formed a half smile. Apparently the situation did not displease him.

"I thought you were getting rid of Clark," Michael said.

"Don't have a replacement yet." Étienne winked at me. "Unless the lady is looking for a job."

"She works for me." Michael stepped closer. His shoulder brushed mine.

Étienne smiled, obviously interested now. "She's yours."

"Yes. She's mine."

I gritted my teeth. He'd made an enormous leap from "she works for me." Michael and I needed to have a serious discussion about the dramatic difference between employees and possessions.

"What's your name?" Étienne asked me.

"Madeline." I didn't see any reason not to tell him.

He inclined his head toward the moaning Clark. "Don't try that with me, Madeline."

"Then don't pull a knife on me."

Étienne laughed—a laugh that I would have enjoyed under different circumstances. "I'll keep that in mind."

I handed him Clark's gun. "You shouldn't let him play with grown-up toys."

"I keep hoping he'll shoot himself." Étienne accepted it and nodded at Michael again. "If you ever get tired of Prince Charming, Madeline, come see me."

Still angry at Michael for claiming me as his property, I gave Étienne my best smile. "I could do worse."

Étienne grinned back. "Honey, you already have."

Michael hissed softly. He grabbed my hand and

started for the stairs. Surprised, I let myself be dragged along until we reached the steps. I certainly didn't want to stay with Clark, especially after Étienne kicked him.

When we reached the stairs, I jerked my hand away and glared at Michael.

"Madeline, I . . ." Whatever he saw in my expression silenced him. He turned and went up the stairs without speaking. I followed because I didn't have anywhere else to go. I sheathed Lillian's knife and glanced back. Étienne smiled at me. For the hell of it, I smiled back.

We walked down a wide hallway on the second floor, softly lit and less spectacular than the entrance, but well maintained. As soon as we were out of hearing distance, Michael stopped. He crossed his arms and frowned at me.

"You like Étienne?"

What was this about? He sounded offended. Jealous, even.

"Yeah, I like him." I would not let him make me defensive. "But it's a shallow first impression. Don't worry." I patted his chest. "I like you best." Act like a child and get treated like one.

He laid his hands lightly on my shoulders. "Madeline, Étienne is an ex-con. He was convicted of three murders."

"Michael, I'm an ex-con. And you've seen my capacity for violence. You think I can't deal with him?" That Étienne was a murderer didn't surprise me, but I wouldn't judge him without knowing his story. "Would you please tell me why you suddenly felt the need to claim ownership of me? Telling me you like me doesn't give you that right." I clamped my teeth together. This was not the time or place.

He wouldn't meet my eyes. He released me. "We should go. This wasn't a good idea."

"Oh please, don't leave," said a smooth, masculine voice. "I rarely have such an interesting guest."

That voice, a deep baritone, caught me and made me turn—compelled me to turn. The source of the voice stood ten feet from us. My mind stopped working. Stunned at the sight of something so strange, so alien, I could not think. I could not speak.

Michael spoke softly. "Madeline, this is my father."

chapter 17

I am not, by nature or training, given to awe or amazement of the supernatural. I have always accepted the idea that humans aren't the only sentient beings in the universe. But I stood, motionless, and gazed at the magnificent creature before me.

The ultimate Drow—Michael's father—stood at least seven feet tall. Gold. His skin was the color of a deep gold coin, his eyes the same. Impossibly beautiful, impossibly masculine, he had a lion's mane of bronzered hair that made him glorious—and an absolute alien in this world.

Even standing frozen in wonder, I knew, beyond a doubt, this was the cause of the Earth Mother's ward around the Barrows. Stunned as I was, I realized the danger here. While I felt no desire to worship him, I knew men and women would fall on their knees if he were to go into the world. He would be like a movie star or charismatic politician or preacher—or, worse, a god.

Good and evil would do his bidding.

There's a demon in the ruins, Hildy had said. *A big, badass demon. The king of the Drows.*

Michael's father gave him a beneficent smile. He spoke with a gentleness that surprised me. "It's been months. I thought you'd forsaken me, my son."

"His name is Aiakós," Michael said to me, ignoring his father. His voice filled with deep emotion I didn't understand—until he spoke again. "He lived in another world, controlling people in the Barrows from afar, influencing them to do his bidding. His powers were limited until my mother, a troubled witch who escaped from an insane asylum with the help of my brother, cut her throat for him and bled out on an altar in the plaza outside. Her sacrifice brought him here to the Barrows, and my mother and brother are now dead."

"And the Earth Mother binds him here." My own voice sounded harsh compared to theirs.

Aiakós stepped closer. He was dressed in well-cut clothing. He wore a cream-colored silk shirt that framed broad shoulders and thick muscles. It had to be tailor-made for someone of his size.

"How are you called, little witch?" Aiakós asked. "Are you one of Innana's?"

Innana, of course, was one of the Earth Mother's multitude of names. To my amazement, I found my voice. "My name is Madeline. I'm not a witch."

Aiakós stepped closer. Too close. Reflex, years of training, or maybe the recent violence sent my hand to the knife at my hip—the one Lillian had called the Morié. It didn't escape me that instinct made me choose the knife, not the gun. The fighting stance I'd learned from Sister Lillian—one foot forward, knife level, ready to strike—also came without thought.

Aiakós stopped.

"A warrior, then." Curiosity filled his silky voice. "Has a new Huntress come among us?"

"I'm looking for someone, if that's what you mean." At least I could still talk.

"How delightful." Aiakós nodded. "Perhaps some new game has begun. This is such a boring prison Innana has constructed for me." He laughed, and the sound caressed me. "The binding between you and my son is strong. Innana must be trying to seduce him away from me."

"What binding?" Michael and I spoke at once.

Aiakós laughed. "Oh, it's nothing. But it will be interesting to see which is stronger in my son—my blood or a witch's spell." He gestured to a room behind him. "Please, come in. I have some wine." He stared at my knife. "Unless you wish to stab me." His voice had an edge, a deadly edge as sharp as the Morié.

I shook my head and sheathed the blade. Having seen Michael's cut heal, my knife would probably only irritate him while he tore my arm off. I suspected that, while he was sensitive to bronze, he was a lot harder to kill than the Drow that attacked Michael.

Curious, though, that he'd seen the strange connection that I felt to Michael. A binding, he called it. But I knew from my mother that a binding was a two-way thing. If the connection was a binding, it imprisoned both of us, not just me.

Michael stepped closer to me. "You're not frightened." His voice carried a bit of surprise.

"You thought I'd run screaming down the stairs?"

"He is dangerous, Madeline."

I glanced at Aiakós, who stood smiling at us.

"What gives it away? The claws?" The danger was not immediate, and curiosity filled me now that the initial shock had faded.

Michael sighed. Relief? Maybe. Had he thought he'd have to defend me? He had a lot more to learn about me.

The surprises kept coming. I stepped into an opulent room filled with red and gold. I immediately went into sensory overload. My parents were not poor, and my mother loved luxury, but even she couldn't fathom this. Walls covered with gold drapes, fine wood paneling, red upholstered furniture, gold vases and bowls, rich rugs scattered across a stone floor—the room screamed of wealth.

I turned to Michael. "This is a prison?"

Michael's face went hard. "He has resources, plus a small cadre of worshippers who import things he can't get in the Barrows. He has each of them convinced that he or she is special, a favorite. My brother created a network for him before he came here."

We sat at the table. Michael sat close to me. Too close. I didn't object in spite of the discomfort. He knew this creature far better than I did.

"Michael, have you been avoiding me?" Aiakós asked. He poured three glasses of wine. I suppressed a shiver. Though I'd noticed them before, his claws looked deadlier up close. Short claws, short enough not to interfere with his use of his hands, but they looked sharp enough to tear through flesh. He was like a big cat, walking carefully and silently through the night, ready to pounce and shred whatever crossed his path.

"No, I haven't been avoiding you. I've been busy."

Aiakós smiled directly at me. "Which reminds me, thank you for saving his life, Madeline. I arrived that night just as the creature attacked. You were magnificent. Michael is stronger than it, but taken unawares, it could have been fatal. Innana requires that I hide myself here. To amuse myself, I walk these empty ruins at night when no one can see. I try to kill those beasts when I can. I fear they might start breeding."

I didn't like that. "You don't kill the gentle ones, do you? The ones with scales."

Aiakós's laughter filled the room. It bubbled and rolled, giving the illusion of true mirth—with an edge. He leaned back, obviously interested. "You feel sorry for the creatures?"

Michael laid a hand on my knee. I shoved it off. He grabbed his glass of wine and swallowed it in one gulp.

"You kill just for fun?" Anger slid through me. "It doesn't matter that they probably don't want to be here? That some of them wouldn't hurt anyone?"

Aiakós stopped smiling. He leaned forward. "I do not wish to be here. But I am. And though I must hide, I will control my surroundings. This place, this prison, is mine. And, yes, Madeline, I have killed many times simply to amuse myself. I warn you this one time: Never come between me and my prey."

"Are you invulnerable?" I don't pray, but I thought I would ask the Earth Mother to keep her ward tight.

Aiakós didn't speak for a moment; then he said,

"Not entirely. You could probably kill me with a bomb or a missile. Your little knife will only annoy me."

I thought about it for a moment. "My mother was a witch. A powerful witch. I did not inherit her power, but she taught me other things. The biggest, most violent creature can be driven to its knees with the right magic."

A smile curled his lips. "True, but you have said you are not a witch. And your Earth Mother will not intervene to save you here in the Barrows should I choose to destroy you."

"No. The holy bitch did not intervene to save her faithful servant, my own mother, the night she was raped and murdered. She would not come for me."

Aiakós laughed, loud and strong. "Well, it's nice to see that not all of Innana's followers blindly worship her. Someday I'll tell you stories about your precious Earth Mother. We were friends before . . . Ah, so long ago. But I wonder, are you one of those fanatical humans who throw their lives away for some foolish cause?"

"Love and honor are not foolish. Destroy me you may, but I would stand between you and those I love."

He stared at me with those alien eyes. I could not read that wonderful face, except to note the similarities between it and Michael's.

He gave a brief nod of his head, as if acknowledging my statement—or judging its veracity. He turned his smile on Michael. "Have you given more thought to my request that you join me?"

"I've thought about it."

"What do you want him to do that he finds so onerous?" It was a personal question that I would not ask in many situations, but Michael had drawn me into an intimate, though possibly deadly, situation.

Aiakós's fingers, his claws, tapped lightly on the tabletop. It sounded like the rattle of old, dry bones. "I wish him to come here, accept his heritage, and truly be my son, not some pretty human. Somehow, I must overcome his reluctance. He blames me for the death of his mother."

Michael shifted. His outer thigh pressed hard against mine. That statement disturbed him. Much of what Aiakós spoke of was indecipherable to me, but I would demand that Michael explain later.

"And if he joins you, what then?"

"With him to act on my behalf, I will find a way to force Innana to free me. Innana lives in the past, rigidly adhering to her ancient principles. She refuses to control the scurrying mass of human animals overrunning her land. Because of her insistence on free will, she's allowed them to breed and create weapons that could destroy every living thing in this world." He clenched one of his great hands into a fist. "I would do a better job." He stared straight at me. "And once I am free of this place, I will."

Michael rose. He offered me his hand. I ignored it and stood too.

Aiakós chuckled. He rose to his considerable height and came to me. He offered me a clawed hand. "Let there be peace between us, Madeline. As a gift to you, I will not kill the gentle beasts."

I glanced at Michael. He looked away.

I laid my hand in Aiakós's. It was smooth and large enough that I could avoid the claws easily. "Thank you. I will harm nothing of yours that does not seek to harm me or those I love."

His other hand closed over mine. "Daughter, you are well matched with my son, even if it is Innana's scheme."

I didn't know what to say to that.

chapter 18

Étienne and Clark were gone when we went back down the stairs. Only smears of Clark's drying blood remained to indicate violence.

Michael didn't start the car right away when we climbed in.

"Madeline, I've given you a great deal of myself, more than I've ever shown anyone. I've trusted you with my only family, abhorrent as he might be. Did I do wrong?"

"He's not abhorrent. He's magnificent. And terrifying."

Michael had let me into the bitter truth of his life. Our relationship, whatever it was, had changed.

So I told him of Justice, and what I'd done there. How I got there. I spoke of the Drows and the Sisters' mission to fight them when they intruded on the Earth Mother's territory. I stopped short of speaking of the role of the Sisters as executioners for errant witches. He seemed rather fond of Abigail.

"Eunice and Lillian, they're Sisters?"

"Yes."

"Well, that explains many things. Would they kill Aiakós?"

"He's the ultimate Drow. But I won't talk about him with the Sisters. Not until I understand more."

"You think they could take him?" He sounded genuinely curious.

I chuckled. "Not alone. It would be a hell of a fight. Would you like us to try?"

"No!" Concern filled his voice. "If it comes to that, I'll be the one."

"Alone?"

"Yes." He started the car and drove away from the Zombie.

"Do you think you could actually kill him?"

Michael shook his head. "No."

I considered. Eunice, Lillian, and I could form the Triad Lillian had spoken of. A tingle of fear twisted through me. Or was it excitement? Is that why they had come? To kill a Drow?

I shifted in my seat, my mind returning to Aiakós's words about binding. The soft leather had suddenly become uncomfortable.

"You consider him a monster?" I asked.

"Yes. He is evil, Madeline. And dangerous. A liar. He not only looks good, but he has the ability to persuade humans to commit vile crimes. They believe they serve a god."

That sounded like most religions to me. Unrestrained zealots. I considered the Sisters' deference to the Earth Mother in that category, too. Given what I knew about them, a Sister of Justice would kill on command, without questioning, believing all the while it was a good thing.

Michael turned the car onto an empty River Street. "As you've seen, I have a similar effect on people. But I'm not comfortable with it. I try to avoid relationships with . . ." He paused, searching for words. I supplied them.

"Fans? Groupies? Worshippers?"

"Yes. But you're not like that. Aiakós said it. You're a warrior. A guardian. You have the courage of a tiger. You saved my life, and actually stepped between me and Aiakós tonight."

I drew deep slow breaths and tried to think. Is that how he saw me? We had a relationship? Yes, we did, but it was threatening to overwhelm me.

Michael pulled up to Harry's and parked at the curb. "That first night, when I held you in my arms, I did not see a scar. I do not see a scar."

"But it's there. It's a part of me. It's a reminder of my duty to my parents. To the Sisters." I turned to face him. I couldn't read him or his intentions.

"You ask what I want from you." He held both of my hands in his now. I was intensely aware of it. "I want to help you fulfill your mission. Let me into your life. Trust me. I can help you. No one knows the Barrows better than I do. Not even the Bastinados."

I realized I was shaking, a fine shiver like a chill before the full blast of winter. Only I wasn't cold. I was hot. The confinement of the car suffocated me.

"I need to think about it."

"May I come for you tomorrow?"

"Come around two. We can talk then." A brief decision and I was on firmer ground. He opened the car door and climbed out. I drew deep breaths. By the time he came around and opened my door, I had regained some composure.

At three a.m., even the most determined of sidewalk people had found some other place to live or maybe sleep. I'd never been in a place where the silence fell as it did in the Barrows. The night seemed to be holding its breath, daring anyone, anything, to disturb its intensity. An hour ago, I'd ridden through dark streets to meet a creature of great power and beauty, something even a woman who grew up with magic could find amazing. What would happen tomorrow?

Michael walked me to the alcove at the front door of Harry's.

He stood close. "If you need me, I'll be at the Archangel. Whatever you need to do, I'll help." He laid gentle hands on my shoulders.

I turned to open the door when he seized me and drew me tightly in his arms. I found myself clinging to the magnificent man, desiring him, needing him—a surge of emotion so sudden I was shocked by the rise of it. His lips touched mine like a whisper, a gentle brush. Then he claimed them, urgent but soft. I had to hold him, draw him closer.

Since that horrific night when I was seventeen, I had desired nothing but revenge. Locked into an obsessive hatred as the Sisters drove me, molded me into a weapon, I had rejected even self-gratification. Now my body's needs threatened to overwhelm me. All that wonderful muscle under my fingers, unbearable sensations running through me, his hands sliding down to drag me closer and—

He stopped.

His breath was ragged as he gently pushed me away. "Forgive me. I keep rushing you."

I stood, reeling from the kiss and its sudden end. What was he doing to me?

I left him there and walked into the building without a word. I was tired, confused, irritated, and dreaded the dreams that would plague me when I finally slept. I trudged up the stairs, trying to turn my mind into a blank wall.

chapter 19

I'd no more than entered my room when a scratching came at the window. Looking out, I saw Spot, my little dragon friend. I raised the window and he jumped from the sill to the bed. He made odd little sounds that might have been a language, punctuated by a high-pitched yap, like a small dog.

"Hush. Harry will hear you."

He fell silent. He understood me.

He hopped from the bed back to the windowsill, where he made another sound. This one came out soft, like a whisper. He sat on his haunches, his wings folded, tail out the window and summoned me with his . . . paws? . . . Hands? I went to the window and he jumped off. I stuck my head out. The building next door was only a single story and had a flat roof. Spot landed on the roof of the other building.

He barked again.

"Okay, Lassie," I muttered. "I'll follow."

I was tired and wanted to go to bed, but this little creature had touched me, just as his larger brethren had at the Goblin Den. I climbed out the window and lowered myself down to the single-story roof. When I reached Spot, I saw his concern. Another of his kind lay there. I dropped to my knees. The second dragon seemed to be hurt. I reached for it. It growled and bared impossible teeth—dragonlike teeth. I knew a warning when I heard one.

"I can't help unless you let me," I said.

Spot made chirruping sounds again. The second stilled. There was a streetlamp near the second building and I could see the problem. Spot's companion had an injury, a tear in the skin across the back near one wing. I had no idea what to do about it. It lay panting under my hand. It must have made a heroic flight to get here, out of harm's way.

I needed more light. I stripped off my jacket and made a sling. "Let's get inside."

Spot mumbled his assent.

The second made no noise as I wrapped it up. I could probably drag myself back up into my room through the window, but not while carrying the little creature. At least my room key was still in my pocket. There was a ladder bolted to the back of the single-story for roof access, probably because of the large heating and AC units there. I climbed down, went around, and walked upstairs to my apartment.

Back inside, I assessed the damage to my new mini-dragon. The cut, while probably painful, was not gaping. It did have dirt in it. The only thing I had resembling a washcloth was a T-shirt. At least Cassandra had given me a supply.

I held the injured dragon in my lap and cleaned the wound. I had nothing to dress it with, and if I did, I didn't know if it would work. I opened a dresser drawer about halfway, grabbed a couple of T-shirts, and made a bed. Carefully, I laid my patient in the drawer. Tomorrow I could get a towel or something.

Spot slid in with his injured companion. "Okay, guys, here's the deal. I'll leave the window open and you can come and go. I'll get you some food, but please be very quiet." I knew Harry wouldn't approve of reptiles in the building. "What can I call you?" I stared at them. They stared back.

There were no visible organs to tell if they were male or female, so I made an assumption. I brushed the injured one with a finger. "You can be Grace." I had a lovely cat once named Grace. "Spot and Grace. Is that okay?"

Spot gave a low bark I accepted as consent.

Then I went to bed and fell right asleep. If my visitors made any noises, I didn't hear them.

The whine and crash of something large being dropped outside on the street woke me at daylight. I ignored it, but it was replaced by shouting. I groaned. I had to go to the window to look. The sun had barely risen, and it gave a soft light across the wide street.

A truck roared and whined as it pulled away, leaving a massive open Dumpster covering two parking spaces in front of Hildy's pawnshop.

Eunice and Hildy stood toe-to-toe on the sidewalk,

by the Dumpster, obviously arguing. Hildy did a bit of arm waving, too. I laughed but understood the futility and frustration Hildy felt. I'd seen it in many of the Sisters at Justice. The immovable Eunice would eventually prevail.

chapter 20

June 23

I showered, dressed, and glanced out the window again. As I watched, Eunice came out the front door of the pawnshop with a large dresser on her shoulder. She heaved it into the Dumpster as easily as if she were tossing a garment into a laundry basket. I wondered exactly how much strength those muscles and sturdy bones held.

Spot was gone and Grace was asleep, snug in her drawer. I went down to the grocery store and bought some sandwich meat and a package of frozen fried chicken. I grabbed a bowl for water. Grace accepted the bologna with delicate bites. I hoped it wouldn't give her the runs. I opened the chicken and left the package on top of the dresser. Maybe it would thaw before Spot came back.

I wore only my knives this morning. I decided I'd better check on Hildy and Eunice. I would not come between them, however; nor would I choose sides in any argument. I crossed the street and walked into a scene that reeked of ferocity and magic.

Eunice had stripped the pawnshop of its contents, leaving lots of open space. Apparently missing her favorite times at Justice, she'd created room for some serious violence. She'd spread a large practice mat, which I was very familiar with, across the floor. Eunice had created her own space, regardless of Hildy's wishes.

Eunice and Hildy stood side by side, and Lillian stood on point in front of them. I realized they formed a triangle. Then I noticed Abigail in the room—and a barrier of magic in front of her that she must've thrown up to defend herself against the Sisters. I rushed to stand between them and the earth witch.

"Stay out of the way, Madeline," Lillian said.

"No. I won't." I threw my hands up in frustration. "Is this what you came here for, Sisters? If it's not, I suggest you stop. I can feel magic, remember? This witch can fry an army of Sisters."

"She came here looking for you." Lillian spoke without taking her eyes off Abigail.

"And here I am." I was neither Sister nor witch and I would not take either side—for now. I nodded at Abigail. "How may I serve you, Innana's daughter?"

"I've come with a message for you," Abigail said. She kept her eyes on the Sisters.

"And that message is?"

"I don't know yet." She stared pointedly at the three Sisters. "Will you keep the wolves from my throat while I deliver it?"

"Of course."

Eunice growled.

"Stand down, Eunice!" Lillian had ceded authority in this matter to me.

Abigail closed her eyes. She drew a deep breath. I knew this. My mother had told me the Earth Mother sometimes communicated through her witches without letting them know what the message was. The assembled Sisters came to stand beside me.

"Greetings, daughter." Abigail's voice had changed. It was filled with power. "I watch you, even if I cannot aid you directly. You have done well. But know this: Time is running out. You have met Aiakós. You understand the danger. He does not know the stone is within the realm of his influence. If he obtains it, he may be able to cross my ward. Then there will be a battle for this world that could very well destroy it. You have only two days. Find it!"

After a moment, Abigail relaxed. She swayed and I steadied her. "Are you okay?"

She nodded.

"What's happening?" Lillian asked. She brought Abigail a chair, and Abigail sat with a sigh.

For the Sisters, the delivery of the message had clarified Abigail's presence and I could see that curiosity had changed their attitude a bit. Hildy brought her a glass of water, but she gave it to me to hand to Abigail. She would not touch the witch. I understood. The last time I touched one it altered my life forever.

"The Earth Mother put the message in her mind," I said. "Humans, even witches, are not meant to carry that kind of burden for more than a few minutes. She's disoriented. It takes at least a half hour to get here. Too much time."

All those lessons my mother taught me about the earth witches and the Mother were finally proving useful.

"Oh, it's a burden," Abigail said. She drew deep breaths. "Cassandra once carried the Earth Mother within herself entirely, allowing her to come into the Barrows without breaking her own ward."

My respect for Cassandra rose immeasurably. "How did she do it?"

"It was painful, to say the least. But does the message I brought serve you?"

I sighed. "Depends. What happens in two days?"

"The summer solstice," Abigail said. "The solstice always brings change, even if we don't know it. This coming solstice is on a dark moon. Evil is always ascendant in the Barrows on a dark moon. The combination could be catastrophic." She raised her eyes to those around her. I was reminded of Cass's reference to a dark moon conjunction. How the last one had changed the Earth Mother. While the dark moon rarely played a role in my life, my family lived by the solstice and equinox, the divisions of time, the Earth Mother's only clock.

"I don't know Madeline's mission," Abigail continued. "But whatever it is, you must help her, Sisters."

"We will," Lillian said. "If we know how."

"If she will let us." Eunice wasn't happy.

"Does it concern the murderer you said you were searching for?" Abigail asked.

"Yes, but there's more to it than my personal crusade."

"I wish Cassandra could help you more," Abigail said. "Only one person knows the Barrows better than she, and that's Michael. But I'm not sure he can be trusted."

"Oh yeah." Eunice laughed. "We met him. Pretty boy has a hard-on for our little Madeline. Who is Aiakós?"

I froze. I had to keep them from going after Aiakós. At least until I figured things out.

"Aiakós is Michael's father. I met him last night. He is a rather magnificent creature, a Drow if you will, from another world."

"Oh, beware of Aiakós, Madeline." Abigail rose from her chair, a look of concern on her face.

"I will. I know deadly when I see it."

I glanced at Hildy and she gave me an I-told-you-so smile. Hildy pulled a pack of cigarettes out of her pocket. Lillian and Eunice glared at her and she put them away.

"I'm fine now," Abigail said. She did look steadier. I needed to get her out of the Armory. While some tension had eased, it could turn volatile again.

"Hey. Witch," Eunice said. "You should come back and play with us sometime."

Abigail smiled. "Sister Eunice, I could have taken your Triad rather easily. You would need the Solaire and Morié to hurt me. I know Madeline has the Solaire, and she's not inclined to do me harm."

The Sisters exchanged glances.

"I have the Morié, too." I flipped my coat to show the knife. "Hildy told me about their power. How do they work?" I asked slowly.

"They are protection." Abigail spoke up before they could. "Having both makes you immune to earth magic. In a Triad, the one with the Solaire and Morié is the protected one. An earth witch of my standing can easily take out two sisters on her own. Two points of a Triad. They're offered up as distractions while the protected one goes in for the kill."

"The base points of a Triad are a sacrifice," I said, catching on.

No one answered, which was an answer in itself.

"So, how did I wind up with the Morié and Solaire?" I stuck my finger in my shirt and rubbed my finger over the amulet.

"Obviously, the Earth Mother wanted you to have them," Abigail said. She frowned. "Though I don't know why."

"I don't either." And I didn't. I was immune to earth magic anyway. Abigail knew I was immune to earth magic. The Sisters did not. I cast my eyes around the room. I wasn't getting any answers from the Sisters. "It doesn't matter." I caught her gently by the arm. "Let's get you to your car."

She hugged me. It startled me. From their faces, I'd say it surprised the Sisters, too. Exactly how much discord was there between witch and warrior?

"Does she know about the Portal?" Hildy asked after Abigail left.

"I don't know," I said. "She's in direct contact with

the Earth Mother, but I don't think the Mother tells her everything. The Mother plays war games with blind soldiers."

"What do you want us to do?" Lillian asked. Was she ceding control to me again?

"Okay." I grinned at them. "I need help. I need copies of a drawing. The man I'm looking for. We can start walking up and down River Street." I figured that River Street was only one block deep in most places. Three of us could cover a lot of ground. "Try to keep the story simple. Long-lost brother who owes me money. Something benign."

It wasn't much, but it was a start. I might get lucky. I figured it would take luck to pull it off.

chapter 21

When I went to my room to get the drawing, I found Spot staring at the chicken.

"Something wrong, Spot?"

He chirped.

"Go ahead." I gestured at the chicken. "I don't have any way to warm it."

Spot snatched a piece of chicken and dropped down to Grace. He served her first. I'd been taught that Drows were dangerous, and certainly Cassandra had experiences with that. I hoped there was some way to help these little creatures, no matter what they were. They had an air of civility that was rare, even in humans.

I retrieved the drawing from my room and brought it to Hildy, who had a functioning copy machine in the back. Hildy glared at Eunice and occasionally glared at her now-empty storefront. Eunice had cleared it to make a fighting practice room, one that I was sure she would demand that I use soon. Hildy probably didn't have much business, but Eunice had battered her with the usual Eunice sledgehammer.

"I'm going to talk to Michael," I told them. "Maybe show the picture to a few people on the way."

He had said he'd pick me up at two, but if I asked the Sisters to go door-to-door, I'd better do it, too.

"What about this Aiakós?" Eunice asked. She sounded eager.

A chill came over me. I held up a hand. "Do not go looking for Aiakós, Eunice. I beg you. I do not know what kind of Drows you have battled in the past, but he's not the same. He is not a mere animal."

Eunice sneered. "Oh, my. Is it because he's your pretty boy's daddy?"

"No." Hildy ignored Eunice's nasty looks and lit up. "It's because he will tear you apart." She sighed and blew out the smoke. "I've seen him, Eunice. Annihilation is the word. Twenty of us couldn't take him. And the Earth Mother wants him here. He's her pet. Leave him be."

"What?" Lillian's eyebrows went up. "He's bronze-proof?"

Hildy chuckled. "Don't know. Don't want to find out." She pulled a deep lungful of smoke.

Eunice grumbled and stalked out.

It was early, so I stopped at a small café and bought a coffee and a sweet roll. I bought a second roll and made a pig of myself—but it had been at least twelve hours since I'd eaten. The way things were going, I didn't know when I'd get to eat again.

I stopped often as I walked on. A few had seen my man. Not often, just occasionally. Day, sometimes night. I might just come across him after all.

As I passed through the Archangel's parking lot, the

number of high-end vehicles amazed me. I bet they came for Michael, just as they came to the Goblin Den to see him. As I approached the place, I saw that it was a high-end exercise studio. I had never thought to ask what kind of business it was. Michael was clearly diverse in his business ventures. Maybe that was part of his success.

The morning exercise crowd stared when I walked into the Archangel. But they quickly turned away. A heavy-duty bouncer type edged closer, studying me, assessing a possible threat. As Cassandra had said, Michael had hired people to protect his exclusive clientele. I didn't think he could see the knives under my jacket, but I wasn't sure. I waited for him to challenge me. He didn't. He didn't stop watching either.

The perky little blonde at the desk did not smile. I'd wager she was barely eighteen. She had a great body and wore a tight, stretchy outfit that displayed it well. Her name tag with its little angel wings said she was Candice. Of course she was. I'd never been blond, but perhaps, for a brief time, I'd been pretty and perky. I couldn't remember. She pushed her upper arms together to enhance her cleavage. Not for my benefit, but it was probably habit by now.

"Do you have an appointment?" Candice, for all her youth, knew how to pitch her voice in a tone that said I was not worthy of such a high-class establishment.

"I'm here to see Michael."

She gave me a look that said I lived in a fantasy world, filled with delusions that I might actually be someone Michael would honor with his presence.

"He's not in." She said it so abruptly she had to be lying.

"Candy, I think you've made a mistake." I talked to her as I would to a naughty child. "Why don't you try to find him?"

She glanced at the bouncer, looking for help. He shrugged. He'd probably assessed that I was no real threat. A bit careless, though, since my jacket covered some deadly weapons. He probably just didn't like her either.

"My name is Candice." She spoke in a tone as tight as her ass, but she picked up the phone. After a moment she said, "Sir, there's a woman to see you."

"It's Madeline, Candy." It seemed petty, pushing little girls around, but I was enjoying myself doing the Eunice thing.

"Her name is Madeline," Candy said quickly. Her face fell as Michael spoke on the other end. She hung up the phone, her face a mask of pure hatred. "He'll be right down."

"Thank you." I spoke politely, but my smile was pure *I told you so*.

Michael's studio, the appropriately named Archangel, was a bright and airy place, filled with machines, green plants, and people. A snack bar was tucked into one corner and the ceiling was two stories high. There were stairs along the back wall to a second floor. Moments later, Michael hurried down them to meet me. As he did, the same collective sigh that had occurred in the Den last night greeted him.

I inwardly groaned. Magnificent as usual, he was as

beautiful as a movie star in a glamour photo. Last night I had kissed him. He had kissed me. But some little worm of doubt still wiggled in my mind. How could it not? From the moment he met me, he had pushed for a relationship, one I wasn't sure I was ready for.

Michael slid an arm around me, drew me close, and kissed me lightly on the mouth.

The crowd gasped. I was shocked as well. He didn't appear to notice.

"I'm glad you came." Michael frowned. "Is something wrong?"

I shook my head. He'd left me speechless again. I had to get over that.

Michael held my hand and led me up to his office. I didn't like the possessiveness, but it was his place and I didn't want to make a scene.

We entered a room where a massive window overlooked the floor. Sleek and modern, his office had a single glass-top desk, a long creamy leather couch, chairs in the corner, and a small bar. I grinned. "You don't work here, do you?"

He laughed. "I don't work at all. I pay people to do things for me."

I shook my head. Humility was not one of his virtues.

I handed him the drawing. He stared for a long time, then handed it back to me. "I've seen him."

I quirked an eyebrow. I wasn't expecting a lead so early.

Michael touched the picture. "He washed dishes in the kitchen for a while, I think. Months ago. I don't usually keep tabs on dishwashers, but we had problems with him. He was unstable—couldn't function and couldn't take care of himself. The manager drove him to one of the homeless shelters. I told the staff to feed him if he came by again. We'll ask them." He picked up a cell phone from the desk and handed it to me. "In the meantime, this is for you. When I'm not around. It won't work deep in the Barrows, but it does work on the periphery and on River Street. I programmed my number and the Archangel's private and public lines. If you need me, you can call."

I dropped the phone when the building's alarms blared like a freight train horn. Michael rushed for his office door. When he threw it open, shouts and screams poured in from the studio floor below. Worse, the crack of gunshots broke the air over the sound of the alarm.

I followed. An ugly scene spread out below me. Six men had the fitness crowd backed up against a wall, lined up like victims of a firing squad. The gunmen appeared ordinary in size and build, dressed in jeans, shirts, jackets; you could pass them on the street without notice—except for the ski masks. Every one of them had a significant pistol in his hand. All I had were knives.

Michael didn't slow. He reached the bottom of the steps and snatched the first man he reached, lifted him bodily over his head, and threw him at the others. The man hit his companions like a runaway truck. He didn't just knock them down; he plowed through three of them, flattening them. Michael snatched up another one and threw him. The force wrapped the man's body around a weight-lifting machine like a contortionist in a circus side show. I stopped and stared in shock. Michael was using bodies like bowling balls.

The sudden eruption of violence—and Michael's entrance—had brought gasps and cries from the patrons still lined up against the wall. Even in the midst of terror, they focused on him, not the true danger, the men with guns.

One of the men still standing turned his gun to Michael. Michael tore it out of his hand and smashed the man's face with his fist as if he were punching a loaf of bread dough. The odors of blood and terror, stirred by the air-conditioning, filled the room.

A single gunshot. Michael's body jerked. A splash of blood appeared in the middle of his back, a scarlet bloom on his pure white silk shirt.

Michael whirled to face the shooter, who held a large-caliber pistol.

Again, the man pulled the trigger. This one hit Michael in the chest. I heard it, a solid smack of metal in flesh.

Enormous silence fell after the sharp crack of gunfire. Michael stood where he should have fallen dead. Then he growled. Not a warning, but the full savage attack of a wolf. More terrifying was the pleasure in that growl. He wanted to kill.

In two steps, Michael had the shooter. He didn't even bother to take the gun away. As with the others, he picked him up, but this one he threw through the front plate-glass window. The man didn't even slow down as he hit the glass. He landed in the middle of

River Street. Tires screeched, horns blasted—I'm relatively certain he was already dead or at least unconscious when the cars ran over him.

The lone remaining would-be thief ran, scrambling out the shattered window since it was closer than the door. Sirens sounded in the distance as the fallen lay there either still and silent or slowly moaning.

Michael instantly whirled and raced through a door in the back wall of the studio.

I followed him into a hallway with multiple doors. I'd been a part of much violence at Justice, but nothing at the speed and level of the last minute.

"Michael." My voice sounded nearly hysterical as I blindly ran after him. A door to my right opened. I faced a rectangle of black, a windowless room.

"Come in," Michael said. He was close. His voice sounded deep and filled with mystery. He sounded like Aiakós. "Close the door."

I did as he asked. Total darkness filled the room; then a small light came on. He stood with his back to me. I laid my hand on his shirt, on the bloody hole where the bullet had struck. His back was solid. It had healed just as his hand had last night.

Michael turned to face me. He had changed. His face was a mask of Aiakós's ferocity, and his skin glowed as if polished with fine oil. His eyes were no longer the wonderful blue I had known. They captivated me, animal gold, intense and predatory. Did anger, rage bring out his inner nature? A bit of a shape-shifter was this son of Aiakós, the demon who ruled the Zombie Zone.

To be with him would be like loving a great golden cat. Not safe, but infinitely exciting.

I laid a hand on his chest. His heart beat under my fingers, steady and strong. As each moment passed, I realized he was everything I wanted in a man—both gentle and brutal by turn, if he needed to be.

"You're not afraid?" Surprise filled his voice, as if he had believed I would run away.

"No. Yes." He was destroying me. My body cried for him. I ran my hand down his chest. He rubbed the back of his hand against my cheek. His claws were not Aiakós's, but they would tear flesh nonetheless.

The gold in his eyes faded and the blue returned. He drew a deep breath. The glorious smile returned. My smile. He smiled at me, truly at me, knowing me. For the first time, I believed, truly believed. He wanted me.

"I was afraid for you. In the studio."

"They were just Bastinados, most likely. Thieves who wanted to steal from my wealthy clients."

I couldn't tear my eyes from him. He took a step closer. "Now you know me." He wrapped his arms around me. "I will change shape like this when we make love. But I am in control in this state. I won't hurt you. Madeline, you are incredibly beautiful in my eyes. You have so much power over me. From that moment you lay dying in my arms, I knew I had to have you, to save you. I don't know what will become of me if you can't accept me."

A tiny fountain of self-preservation rose in me, followed by the briefest second of panic. "Don't try to control me. That is something I cannot bear."

"That is a battle I'll fight every day because I want to protect you." He stood a little straighter. "I will protect you. I will kill for you—"

"Stop. I don't want that. I'll do my own killing." I turned away from him. It wasn't what I meant, but he needed to know I wasn't defenseless.

From the first moment I saw him, I wanted him. I would, however, at all costs, protect my independence. No matter how difficult, arrogant, and controlling Michael proved to be.

Blaring noises came from outside the room. Michael glared at the door, as if his anger alone would make everything go away. It didn't work. Approaching sirens shrieked, coming closer.

"We need to take care of this immediately," he said. In a second he had stripped off the bloodied shirt and handed it to me. "Will you dispose of this?"

I accepted the shirt.

He gave me a quick kiss. "We can talk later."

"Talk."

"Well, maybe we can do some other things, too."

"Other things?" Damn, I sounded like a parrot.

He laughed softly. "Only if you want to."

"Yes. No. I can't decide that right now." Oh, hell, I couldn't even think.

He left me there and I went on autopilot. I rolled the shirt in a tight bundle and held it close. The front of the studio was filled with police and EMTs, people I didn't want to see. I hurried out the back door.

Chaos churned in my mind, stirring everything into an emotional soup. Relationships. Sex. I didn't know what I thought, and I didn't know what I wanted. So I fixated on the thing I was here for. The Portal. I had to find the Portal. And the man who had killed my parents. I couldn't be distracted by any other man—or whatever Michael happened to be.

chapter 22

The alley behind the Archangel stretched a good three blocks parallel to River Street. I walked away at a steady pace, past the foul-smelling Dumpsters. No hurry, no rush. I wouldn't attract attention, not that there was anyone around to see me. After I scanned the area to be sure I was alone, the shirt went in a Dumpster filled with food waste. I found a piece of pipe and jammed it deep.

I cut back to River Street and caught the uptown bus. I had to think. I wanted to think, try to make sense of things. The magical things I had seen in my early life seemed tame compared to the last few days. I had a man, a half-human man, whom I desired enough to die for; a killer to find; the Portal to find. No matter what action I took, it got sidetracked in another direction.

The bus crossed the Sullen River and rolled into the downtown transfer hub, where it parked with at least ten others of its kind. I climbed off and the buses around me rumbled and pumped out toxic diesel smoke like mechanical versions of Hildy. It left me disoriented and longing for clean air.

The sun warmed the day, but a breeze kept the temperature from rising above a moderate spring morning. Benches placed amid planters of multicolored flowers decorated the small urban park. I sat under a lovely maple tree.

Earth magic shimmered around me, as it did with all living things. I breathed in and let it fill me up. I loved the life I could sense in this world, even if I couldn't use it to create potions and spells. The Earth Mother came, sliding in on a breeze. She remained invisible this time, but I could feel her. A single tiny flower drifted from nowhere and landed in my hand.

"Tell me why you let them die. Why you didn't help them." I spoke in a whisper, one filled with bitterness. "My mother loved you, trusted you." There was no answer. I hadn't expected one, but I suppose I could hope.

I tossed the flower away and walked back to the transfer station to catch the bus back to the Barrows. Answers to all my questions would be there, including what to do about Michael.

I caught the next bus and the driver was my new friend Jim.

"Thought you worked four to twelve," I said.

"Working a double today. Driver out sick." He glanced over his shoulder at the almost empty bus. "Hey," he said quietly. "Got three hundred for that piece. You want part?"

The gun I'd given him was worth more than I'd thought. "No. You keep it." I did need money, but I suspected the disabled vet needed it worse. Three little brown prescription bottles of pills sat in a tray by the steering wheel.

I showed him my murderer's picture.

"Yeah. I see him. Sometimes he begs a ride. I let him on if we're not too crowded. Kinda pitiful. Always looking over his shoulder. 'Course, that happens a lot here."

Now I had a picture of a timid, pitiful man who worked in kitchens and begged for food and transportation. Certainly not the vision of a killer my mother had left me.

When the bus passed the Archangel, police cars still filled the lot. I didn't get off.

"Wonder what happened there," Jim said.

"An attempted robbery, I think."

When I climbed off at Harry's, the pawnshop across the street had a CLOSED sign on the door. There was no sign of activity. I went back to my room.

Grace slept and Spot was not around. They'd cleaned up the chicken. I really didn't know what to think of these strange little creatures, other than they were harmless and relatively intelligent. But some communication had passed between our little trio on an extrasensory level, though I'd never thought of myself as sensitive to such things, except earth magic. Spot and Grace were capable of some humanlike emotions. I hoped I could protect them. I'm not sure what arrangements they made about personal hygiene, but I hadn't had to clean up after Grace.

Two o'clock passed and no Michael. He was probably dealing with cops. I figured I could kill some time, ask more questions, and look for my man. This time, though, I put on the gun. The shoulder harness fit well enough with some adjustments. It would be okay unless I hesitated on whether to draw the gun or the knife.

Cassandra had loaded the gun and given me an extra magazine with bronze-coated bullets. Handmade, she said. Maybe they wouldn't blow up in my face. I shoved the extra magazine in my jacket pocket.

I thought of the cell phone Michael had offered to me. I'd left it at the Archangel. I hoped I wouldn't need it.

I worked my way down the street. The grocery store, hardware store, nothing. One possibility formed in my mind. What if my man no longer had the Portal? Michael had mentioned that he was unstable.

The Earth Mother was sure it was here somewhere. The endless possibilities frustrated me. Why couldn't she see it if she could see into the Barrows? Why wouldn't she lead me directly to it?

A few doors down from the hardware store I went into Amalee's Bakery. Red-checked cloths covered a few small tables for patrons, and the smell was heavenly. The woman behind the counter gave me a glorious smile. She wore a pink dress trimmed in lace, hair as white as mine, with soft green eyes and only a few wrinkles.

"Welcome. Come in. I just made coffee." She pointed to a small table in the corner. "Oh, sit, please. I have fresh donuts. I'm Amalee, by the way." The words came out in a rush, as if she feared I'd leave before she served me. Her bakery case had very few items for sale. I hated to tell her no. I asked about the sesame rolls and the next thing I knew I was sitting at the table with them, butter, and a few fresh strawberries. She also set me up with a glass of lemonade. I asked her to sit with me.

Amalee had seen my man, fed him because she pitied him. She couldn't remember when. "He was very timid," she said. She smiled with kindness I couldn't feel.

So many people had seen my man, but no one could say where he might be at any given time. How frustrating.

Étienne met me as I walked out the door. No visible gun, but he too wore a vest over a T-shirt, probably concealing one. He was a fine man. Slim, tight, graceful.

I smiled at him. "Hi. What are you doing here?" What else could I say? Oh, by the way, how's old Clark?

"I understand you're looking for someone," he said.

"I am." I pulled the drawing out of my jacket pocket and handed it to him. As I did, I flashed the gun.

He raised an eyebrow, skeptical and slightly amused. "Can you use that piece?"

"Yes."

"Are you good with it?"

I grinned at him.

"Why didn't you use it on Clark?"

I shrugged. "Didn't want to waste a bullet, makes too much noise . . . the usual"

Étienne smiled before he stared at the photo I offered to him. He frowned. "He's been around."

Damn, damn. *Been around.* Why couldn't he *be around* when I was?

"What do you want with him?" Étienne asked.

I decided I had little to gain by lying here. Everyone in the Barrows had experienced violence in their lives, some as victims and others as aggressors. "He killed my mother and father."

Étienne gazed at me, his face blank. "Haven't seen him in a while. I'll keep an eye out for him. May I walk with you?"

"Sure."

"What do you plan to do if you find him?" Étienne asked.

I narrowed my eyes. "I'd think it would be obvious."

He was silent a moment. "His name is Hascomb. Kenny Hascomb. He worked for me for a while last year."

I stepped away to face him, a bit shocked. Étienne offered the information a little too late in the conversation—and too casually—for my taste. "Is he a friend of yours? Is that why you're protecting him?"

"No. He's a homeless vagrant." A soft accent rolled through his voice. A cultured accent, one that might have come from an education and refinement associated with wealth and privilege. Whatever he did now, it stood far apart from his earlier years.

"It sounds like you feel sorry for him," I remarked. "What if he'd killed your mother?"

"I would stake him out somewhere in the woods, soak him in syrup, and let anything that wanted to come along munch on him. Of course, I'd be sure he had plenty of water. He'd last longer that way."

I swallowed hard. "Okay. Speaking from personal experience, are you?"

Étienne chuckled. "Maybe. Does it bother you?"

"Not really." This place was filled with violent creatures, myself included.

I noticed that the few pedestrians on the streets stepped wide around us. People in the Barrows seemed preternaturally aware when danger walked in their midst.

"How long have you been looking for Kenny?" Étienne asked.

"Awhile." Silence followed. I didn't feel like elaborating on my story.

"Did you see what happened at the Archangel today?" The way he asked the question made me think he knew the answer.

"I did."

"So, you saw Michael take several bullets without harm."

"Yes." I tightened up. "Only two bullets. Not several."

Étienne stopped and turned to face me. "You care about him, don't you?"

I didn't answer. I didn't have time. A noise, footsteps on the sidewalk, made me look back. At least ten Bastinados were closing in on us.

"Étienne," I whispered.

He followed my eyes and turned to look over his shoulder.

"Run," he said.

chapter 23

As Étienne and I raced away, I quickly realized these were not undisciplined animals barreling into the ruins behind us. I risked a brief glance back. They advanced quickly but purposefully, like stalking wolves. The clinking chains that might have exposed them were tucked into their T-shirts. Athletic shoes muffled footsteps.

Étienne rushed through the open door of a crumbling building. I followed close behind. The single-story building had reached its final stages of decay and would not afford safety for us. Significant holes in the roof produced a patchwork of sunlight on the floor. Great blooms of mold spread on the walls in places never blessed by the sun. Seepage made the carpet under my shoes fray and tear at the slightest hint of friction. It seemed less a place for demons than for disease and putrefaction.

Étienne set a sure, effortless pace. Did he know this desolate place so well? We exited the back of the building into an alley. We crossed into the next abandoned building, a multistory, drier at least on the bottom floor. Upholstered furniture appeared substantial, but I'd bet dry rot would make it burst into lung-clogging dust if touched. The furniture was lined up in orderly rows, as if someone had planned to move it, then ran out of time.

"What happened here, to this place?" I whispered. I knew I shouldn't be talking. The desolation disturbed me to the core. The businesses and streets in this section of the Barrows looked as if some approaching catastrophe had caused people to abandon them overnight. But why hadn't they returned for their belongings? Had their memories of their lives in the Barrows faded once they left? Was the Earth Mother's spell that powerful?

Étienne drew me close into an alcove.

"In 1947 and '48, a lot of the supporting infrastructure of the Barrows collapsed. Parts of the sewer system caved in. The water supply was cut off, and people left, abandoned everything. Then the inevitable atrophy set in."

I thought about Michael's story of the earthquake. But when I looked around, most of the objects in the room looked newer. They couldn't have been here for fifty years.

A faint scrape caught our attention. Étienne motioned across the room. "Run to that door over there."

I ran.

Gunfire rang out behind me.

I raced through the door and slammed right into one of the pursuers in a spectacular collision. I bounced back and crashed ass first into a table, then to the floor.

I raised my head to see the man climbing to his feet, staggering. He had a gun in his hand. Thankfully, Eunice had taught me to shoot lying flat on my back.

I drew and pulled the trigger first. A single bullet slammed his chest. The shock knocked him off his feet backward and into a chair. At impact, the chair sent billows of toxic dust and mold spores into the air. The echo of the shot reverberated in my ears like a monster firecracker.

Étienne arrived. He offered his hand to help me. I accepted it, but he had to grab me to keep me from toppling over.

He held me steady. "Are you hurt?"

I shook my head. I stared across the room at the Bastinado. "I had to shoot him."

"Of course you did." He started toward the door.

I didn't follow. I went to the man I had killed. The intensity and chaos of the moment had stunned me, but not enough to blind me and keep me from observing things.

My assailant slumped in the chair, his arm casually falling across his lap. Blood poured out of his chest and down his clothes in a gruesome dye job. As I watched, his fingers relaxed and his gun clattered to the floor. A bit of unease shimmered through me. This close, he didn't look like a gang member. His clothes were new; he was clean shaven, as if he were a professional hit man dressed in a Halloween costume. A brand-new villain, not like the Bastinado on the bus.

"Madeline?" Étienne called from behind me.

I went to him. "That's not a Bastinado."

"If you insist." Étienne sounded annoyed, not surprised. "Let's go."

He avoided my direct gaze. What was he hiding? The bastards had been shooting at him, too.

We played musical chairs with buildings—until we found four of our attackers climbing into a window to get to us. Two for each of us. I nailed my two, Étienne one, but he missed the second.

Étienne stepped in front of me. Two shots fired simultaneously. He staggered back. Blood smeared down his right arm.

"Go!" he said.

We hurried on. His breathing grew ragged. We had to stop. He leaned against a wall, eyes closed. He held his injured arm tight and I could see him fighting the pain.

"Let me see."

I tore the arm of his shirt and peeled the bloody mess away to survey the damage. The bullet had skimmed his upper arm, close to his shoulder. Nothing that would kill him, but it left a nasty trail of broken flesh across one of his intricate tattoos.

"Screwed up your tat," I said.

"That's okay. I don't need it anymore." Strain filled his voice.

He wrapped his good arm around me and drew me close.

"You okay?" He spoke softly in my ear. "You're a little pale."

"I'm fine. You're the wounded one, not me."

"First time in battle?"

"Yeah. It's not the same as training."

"Now you know. Good lesson."

It was. Practiced as I was, it surprised me. I thought I performed well enough, but I was glad he was with me. I would live and learn.

He winced with the effort to reach his back pocket. "There's a cell phone there," he said. "Get it out for me."

"Will it work here?"

"Maybe. We ran parallel to River Street. We're not too deep." Shouts and curses came from outside of the building we were resting in. I got his phone and he made a quick call. He gave a set of coordinates to the person on the other end. "Hurry," he said. He closed the phone.

We stood there, silent, waiting. He held me close and I let it happen. The man had, in any case, stepped between me and a bullet. After an indeterminable amount of time, his phone buzzed faintly in his pocket. He answered it.

"That's it," he said. "Come in, but be careful and ready to fire."

After a moment there came a shout, followed by a burst of rapid gunshots.

"Down!" Étienne commanded.

We dropped to lie on the filthy ground. He grunted as he moved his arm, but he covered me with his own body.

"Get off of me," I muttered between clenched teeth.

He chuckled and rolled off.

"Étienne." A male voice shouted outside the building.

"Over here." Étienne and I climbed to our feet and headed to the front room.

Five men waited for us, all dressed in fatigues, much like Eunice often was. All carried automatic rifles. Eunice had let me shoot one once. The rifle had felt powerful, noisy, and lacked finesse. A little practice would probably change that. I'd bet these men practiced often.

Across the street I could see a couple of others dragging bodies out of sight and deeper into the deserted buildings. None of them spoke, and neither did Étienne until we walked outside and climbed into a giant SUV. Étienne ordered the driver to take us to Harry's.

chapter 24

"Who are those men?" I asked after we climbed out of the car and walked to the doorway of Harry's. The SUV remained parked, waiting for Étienne to return.

"Part of my security force."

"Aiakós's security force?"

"He pays for it."

"And the fake Bastinados? Who was the target? You? Or me?"

"I don't know, Madeline." He sounded irritated. "But I'll try to find out," he said, recovering his calm composure.

Sure he would. He knew things, or suspected things that he wouldn't tell me. "How's your arm?"

"It hurts. I'll get a bandage and some antibiotics. Will you take this?" He handed me his cell phone.

I took the phone reluctantly. I didn't really want it. I am not a technology fan. I grew up with far more subtle communication and a slower-paced life. "I don't know anyone's number. Who would I call?"

"You could call me."

I shook my head and handed the phone back to him. "No. Michael gave me one. I just forgot to pick it up."

He flipped the phone open to show me a number. "Can you at least remember this?"

"Sure."

I stared at the screen, then looked up at him. "Étienne?"

"Yes, Madeline."

"Thank you for sparing me a bullet. But your leave-things-to-me, mysterious-man act is shit."

He laughed and a kind of warmth filled me. "My pleasure. You're worth saving. Please get that phone from Michael."

I paused. "Why am I worth saving?" He'd completely surprised me.

"You're the most interesting thing that's happened to the Barrows in a couple of years. You have an aura of importance about you."

He caught my chin in his fingers and kissed me lightly on the lips. A sweet kiss, but while I liked him, I felt no desire.

He knew it. He sighed and released me. "Maybe in another life."

I nodded. "Maybe."

He grinned and waved good-bye with his uninjured arm.

I started up stairs and then remembered Spot and Grace. Tony's Grocery had some meat, and I bought two nice-sized steaks. Cheap cuts, but it had to be better than rats. I was filthy and desperately needed a shower, but I'd accepted responsibility and they needed to eat.

There was no sound when I entered my room. "Grace?"

Grace stuck her head out of the drawer and barked.

I lifted her out and checked her wound. It seemed a little better. The skin had not split and the wound had a dry hardness to it. She was healing, I hoped. She crawled up and nuzzled my neck. I remembered that mouthful of excellent pointed teeth. "I like you too, Grace."

I set her on top of the dresser and gave her the steak. She picked it up with delicate paws and tore off a mouthful. She barked again, then made little chirping sounds.

"Quiet, please." I tapped my finger on the dresser.

She immediately fell silent as she continued to eat. Spot popped in the window and I gave him his steak. He wasn't as delicate, but he seemed to relish it.

I knew I shouldn't feed them. It brought them closer to people and they needed to be wary. Anyone with a gun might kill them, never knowing or caring that they were intelligent creatures. "You need to hide," I said. "You remember that, don't you?"

Spot made a little chirp, which I accepted as assent.

While they ate, I washed up and changed clothes. Not a shower, but I felt better. Then I cleaned the gun. A tap came at the door.

"Madeline?" Michael called from the other side.

I opened the door and let him in.

He drew a deep breath. His eyes narrowed. "You smell like blood."

He smelled it? Even after I'd washed it away? I should have showered.

Michael seized my arms. "Are you hurt?"

I jerked away. "Don't handle me like that."

He winced and let me go. "What happened?" His eyes roved the room until they landed on Spot and Grace sitting on the dresser.

"Those are my friends. Stay away from them."

He stared at them, then back at me, and nodded. If he'd lived in the Barrows his entire life, I was sure he'd seen many strange things.

I stepped back to keep a little distance between us. "To answer your question, no, it's not my blood. I was walking down River Street with the drawing of the guy I've been looking for and I ran into Étienne and he—"

"Étienne!" He tried to grab me again. I jumped away.

"Do you want to hear this or not?" I gave him a stiff arm, trying to keep him from closing in. He gave a slight nod. Those beautiful eyes focused on me so hard I could almost feel their weight. "I met Étienne. We walked together. And talked."

"About what?"

I threw up my hands. "The weather and traffic and world politics. What else?" He sounded jealous and I hated it. "Michael, stop it or leave."

He rubbed a hand over his face. "I just worry about you. Tell me. Please." He appeared more frantic than worried. He wasn't used to asking for things nicely. I really didn't want to tell him about my doubts about the attack. I wasn't sure the attackers were actually Bastinados. And I still didn't know if the attack was directed at me or Étienne.

A thought occurred to me. "Yesterday afternoon I rode the bus to the Den. There was this Bastinado. He tried to hurt a little kid and I threw him off the bus. I wonder if he got a bunch of his best buddies together to come looking for me."

Michael remained silent.

I looked at him hard, scrutinizing his face. "Étienne is a good man to have at your back, Michael."

"I could stand at your back."

"You weren't there. You can't always be there." I thought about Étienne stepping in front of me and the bullet that grazed his arm. "But unlike you, Étienne is not bulletproof. It's his blood."

He drew a sharp breath. "Is he . . . ?"

"He'll be okay. It skimmed his arm."

"I'll thank him." He sounded grim—and bitter.

"Why? He didn't do it for you." I was frustrated and backed up a pace. I needed more space.

It didn't go unnoticed. "What are you thinking?" he asked. He stared into my eyes with grave intensity.

"Okay, we need to talk. Sit over there. Away from me. You mess with my mind when you get too close."

"I do?" He gave a wry grin and sat in the one chair in my room. It squeaked and protested a bit. Not a small man, Michael.

"Don't be a smart-ass." I sat on the bed. "There's something between us. I don't know about Big Daddy's pronouncement of a binding, but the first time I saw you, I felt it. You did, too. You were helping Cassandra into the Jag out front."

"I remember." He didn't sound surprised. "If it

hadn't been for her, I'd have gone to you. I couldn't see you, didn't know who watched. All I knew was that I had to find you. I went back later, but you were gone."

"I'd have run like hell, Michael. If you came toward me at that moment . . . I wasn't prepared to meet you that morning. I wasn't prepared to meet you when I did."

He leaned back, seemingly relaxed. A facade, I'd bet.

"Madeline, I don't have words to tell you what you are to me. But today, you accepted me. You accepted what I become when I get angry or overexcited. There's nothing I wouldn't do for you."

"Why? I am not beautiful. My soul is stained with a curse placed upon me by my own mother."

"My mother damned me too," he said quietly. "I cannot be human, but I cannot be what he is either."

"So we're two damned souls who have to get together because no one wants me and everyone wants you?"

"Maybe we're two souls that were created to be together." He started to rise, but relaxed when I held up my hand.

He clenched his hand into a fist and pounded it softly on the chair arm. "Cass and Abby say that the Earth Mother doesn't interfere with ordinary people. Only her chosen. Our mothers were her witches. It appears that our lives are hers to meddle with as she pleases. My mother defied her. Left her for my father."

"And my mother defied her by placing a death curse on me."

I rubbed my hand over my scar.

"Stop that. Your scar is as much a part of you as your courage."

I lowered my hand. "If I can accept you, will you stop claiming me like a child with his favorite toy?"

"Once I know you're mine . . ."

"Michael, I've been yours since the first time I saw you."

He drew a breath to speak, but didn't. Finally, he leaned back and relaxed. His hands unclenched and he spread his fingers on the chair arms.

"Is that enough for you?" I asked.

"Yes. Now, let me tell you the story of the dark moon conjunction two years ago. It's a story of Cassandra, the Earth Mother, and how Aiakós arrived in this world."

And spin a tale he did. Of a web spun by the Earth Mother designed to lessen Aiakós's power in the Barrows by dragging him against his will into this world, where she believed she could control him. But was she controlling him? It was the people in the Barrows who bore the brunt of a demon in their midst.

"My mother cut her throat across an altar of concrete blocks, there in the plaza, the center of that giant pentagram created by the streets of the Barrows. As she bled out, he arrived from . . . somewhere. Another world, I guess. I watched. I could do nothing. We were all the Earth Mother's pawns. She called us her warriors, but Cassandra lost a dear friend; I lost my mother and brother. Flynn got his sister back safely, though— and he got Cassandra."

"The Earth Mother." The damnable female had

caused incredible suffering with her games. I rubbed my eyes. Would the holy bitch never be done with me?

But I did realize one thing. According to Abigail, if someone wanted to use the Portal, the solstice and the dark moon would certainly be the perfect time. Two days. I had two days to find it—and one of those was almost gone.

He stood and I let him come closer. He sat beside me. "Come with me. Back to the Archangel. I have an apartment upstairs, wine, food."

It was tempting, but I had more work to do to locate the Portal. The summer solstice was drawing near. I had to keep up the search. "I can't. There's still so much to do."

Michael kissed me gently on the mouth. "When you're ready, Madeline. I won't push you." He opened the door, reached into his pocket, then tossed something my way. "Here's your cell phone. It won't work if you go into the ruins, but it will be fine on River Street."

I watched at the window until he drove away. I felt the pull to be with him but pushed it down. I had work to do.

At sunset, I went out and caught a bus. I wasn't going anywhere in particular, but the ride would clear my head. The driver wasn't my new friend Jim, but a rather dour woman who kept her eyes straight ahead. The bus was headed south and I knew it would make a turn at the cul-de-sac at the Goblin Den. I simply rode and tried to think.

Michael wanted me, but he was distracting me from

my mission. I would do well to remember the threat of prison if I failed. Étienne and Oonagh thought they were hiding in the Barrows, and maybe they were. Maybe no one wanted them enough to dig them out. If Oonagh had offended enough, the Mother would sic the Sisters on her. Would they do the same to me? Now, there was an interesting thought. Would Eunice or Lillian drag me to prison if ordered to do so? My thoughts bounced from one place to another. I had to stop thinking.

It was a good thing I did, because after the bus made the turn at the cul-de-sac and started its northward run, I spotted him. The third murderer. Kenny Hascomb. The man who had strangled my mother. For years I'd fought a vicious need to kill this man. For years, I'd beaten it down, like a raging fire burned down to an ember. Now, it sparked to life and burst free.

He leaned against a boarded-up store-front building, shoulders hunched and hands in his pockets. He stared at the sidewalk. A couple of prostitutes walked by, stepping wide around him as if he were something filthy. Filthy, he was, and I planned to toss him in a Dumpster after he told me the Portal's location. I'd show him what my mother's life meant to me.

chapter 25

I forced myself to be calm, but I immediately rose and headed for the front of the bus. The driver wouldn't let me off except at the marked stops, but one was just ahead. I could still see him, a block and a half away, when I stepped down from the bus. I walked slowly, searching all the possibilities.

Excitement rose in me. Could closure be coming so quickly?

A few people wandered down the sidewalk, a drunk weaving back and forth, a prostitute at the corner. The drunk was headed back toward the bars. The prostitute wasn't going anywhere. She stared at the few passing cars without any hope. Neither would be a problem. The cars? Some Good Samaritan might stop if I had to take him down in public.

I shoved my hands in my jeans pockets and copied his posture as I walked toward him. Shoulders hunched, face down. Slow, I had to go slow, not spook him—though I didn't know where he would run.

Closer. I had to let him know why he was going to die. He remained stationary. Michael and others had described him as rather pathetic. But the last face my mother saw was not pathetic. It was hateful, twisted in cruelty. This was the face I needed to keep in mind as I did this final deed for my parents. I would not let him live.

I was within twenty feet of him when he raised his head. He saw me. Recognition came alive in his eyes. He'd either seen me on the news as the killer of his two partners, or seen me as I asked about him along River Street. My face wasn't one to forget. He whirled and ran.

I raced after him.

Running downhill, back toward the Den and the cul-de-sac, he howled in terror. I shortened his lead on me. I could hear him now, huffing and puffing, his soles slapping the concrete in shoes far too large for his feet.

Closer, ten feet. I almost had him. He ran in terror, but I ran easily, alert, alive and . . . damn!

He staggered, almost fell as he turned left, into an alley. I was right behind him. I slowed down. Some light from a streetlamp penetrated here, but not much. I'd lost sight of him, but all I had to do was wait for him to fall. Then I'd be on him.

It occurred to me that I was close to the Den, close to the place where the Drow had leaped from the roof. I stopped. He had to be breathing hard. I'd hear if he were hiding, if only I could shut out the noise around me. The hiss of cars behind me filled the air.

I glanced back toward the street, toward the light. I should go, I thought. Surely a Drow would find him. But if I didn't kill him, the curse would never be broken—and I'd never find the Portal. A familiar scratching sound. I glanced up. Drows, two of them, like the one that attacked Michael, crouched twelve feet above me on the roof of a single-story building. Silhouetted against the ambient light of the night sky. They'd be on me before I could reach the light of the street behind me. I swallowed, remembering the pain, the incredible pain. These two would probably tear me apart. This time, though, I was prepared. I drew my gun and slowly started backing toward the light. When the Drow attacked Michael, it had unfurled its wings before it leaped. These remained still, simply staring at me.

Footsteps approached from my right. Odd, shuffling footsteps, so I didn't think it was my man. I suspected he was gone or so well hidden I'd never find him in the dark. A great scaled Drow stepped out of the total darkness. His posture wasn't threatening. I didn't know if it was the one I'd fed or not. The minimal light gave a slight sheen to his scales and his wide eyes had a bit of a glint to them.

"Hey, big guy." I spoke softly.

He grunted, held out an enormous clawed hand, and beckoned me to come closer.

He wasn't a carnivore—I could tell because I was still alive—and didn't seem to be fearful of what hung over us on the roof. He lay that fearsome hand on my shoulder, drew me closer. He tugged gently, leading me deeper into the ruins. I planted my feet and he stopped. He released me. No force. He would take me somewhere or let me go. I glanced up. The Drows on the roof were gone.

Decision time. Did I follow? Or run away? I had entered this world and I had a mission. Yet I couldn't afford to run blindly, and alone, through unknown parts. Having lost my man to the darkness, I would go where circumstances led me. I holstered the gun and laid my hand on his arm.

The scales felt smooth, hard, and slightly warm under my fingers. I allowed him to lead me. In a few minutes the darkness became complete and I was hopelessly lost. Clinging to him was my only hope.

As if recognizing that he could see and I could not, he stopped often to lead me around some invisible obstacle. Progress slowed. Finally, he slipped a massive arm around my shoulders and the other under my knees and lifted me with ease. A little scary, but much faster.

He carried me for a while, then set me gently on my feet and again led me by my arm. He opened a door. Inside, another door, then another. Light, dim light, filled a large, high-ceilinged room.

A room filled with Drows.

chapter 26

The scaled ones, like my guide, sat on the floor; winged ones perched on exposed beams above me. Several little dragons were there, though I didn't see Spot.

I stared around me. If they attacked, I'd be dead . . . but they didn't move. A wise person would've been terrified. I had no claims to wisdom, but I did believe in intuition, and intuition told me there was no immediate danger.

"Good evening," a deep voice said from across the room. Aiakós walked into the light.

Or so I thought. But after examining him for a moment, I noticed subtle differences. He was almost as big as Aiakós. Hard to tell in the light, but his hair seemed a little less red and he had some, but not all, of the majestic presence of Michael's father. He wore a cinnamon-colored, oddly draped robe that covered him from shoulder to ankle. Strangely enough, I did not feel threatened by him as I had by Aiakós.

"My name is Kyros." Aiakós's look-alike came closer. "Please, sit down for a moment." He gestured to an industrial-looking table with mismatched chairs.

They must have scoured the ruins to find them. His voice was deep and soft, but lacked Aiakós's beguiling honey-and-cream texture.

I went to the table and sat. Kyros's chair protested as he carefully lowered himself.

"You are not afraid?" he asked.

I glanced at the winged things in the rafters. "Not yet."

"Nothing in this room will harm you." He laid his hands, palms down, on the table. He had claws, too, but somehow they looked smaller and less lethal than Aiakós's.

I nodded, but remained cautious. "So, who are you? Why are you here?"

"I am what you would call a wizard or a warlock, though among my people I am a priest. These are the Beheras." He pointed at the scaled giants. "These are the Custos." He smiled at the winged and fanged creatures above us. "The little ones are Tektos. Nine of your moon cycles ago, we were together for a celebration in our realm in a place we call an Apex of power. An Apex is difficult to describe, but simply put, it is a place where the walls between worlds are thin."

I remembered what I'd been told by the Sisters. "I've heard that there are places like that."

"The Apex is a doorway. Difficult to master, but it can be done. At the height of our celebration, there was an inexplicable shift in place and time, and we found ourselves here, far from home. We have no way of returning."

"That's terrifying."

"Yes. We survive. Barely. We hide in these ruins."

"You speak good English. Little bit of a British accent."

He laughed softly. "I've been here before. There was a time, long ago, when we and others from this world communicated. Not here, but in another place. I don't know where it is in relation to where we are now."

"Do you know what happened? What brought you here?"

He leaned forward, arms on the table. "I believe I do. Someone in this world has acquired and is using a powerful talisman that facilitates travel between worlds. Using such without the proper skill and knowledge can create great destruction. If the worlds get too close, they could destroy each other."

I sighed. I knew what it was. How completely idiotically obvious. The Portal. And someone without the power or skill currently wielded it.

"Will you tell me why you are here?" he asked.

"I'm looking for someone."

He nodded, but I could not read the expression on his face. I'd need to be careful how much information to share.

"I followed the man tonight, down the sidewalk. He ran down the alley where I met . . ." I glanced at the larger creatures. One stepped forward, but they all looked alike to me.

"Termas. You found food for him and his young a few days ago. They are most likely indistinguishable to you."

I smiled. "Termas, it's good to meet you."

Termas nodded. His mouth widened in what I thought might be a smile.

"I've met Aiakós," I said. "What is he to you?"

"I am his youngest brother. Aiakós is an exile, a rogue and an outlaw. In our realm, we live in a peaceful matriarchal society. We are sons of the queen, and as the eldest, Aiakós was destined to be a great leader himself. But he did not want to lead alongside a queen—he wanted complete dominion. He thought his mother too benevolent. The queen chose a younger son to be her heir. Aiakós killed our brother. Then he ran away. He is an . . . aberration."

"You're hiding here. You haven't talked to him."

"He would kill me on sight. I was the one who stood witness at the inquest for our slain brother. Aiakós wanted me to lie, but I would not. He is far stronger than I am."

"Wow." An interesting story, but why was he telling me all of this? And could I trust him? How had he known where to find me to bring me here? Did he have Drows positioned near the Den, watching for me, waiting for me?

Kyros laid a hand flat on the table. Why would a nonviolent race have claws? It seemed to work against the laws of nature . . . But I lived under the Earth Mother's laws, the laws of this world. I realized things could work differently in other realms.

"I am curious," Kyros said. "What is the young prince to you? I see him with you. There is something there I don't understand."

"Young prince? You mean Michael?"

"Yes. It is not common for our race to mate with yours, and even more rare that such a mating would produce a child. Michael, were he in our world, would not be eligible to take the throne, but he would be a prince and most welcome."

"I'm not sure what Michael is to me. I'm still working that out." I bit my lip, but I had to ask. "One of the Custos tried to kill him the other night."

"And almost killed you. The Custos of which you speak was named Azema. He was grieving. Aiakós hunts them, kills them for sport. He is a very efficient killer and he killed Azema's mate. Azema saw Michael as an extension of Aiakós. It is a tragedy."

"I'm sorry I had to kill him. I couldn't let him hurt Michael."

"I understand."

The young Beheras from the Dumpster bumped against my knee. He was as big as a St. Bernard. I laid a hand on his shoulder. "Who is this?"

"Termins," Kyros said.

"How many of you are there? How do you survive?"

"There is myself, eight adult Beheras, a young Beheras, six Custos, and ten Tektos."

"Wow, that's a lot to feed. I believe I have two Tektos under my protection right now. There was a wound on one's back. I did the best I could."

Kyros smiled. "I know. The others told me. The Tektos can be endearing—and infuriating. They are sentient, but have limited reasoning capability. Don't worry too much about the wound. They are very hardy creatures."

His claws tapped lightly against the table. "As for survival, food is difficult. The Tektos eat rats, but it's not a good diet. The Custos hunt over the marshland at night. Small things, but occasionally they catch a deer. The Beheras go into the swamps and gather plants, but there is little sustenance for them there. It will be worse when winter comes."

Since he seemed to be forthcoming, I had to ask. "This talisman that was misused to bring you here, can you use it to go home?"

"Absolutely. At the proper time."

Of course. I knew the time: the summer solstice, two days from now. And the place . . .

"The Zombie Zone," I said quietly. "There's a plaza there that forms a giant pentagram." The place where Michael's mother had sacrificed herself for Aiakós.

"Yes, that is an Apex in this world. I have traveled between worlds many times. Even I can feel the correct hour approaching."

I had no way of verifying anything Kyros told me. No reason to trust him.

"Thank you for telling me all this. Few people I've met here have given me straight answers. But why did you bring me here? Why share your history with me?"

Kyros smiled. "You have shown kindness to us. We hope you can help us obtain food. We simply implore that you not tell Michael of us—or at least of me. I fear he will speak of us to Aiakós."

"Okay. Let me see if I can get some money." Maybe I could get the Sisters to fork over some if I didn't tell them what it was for.

"I have what you consider currency." He drew a wad of hundred-dollar bills out of his robe. He registered my shock. "I have seen how your people kill each other to obtain them. I recovered these from a man who came into the ruins. He had a young woman with him and he hurt her. I killed him. She ran away."

He killed him. So casual, so cool . . . or was it? I knew nothing of him other than what he had told me.

"And you stole his money."

Kyros laughed softly. He might be no danger to me, but he was not totally benign. "Yes, and when others like him have come, I have done the same. They don't come here very often anymore."

I accepted the money. Several thousand dollars, from the look of it. Must've been a lot of visitors in these parts before they were chased out. I could buy a lot of food with this. Not just vegetables, either.

"I'll get it delivered as soon as I can. Near dark. You'll be able to get to it easily."

"Why should darkness matter?"

"I was told the Drows . . . your people don't come into the sunlight."

He shrugged. "You are misinformed. There are some that cannot bear the light. We go out in the dark only because we must hide, not because we don't enjoy the sun. Your sun is not as bright as ours, but it is warm."

As I left with the money in hand, I thought about all that Kyros had shared with me. I needed to rethink my assumptions about the Drows. Perhaps the Sisters did not have all the answers.

chapter 27

Termas escorted me until I could see River Street. Kyros told me how to tell them apart. There was an odd marking on the scales near the shoulder, individual as a name for all of them. I memorized all eight. I was respectful of the Custos, as I had killed one of their own, but cautious. It was difficult to get beyond the memory of pain. They seemed to understand.

We had come north toward the bars, which were just letting out for the night. I emerged from the alley into a small crowd of the younger prostitutes. They stepped out of my way, backed up, and skipped away. I'd only startled them, though, and they quickly recovered.

I walked north on River Street, back toward my apartment. Kyros and his Drows had offered me no harm, but I had no way of judging the truth of what I was told. I certainly had compassion for those I had interacted with personally. I cared for Spot and Grace, caught in a trap for snake food, and Termas, digging through Dumpsters to feed his child.

No matter how much it hurt, I couldn't help the Drows until I found the Portal. But what would I do with it? Return it to the Sisters and leave the Drows to suffer in a place they didn't belong? I didn't know.

My new phone gave me the time. Two a.m. I picked up my pace. Tired and uncomfortable, I wanted to be inside, away from this street.

"Madeline?" A voice came from a doorway.

I stopped and was startled to see Riggs.

"What are you doing here?" He stepped out onto the sidewalk. "I thought you were with Michael."

"I was for a while. I had something to do."

A boy erupted from the doorway behind him. "Hey, Father Riggs, can I . . ." He had seen me. "Sorry," he said and slipped back through the door.

"Father Riggs? You're a priest?"

"I was once. I fell from grace. Not pious enough, apparently. Or obedient."

I shrugged. "That's okay. I'm not good at rules, either."

He grinned. "I've noticed. I try to get these kids off the street. Sometimes it works. Come in for a moment." He gestured toward the door.

I walked into a room full of light and laughter, laughter that died as soon as they saw me. Boys and girls, five of them, as young as those on the street outside. A dartboard hung on the wall and a well-worn pool table sat in the middle of the room.

"This is Madeline," Riggs said them. "She's a friend of mine."

They didn't speak, and their silence held until he led me toward a back room, an office. As he closed the door, the laughter picked back up behind us.

"They're wary. I keep this place as a sanctuary at

night. Any runaway who wants to go home can come here and I arrange it. No one bothers us because of Michael. Michael will come protect us if we need it." He gestured toward a chair in front of a shabby desk covered with papers. A rusty file cabinet sat against the wall. One drawer was partially open and cocked to the side as if defying anyone to close it. A crucifix decorated the wall behind the desk.

I sat in the chair and it sank down an inch or so. "When do you sleep?" I knew he spent long hours at the Den.

"When I can."

"No wonder you were grumpy when Hildy called you the morning I arrived." I thought a minute. "But you did what Hildy told you to do. Why? Is she important to you?"

This was a night for revelation. I basked in it.

"Hildy, as well as Michael, provides me with money to keep this place going. Hildy asks—or orders—and I do my best to get what she wants. Hildy has helped many people. We are all grateful."

He was grateful. I wondered where she got the money. Unless she was trading in weapons or drugs, it didn't come from the pawnshop.

Riggs frowned. "But I'm more interested in why you're down here and not with Michael. You should be together. You'd be good for him."

"It's complicated, Riggs. I have something to do here and I don't have time for a romance."

"And you're afraid of it." He smiled and his eyes glittered.

I grinned. "Terrified."

"Have you considered that he might help you?"

"Possibly. I've known him only a few days."

Riggs sighed and shook his head. "Years ago, in the church, we had a celebration of long-term marriages. Twenty couples married more than thirty years told their stories. Over half said they fell in love from the first moment they saw their partners. Could that not be true for you and him?"

He reminded me of the first time I saw Michael. The first time he saw me, I was dying. "It doesn't matter, Riggs. If I get involved with him, my mission here might not get done."

"You think that simply accepting love from a man will deter you from a goal?"

"No, but the man himself might stop me. He's controlling. It would be a constant battle if I give in."

"How much do you know about him?"

"I met his father."

Riggs rubbed his hand across his mouth. "That creature is evil incarnate. He would destroy everything, a whole world, to get his way."

"He wants Michael to join him."

"Michael has confessed many things to me. I will not speak of them. But he is one who needs love desperately. True love, not the adoration of the masses. If he does not find it soon, he will fall to the only person—or thing—that even moderately cares. I believe Aiakós does love his son in many ways. But Aiakós will destroy him. Or at least the part that is human."

"And I'm supposed to be his salvation." I didn't like

that. I had my own problems. And I wasn't sure Michael wanted to be saved from anything.

"I don't know what you are supposed to be, Madeline. Beautiful women throw themselves at him constantly. You are what he wants."

I stood. "I don't think I'm that strong."

"You don't think you are beautiful, either." He stood, too. "You are wrong. Simply and tragically wrong."

I left Riggs's sanctuary with a lot to think about as I walked back to Harry's. I wanted Michael as much as ever. I'd told Riggs I was terrified, and that was the truth. One of Lillian's lectures came to mind. *A Sister of Justice always faces and conquers her fears. It is a measure of her worth.* How much was I worth?

As I approached Harry's, I could see Michael sitting in his Jag, waiting on me. It was exactly what I wanted.

I opened the door and climbed in.

chapter 28

"Are you okay?" he asked. "I wanted to go up, but the light was off. I thought you were sleeping."

"No. I'm not okay."

"Has something happened?"

"I saw him. The man who killed my parents. I chased him, but he got away." I'd say that much.

"I see. And if you had caught him?"

I didn't speak. The notion that I had come here to kill a man seemed far away right now.

"Can I do anything? Help you?"

I remembered Riggs's words. Would being with Michael deter me from catching my man? Certainly he had kicked me off track. Love? No, not yet. Desire? I'd take a chance on that.

I slid my hand in his. "Take me home with you. I need a shower."

"You're sure?" He hesitated. "I'll take you to Étienne, if you want."

That pissed me off. "Why are you so jealous? If I wanted Étienne, I'd be with him, not wandering the damned streets of the Barrows." I jerked my hand away, made a fist and pounded it on the seat rather than his hard head. How could someone so adored be so insecure? Was Riggs right? "I want you, Michael. I'm terrified of you."

"Will you tell me what frightens you? I've told you I'm in control when I change."

"It's not that. I've already said it. I'm afraid you'll own me. You're so intense. If I relax, I could be over-whelmed."

He didn't say anything.

It didn't take long to get to the Archangel. He drove around to the back, where a door slid up to let the Jag glide in. The interior lights came on in a large garage and he turned off the engine.

I wanted to share everything I'd seen that night. I wanted to speak of Kyros, his uncle, the Beheras, the Custos, the Tektos, all new and wondrous—and terrifying—to me. But no matter how much I wanted to tell him, he was still a stranger. I simply couldn't turn desire into that kind of trust. If I didn't trust him to let me keep my freedom, how could I trust him to keep the secrets of Kyros and his kind? Their lives depended on it.

Michael drew a deep breath. As if he could read my thoughts, he said, "Madeline, there are many things about me you don't know. Some of them are pretty bad. When I was a child, my mother was in and out of institutions. She'd gone insane after she'd returned from the world where she met my father. We had no money. She'd have been better off in a regulated state facility, but her family wanted to keep her hidden in a squalid cell. They had no use for me or my older brother. We were both bastards of little significance." He spoke with contempt—and hatred. I don't know if it approached my compulsion, but he could probably empathize. He continued.

"I knew I needed money. Fast. As soon as I turned eighteen, I tried to go to work. It was impossible. No one would hire me. My presence was too distracting. I did odd jobs, yard work, things like that. One day an older woman offered me a considerable bit of money for other services. After that, I found others like her. When one client ran out of money, I went on to the next. I was deeply ashamed, but I finally had enough to go to court and get custody of my mother from her family. The facility I placed her in wasn't the best, but it was better. Things were good for a while. Then her illness began to take hold of my brother." He stopped and breathed deeply. Whatever had happened to his brother had affected him profoundly.

He leaned back against the headrest. "I went to New York. Much more money there. I worked as a very expensive, very private escort for very wealthy women. And men."

Michael laughed softly. It sounded more like irony than mirth. "I made good investments. Once I had enough money, I came back to Duivel and placed my mother in an expensive asylum, where she stayed until two years ago."

I shivered. I knew what came next. Part of Michael's past disturbed me. I tried to keep my judgment in check. Michael had sold himself for his mother. I thought about my ruthless quest to avenge my parents. Perhaps her insanity and poverty had been a curse of a different kind for Michael.

Michael sighed. "In some ways, I'm as chained to the Barrows as he . . . as Aiakós is. I can pass as human most of the time, but my true nature will show occasionally." He gripped the steering wheel. "When I first came back to the Barrows, the vice was incredible. Prostitution, sexual slavery, the Bastinados. There were eight gangs, then. They used the Barrows as a base to raid uptown."

"What happened to change things?"

"I saw the possibilities. I killed most of the pimps along River Street and set up my own men as protection specialists for the girls, at a fee much smaller than the pimps' ninety percent. I had managers at several houses. Uptown Duivel sent its rich and poor to me for sex and games. The backroom gambling made a good profit. Vice in the Barrows made me very wealthy. I slaughtered several Bastinado gangs."

"Slaughtered?" I swallowed hard. *Demon*, they called him. "Personally?"

"Yes. Five, ten at a time." He shrugged, as if he spoke of stepping on roaches. "You saw what I can do. It was brutal, but necessary. I . . ."

I sat silent and waited for him to continue.

"I will admit to you and no one else, I enjoyed it. Killing them. I suppose that is my father's side of me."

My mind stopped there for an instant. Michael enjoyed killing. I couldn't quite assimilate those words. I continued to listen in silence.

"Because I enjoyed it, I stopped. About twelve years ago. Started making money in more legitimate ways. Then Cassandra came. Cass was erratic, unpredictable. But effective. She cut a path through vice in the Barrows like a bulldog on speed. Not intentionally or as effectively as I had, but nothing stood between her and a child."

"Did you tell Cassandra all of this?"

"No. Cassandra never let me get that close." The irony that filled his voice must have tasted bitter. It showed on his face.

I had a happy childhood. I had deliberately planned and executed murder in my youth and spent the last six years as an acolyte to assassins. While I would not like to see Michael tear men apart, I had no doubt he could do it. I thought of the bus and the little boy's burns. The Bastinado I'd savaged. There was a darkness inside Michael that mirrored the darkness in me. For now, I would accept him as he was.

"Michael, I've known you only a few days. I've seen what you are. I want you, but if you ever try to control me, I'll die fighting."

He chuckled wryly. "I seem to be doomed to desire independent women."

I thought of Cassandra and felt a twinge of jealousy. As if he read my mind, he leaned in to brush his lips across mine.

I pulled back. "There's something you need to know. About me."

"And that is?"

I swallowed and bit my lip like a kid. "I was seventeen when my mom and dad died. After that, I was in jail and I never . . ." I couldn't say the word *virgin*.

"You've never had sex before." He laughed softly.

"It's not funny." Then, inexplicably, I started to laugh. "I've pretended to be a prostitute. I've seen people have sex. I'm not shy or afraid. I'm athletic and you probably wouldn't know the difference—physically. But in other ways . . . I guess after all I've been through, it is amusing. I just didn't want to surprise you."

"We can wait, if you'd like," he whispered against my neck.

"No. I've waited long enough."

He brought his lips back to mine. "I love you."

My heart filled. Part of me wanted to return his words. That same part knew I wasn't free to commit until I located the Portal. Good excuse anyway. He didn't frighten me.

Love did.

chapter 29

Once in the elevator that led from the garage to his apartment, he pushed me up against the wall and kissed me. His mouth was hot and warm, demanding, and I wanted to grind my body against his. I gripped his shoulders. I am not a petite woman, but I felt small beside him. I'd never had such a kiss. My knees went weak and I had to cling to him to keep from collapsing. I had never felt such primal attraction to a man and I wanted him with an intensity that terrified me.

I barely felt the elevator move, didn't know it had until he urged me out and into a room filled with red and gold, like his father's place. There were plush couches and chairs scattered everywhere. Not that I had time to admire the furniture. He drew me away and into a bedroom with a massive platform bed. Purest white, it sat in the middle of a sea of pearl carpet. I had never dreamed of the first place I'd have sex. Now I would lose my virginity, if not my innocence, to a half man, half . . . what? I couldn't bring myself to call him a Drow. I shivered. When he kissed me, it didn't matter what he was. This was my man.

I gasped as Michael scooped me up in his arms and carried me to the bed, set me down, then dropped to his knees beside me. He wrapped his arms around my waist and buried his face against my throat.

"Do you know how hard it's been to watch you walk away from me each time, not knowing if you would return?" His voice was husky, as if he uttered his deepest secret—or sorrow. "Knowing how strong you are but knowing, too, how much evil there is in the Barrows?"

I touched his face, brushing his corn-silk hair, smoothing the fine wrinkles on his brow. I wanted him to understand. I needed him to understand.

"If you hadn't given me space, I wouldn't be here now." These were the truest words I could speak.

Flames rose in each of us. Driven by desire, each with our own needs, we couldn't undress fast enough. Wild, uncontrolled, we tore at each other's clothing until we found bare skin to kiss and caress. The heat of him burned my skin as I fell into the oldest and most primitive longing.

As the last of our clothing fell away, the connection to him I'd felt the first time I saw him flared and I felt what I'd been denied before—passion, desire, desperate need.

"No one else could give me what you offer." He spoke in a low voice, deep with emotion. "You make me feel like a man, not a beast." He drew me closer. His breath caressed my skin as he left a line of kisses down my body. His skillful hands played along me, touched me, sent me shivering out of control. He was a master

of seduction. Everywhere he touched, he sent shock
waves of pleasure over me.

When he moved over me, I spread my legs to welcome him. He stopped. "If I hurt you, I'll stop."

I didn't want him to stop. My whole body ached to
have him inside of me. There was no pain. Nothing in
my life prepared me for the searing intimacy and the
silken slide of flesh into flesh. The sensation blinded
me and the room ceased to exist. I clung to his shoulders and arched my back to meet him. I licked and bit
his skin. He tasted so hot and male. I slid my fingers in
that flowing hair. I strained against him, couldn't get
enough of him. My sudden, unexpected loss of control
frightened me, but I soon forgot it as ripples of pleasure
rolled through me until . . . I cried out when that final
wave struck.

When I came to myself again, my lungs gasped for
breath and my body trembled. I'd touched myself before, though only occasionally. I knew my body and
gained minor pleasure from it. It was relief from stress,
from sorrow. This was something different. Even the
slow easing of our breathing in the aftermath seemed
to consume me. He trembled, too, but I could feel him,
still hard, apparently holding back. I realized that he
had withheld his release to protect me. He had not
wished to shift into his other form, to hurt me, to
frighten me. Part of me warmed at his kindness and
generosity. That part warred with dismay at his ability
to control his own body when I could not.

He rolled off of me. A gentle hand slid from my

cheek, across my breast, and stilled on my stomach. I shivered when his finger circled my navel.

I turned and touched him then. My fingers explored his body and I tasted the salty sweetness of his skin. My hand closed over the part of him that pleased me so much. He groaned. Half human? No, this was a man.

I rolled over to straddle him and let that magnificent erection slide into the slick wetness of my sheath. His body arched, golden and glorious, below me. His eyes glowed, blue as the daytime sky. I caught his hands. They were ordinary hands, not the clawed things he'd shown me the other day. I kissed his fingers, then held his palms against my breasts as I moved slowly, wanting to draw things out for him. I could feel the orgasm building in him, feel it in the tension of his whole body as he began to move with me. It was easy enough to remember the way he looked after the attack at the Archangel. I waited for him to change shape as he'd told me he would. I waited for him to lose control.

His breath grew ragged and he closed his eyes. I was untrained in the art of lovemaking, so I kept my movements slow and steady. Pleasure rose in me again, but I had no time to build to a climax before he gasped and his arms dragged me down toward him. His mouth locked on mine and his body jerked. He shook, eyes closed, and it was all I could do to hang on until the waves of pleasure within him subsided. He groaned when I slid off of him. I sat by him and waited. When he opened his eyes, I frowned and said, "You didn't change."

He laughed. He tried to push himself up, collapsed, and continued laughing, breathlessly. When he stopped, I laid across him, my face against his throat.

"No, my love. For the first time in my life, making love, I didn't change. I guess it's you. You make me human."

I didn't know what to say. I was overwhelmed by the idea of it. I made Michael, the beautiful angel with a dark side, feel human.

We didn't sleep. We made love again, slowly, more completely. When sunlight spread through the room from windows above, we rose and showered and made love a fourth time. He easily held me as I wrapped my legs around his waist and the warm water flowed over us. There was an advantage to loving a very strong man.

"Will you stay with me?" Michael asked as we dressed.

"Eventually. But I have only two days to find the Portal. I'm close to finding the killer. I know it." A sense of unease, maybe guilt, flowed through me. I'd just had the experience of a lifetime, and I couldn't tell the man who gave it to me that I'd commit myself to him. As wonderful as the night was, it hadn't changed me in deeper ways—or the way I felt about him. I wanted him, but I couldn't do anything until I fulfilled my mission. It wasn't just about vengeance. I needed to free myself from the bonds of this curse before I could wrap my mind around . . . whatever this was.

"Okay." He hesitated as he spoke. "I'll wait for you." We kissed for a long time before I left. Everything swirled in my mind. Perhaps the simple existence at Justice had prepared me to fight, to kill, but not for the complexities of life outside its walls.

chapter 30

June 24

Michael didn't ask where I was going, but I could tell he wanted to. I wanted to get out of the Barrows and think for a while. I wanted to do something different. I waited at the bus stop, and when the bus pulled up, the door opened to reveal my friend Jim. "Hey, girl. Where you headed?"

"Hey, Jim. Headed uptown." I climbed on.

Jim had worked a double run and was off shift at eight. I rode with him until he left the bus at the transfer station for another driver and offered to buy me breakfast. We walked down a tree-lined side street to a little diner with stools at the counter and a row of booths along the front. A beguiling fragrance drifted through the pass-through to the kitchen.

"How are you getting along?" Jim asked, after the waitress brought us coffee and we gave our orders.

"Still looking for my man. Have you seen him again?" I asked. "The one in the photo?"

"I saw him yesterday, about noon. On the street. He

was hanging out close to the Den. He's not going anywhere, if you ask me. This place is the end. Most never get out—including me."

"Where would you like to go?" I asked between sips of coffee.

"Maybe to a beach." Jim grinned. "Long as it was close to a VA hospital."

I decided to ask Michael if he needed a chauffeur. It had to pay better than the city transit system, and might be safer. We laughed a lot, and when two other transit drivers came in, Jim introduced me like a daughter home from college. He made me feel like family. Jim told me about two stores I could walk to that might have good clothes.

After breakfast I bought a basic, well-fitted black suit with a jacket that would cover the gun and knives. The jacket had inside pockets to hold ammo. I matched it with a silky pale blue shirt, one that matched my eyes. The shirt had a V-neck, fancier than the button-up, but the jacket would keep it from being too sexy. Nicely tailored pants, also with good pockets, and killer black leather ankle boots made the outfit just right for a bouncer.

I caught the bus again and arrived at Harry's at noon. I carried my new clothes to my room. Then I walked into Tony's Grocery Store, two buildings south of Harry's, where I'd purchased the sandwich meat and steaks. It served the small community with the basics.

Tony, the owner, was gray haired and tired, but

friendly enough. He'd seen me, of course, but we hadn't spoken. I needed something special from him, though, and managed to get him talking about himself: retired, put too much of his retirement savings into the store, barely getting by, unable to sell the business and get out. He had no problem with my request for wholesale boxes of veggies and cases of chicken. He had a truck and would deliver the goods where I wanted, but then he surprised me.

Tony glanced around the store. There were no other customers. "It's for them things. The ones who live out there."

I nodded. It didn't surprise me. People in this place always seemed to know more than they let on. What a mystery. Hildy feared these Drows, and yet other people seemed to accept them as part of the neighborhood. My own experience was, of course, mixed.

"I'll take care of it," he said. "When I have it, I leave clean stuff outside by the Dumpsters. I just don't make much money here. Try not to have too much waste."

"You know they won't hurt you?"

"I know. They take care of those filthy Bastos." He grinned and his tired eyes came to life.

It seemed that Tony was more in touch with the Barrows than Hildy. I smiled back. "They do indeed."

They called the Barrows a place of evil. It was. And yet I had found much good here, too. It seemed to be the perfect battleground between chaos and order.

I did purchase some sandwich meat for Spot and Grace. Spot sulked a bit, but then he ate when I told him I couldn't afford steak every day. I changed into fresh jeans and a shirt. Spot was gone when I came out of the bathroom. I went down and paid Harry for another week. After I paid Harry, I crossed the street to the pawnshop. I needed to talk to the Sisters about finding my man.

As I started to open the door, Spot landed on my shoulder, almost knocking me to my knees. Oh, well. I had walked down the street with him on my shoulder the day I rescued him. What would it hurt now?

I went into Hildy's shop.

Eunice, having taken over Hildy's business and completely emptied the pawnshop's main room, had placed a large practice mat on the floor. I shivered. How many times over the years had she slammed me down on one just like it?

I didn't see Hildy. Eunice amused herself on the mat with furious push-ups. She'd forsaken her usual fatigues for shorts and a tank top. She was a woman, yes, but her relentless physical activity and substantial muscles would make a female bodybuilder proud. All solid muscle and bone, covered with a shiny sheen of sweat.

"One hundred, damn it," Eunice muttered under her breath. She popped to her feet like a champagne cork from a bottle and spotted me.

"What the hell is that?" Eunice demanded. She planted her hands on her hips and focused on Spot.

Oops. Trouble. "My pet iguana."

"Iguana, my ass. Fucking thing has wings."

"Come on, Eunice. Don't you have a pet?"

"I got a pet. Her name is Madeline. Come on, little

Sister." She beckoned me to join her. Other than the moisture on her skin, there was no tangible evidence that a hundred push-ups cost her any more effort than a stroll to the refrigerator for a beer. She wasn't even breathing hard. "Let's you and me go a couple of rounds, girl."

I shook my head. I didn't need bruises today.

"What? You leave Justice less than a week and go soft. Lazy." She grinned, taunting me.

"I wouldn't want to embarrass you again."

Eunice bellowed out a laugh. "Ah, poor baby. Come on. I'll go easy on you."

I had my newfound speed, but if she ever got a hand on me, I'd go down. She wasn't likely to leave me alone, though. I hadn't practiced in days. Maybe she wouldn't hurt me too bad.

I removed my jacket and weapons and shoes. Spot flew to the counter.

Eunice stared at him, narrow-eyed and suspicious, but she quickly turned her attention back to me. She grinned and her eyes lit up. Before I could move, she had me locked in her huge arms.

"My pet's name is Madeline," she shouted as she tossed me onto the mat. I landed on my back with a force that racked sharp pains up and down my spine. I rolled to my feet. "Pet abuse," I shouted. "Someone call the Humane Society!"

She tackled me and slammed me down. Oh, it hurt. I had forgotten. Then she bounced on top of me, all two hundred and forty pounds of her. She straddled my hips and caught my wrists in her hands.

"Now," she said. "Maybe I should steal a kiss."

I gasped for breath. "Steal is the only way you'll get one." I twisted, but I couldn't budge her. "What's the matter, Eunice? Your little girlfriend abandon you?"

Eunice chuckled and rocked her body. I groaned as my hips protested.

"You know," she said, "that's the problem with some women. Too soft."

Her weight eased and I shoved her over. She let me do it, releasing my wrists, probably sure she could get me again. I made it to my feet and found her staring at me in surprise.

"How the hell did you get that fucking fast? You were good at Justice, but . . ."

"Things change, Sister."

She crouched and circled, then charged. I stepped out of the way in plenty of time.

"You gonna run, bitch?"

"Of course I am. I'm not stupid." She charged again. Again, I stepped away.

She tried something different.

"I hear you spent the night with your pretty man." She leered. "Is he big and blond all over, or is he just a pretty face?"

How did she know that? A picture of Michael in the shower flashed through my mind. She had, as she'd intended, distracted me. Only a fraction of a second, but that's all it took. Eunice slammed down on top of me.

I landed butt first, and she straddled me again. It drew a painful cry from me.

"Shit, Eunice. You're going to break something."

"Naw, I'm a professional. I only break when I want to."

With a flap of wings, Spot landed on her head.

She roared. She lifted her weight and threw her hands up to grab him. He flew away. I shoved her off and pushed myself to my feet.

Spot had landed on a low-hanging fluorescent light just out of her reach. He barked like a rabid Chihuahua attacking a pit bull. He danced the length of the light, wings pumping, feet stomping, furious, obviously challenging her.

"What the hell!" Eunice roared. She slapped her hand across the top of her head. Her eyes popped open. She whipped the hand down. It was smeared with green stuff.

Eunice was on her hands and knees. She gagged and heaved over the mat, her body undulating like a fish on dry land.

The odor spread. I gagged too.

Spot flew down to my shoulder. I stumbled, but managed to stay on my feet. Retreat seemed the best course of action at that point. I grabbed everything up in my arms and ran. I dodged Hildy and Lillian as I burst out the front door.

"Better wait to go in there," I yelled at them. I trotted down the street in my socks, carrying all my possessions in my arms and Spot on my shoulder. Eunice had treated me a little better since the day I left Justice, but she still scared the shit out of me. Years of fear did not dissolve with a few kind words. I had no desire to

spend the day scrubbing and deodorizing the pawnshop.

"Madeline," Hildy screamed after me.

I kept up the pace until a quick turn told me no one
followed. I slowed.

A black SUV pulled up to the curb beside me. Étienne.

"You need a ride?" he asked through the open window.

"Yes." I opened the door and tossed my stuff in. I
climbed in and closed the door behind me. I snatched
Spot off my shoulder and held him in front of me.
"Damn it. Why did you do that?"

I glanced in the side mirror. Still no pursuit. "I suggest we leave—now," I told Étienne.

"Why the hell do you have that thing? Is it—"

"This is my pet iguana. His name is Spot. But right
now, I have a few other names I'd like to call him."

Étienne stared at Spot, then at me. He shrugged.
"You always surprise me. I take it that Spot misbe-
haved."

"He took a shit on Eunice."

"Eunice. That's the big one with an attitude?"

"You know her?" I was surprised. I hadn't introduced them.

"Only by reputation. She beat the holy hell out of
two of my men the other night. I'm sure they deserved
it, but they're out of commission for a few weeks."

"That's Eunice."

"They're your friends? Those women?"

"I've known them a long time." I hedged, not sure if
I wanted to claim them as friends.

Étienne chuckled. "She and the other one . . ."

"Other one? Lillian? Or Hildy?"

"Not Hildy. I know her. They've been walking River Street at night, beating up pimps. And I hear some Bastos are missing."

"Uh . . . I didn't know about that." Oh, damn. Couldn't they lay low?

Étienne seemed unbothered. "You have someplace you have to be, or do you want to ride with me?"

"I'll ride. I'm still looking for my man." I looked askance at him. "You seem to be around a lot. Are you following me?"

"I like to keep track of you. I have lots of fun with you. However, I suggest Spot behave himself in my vehicle. I am armed."

Spot chirped and huddled closer to me. I wasn't distracted by the joke. Étienne was following me. I just didn't know why.

Étienne turned around and headed back north. As we passed the pawnshop, the door stood open but a huge industrial fan blocked it, blasting the air in the shop onto the sidewalk. A couple of men started to walk by but they backpedaled and rushed away when they caught wind of the scent. I hunched down in the seat. Étienne grinned.

He drove north, then turned into the Barrows. He didn't speak for a while, but he frowned as if deep in thought.

"What's going on?" I asked.

Silence filled the car. "Before I tell you, you have to promise to trust me."

I paused. My curiosity got the better of me. I had absolutely no reason to trust Étienne. Yes, he had taken a bullet for me, but he was being shot at, too. "Trust is a lot to ask from a stranger. At least in the Barrows."

"I know."

He eyes turned from the road to stare at me.

"I've found Kenny, and I'm taking you to him."

chapter 31

Something twisted inside me. For a moment, I saw that hateful murderer's face, felt my mother's terror. Her agony. I heard my father screaming as they— No. I wouldn't conjure these images now. The battle that went on in my mind and body shredded me. I swallowed my nausea, but my muscles trembled. I could not move. *Control makes me stronger,* I recited over and over in my mind. *Control permits intelligent action . . .*

Slowly, one at a time, I closed the doors of my memory.

What would happen when I killed the man? Who would I be? What would I be? I'd never asked those questions when I killed the first two. Why ask them now? Had the years at Justice changed me that much?

The Portal. I had to remember the Portal. My killer had the Portal. It was why I had been released from Justice in the first place. And Aiakós. If he obtained it, what would happen? Kyros and the others, how would they get home?

My mind churned with questions, possibilities—and dread.

"Madeline?" Étienne's voice carried concern. You'd

think he actually cared for me. Étienne had his own plans and I didn't know what they might be.

"I'm okay."

"I'm not sure I should take you to him."

"Why not?"

"You seem disturbed. What will happen when you see him?"

"I'm going to kill him." My heart thumped in my chest.

Étienne kept to the ruins, often driving around obstacles onto the sidewalk. Finally, he made a turn and stopped in front of a building. Like most in the Barrows, it once had another use. People had called it home. It stood two stories—it had probably been an apartment house—with windows on the second floor.

Étienne opened the center console and lifted out a brown paper bag. We got out of the car and I followed him inside to a hall with floors that creaked ominously under our feet. The stairs leading to the second floor had missing steps and no railing. He went to a door on the right and knocked.

"Kenny. Are you there?" He didn't wait for an answer. He opened the door and we went in. The odor of an unwashed body hit me first.

A man sat on a dirty cot staring at the wall.

"Kenny?" Étienne spoke with soft concern.

The man jerked, eyes wide in terror—until he saw Étienne. Then he smiled as if his best friend had arrived. He didn't even see me.

Étienne handed him the bag. "Here now. Go slow. Don't spill it this time."

"Okay." Kenny accepted the bag. He smiled at Étienne like a boy smiling at his father.

This time, he had said. Étienne had been feeding him on a regular basis—like I fed the creatures in the Barrows. Did he pity Kenny? Obviously, he'd known where the man was all along and hadn't told me. This was my man, my killer—or the shadow of my killer.

Kenny carefully opened the bag and lifted out the food—sandwiches wrapped in paper. His hands shook. Stringy hair fell across his face as he gulped large bites of the sandwich. Then he raised his face and chewed, eyes closed, with an expression of simple pleasure—or a prayer of thanksgiving. Ragged clothing, bare feet, this vicious murderer had the mind of an abused child, grateful for any crumb of kindness thrown his way.

Étienne turned to me and smiled. "He's all yours."

Was this the killer who had strangled and raped my mother? Who had tortured my father? The face was the same, even though the expression was horribly wrong. The hands clutching a simple sandwich were the same hands that had wrapped around her throat and squeezed.

One part of me was urged on by the demand for vengeance. I drew my knife. I wanted him to fight me. I wanted him to know how much he'd hurt me.

I stepped toward him.

"Mmm . . ." He bit off more of the sandwich.

The scar burned, but my mother's demand that I kill warred with the logic that told me he would not know why he was dying. He would die as a child, asking why I'd hurt him, why I was killing him. Would that give me peace?

I don't know how long I stood there. Some decisions are easier than others. This was not one of them. As I watched him eat, I knew the man who had raped and strangled my mother and killed my father would not be punished for his crime—at least not by me. I sheathed the knife. Part of me cried out that I was a fool, but another part knew I was a better human being for it. I'd probably regret the decision later.

"You think I could ask him some questions?" Information in lieu of a bloody death.

Étienne tensed. Only for a brief second, barely noticeable. "I don't know if he can answer, but you can try. Try not to upset him. If you aren't going to kill him, that is." I detected a warning there. Étienne had brought me here but had no intention of allowing me to kill. He'd simply tested me. I'd deal with that later.

I knelt in front of Kenny. I didn't want to tower over him. He was eating the last of the sandwich Étienne had brought him carefully, smiling with pleasure, savoring each bite.

"Kenny?"

He froze.

I smiled and tried to speak gently. "Hi, I'm Madeline. I'm a friend of Étienne's. Could I talk to you for a minute?"

He slowly began chewing again. He nodded. I

thought he had recognized me on the street, but I think he was simply responding to my body language, my intent. He'd run because in that moment I had a murderous aura around me that terrified him.

"Kenny, I'm looking for something. It's a pretty jewel—black with little lines of gold running through it. Do you remember it?"

He slowly nodded. "I remember." He stuffed another bite of sandwich in his mouth. "It's gone. I'm glad. Burned, burned me. Made me hurt inside."

Excitement filled me. Was I close to at least half my goal? I kept a neutral expression on my face.

"Where is it now?"

"It was pretty." He slowly smiled, looking even more childlike. "I carried it for a long time. Then it made me come here. I hate it."

For a fraction of a second, his face became the face of a true killer, the face that haunted my dreams. The image crashed in my mind of him leaning over my mother, his hands around her throat as she struggled to breathe. I fought the urge to kill again. Kenny had paid for his transgression—not the ultimate price, but a living death of sorts.

Kenny looked up at Étienne, then back at me. "I did what she told me. She drove us there. I splashed her with the stuff first. I choked her good. I made sure she was dead before I took it off. Then I ran away. For a long time." He leaned forward and rocked back and forth, arms crossed over his stomach as if his meal had turned to poison. "Hate her, HATE HER!" The last words came out in a scream.

At first, my mind couldn't process what he said. *She* drove us. Who? Surely not a common thief. It had to be someone with power, someone with something to gain from stealing the Portal—or allying herself with someone who needed it.

My fragile control shattered. I jumped to my feet, but before I could draw a knife, Étienne was dragging me out the door and onto the sidewalk.

I fought him, twisting. Had I not been almost out of my own mind, he wouldn't have been able to hold me. I stopped struggling. He released me and I dropped to my knees. There on the sidewalk of a dead city, I did what I had never done. I cried for my parents. With great, heaving, racking sobs, I cried for everything I had lost. I had gained the knowledge that the men who killed my parents were lackeys, hired hands, and nothing more. I still had no idea who was really behind all of this. I don't know how long I went on with my belated mourning, but when I came to myself, Étienne was crouching beside me.

I had chosen not to kill. My mother would haunt my dreams again, but I would deal with it. For the millionth time, I asked myself: How could she not have defended herself against someone else's potion?

Étienne helped me to my feet and walked with his arm around me as we went back to the SUV. He didn't start the engine when I climbed in. I was still shaking. Spot patted my arm with his tiny paw and made soothing noises.

"Your iguana seems rather intelligent," Étienne said.

"Yeah. He is."

"So, have you made friends with all of those things in the ruins?"

"I've met them. I wouldn't call them friends."

"Will you talk about it?"

I used my shirtsleeve to wipe my eyes. "Why? So you can tell Aiakós and he can kill more of them?"

"How do you know he kills them?"

Didn't seem like a secret to me. Aiakós was his employer, after all. "He told me the night I met him."

"What do you think of him? Aiakós?"

"First impression is that he's incredibly dangerous. Volatile, deadly."

Étienne didn't disagree with me.

"Why do you work for him?" I asked. "You know a lot about me. Maybe you should give a little in return."

Étienne didn't reply right away, maybe deciding how much and what to tell me. When he did speak, he sounded steady. "He was hiring. Clark was in charge. Aiakós isn't stupid. He saw and gave me a promotion. He told me what he wanted and I started building the security force."

Too deliberate, too casual. He was leaving a lot out.

He abruptly changed the subject. "Would you like to see what I do to earn Aiakós's money?"

"Sure." I needed to hide from Eunice for a while. Take my mind off the confusion still twisting within me.

He laughed, reached over and ruffled my head like I was a kid.

Kenny didn't have the Portal. He'd apparently stolen it at the behest of someone, maybe a witch. He hated witches, but he didn't specify one in particular. I needed to go back to Abigail. I didn't believe she had taken the Portal. She had saved me, after all. But maybe she could help me find it.

I couldn't deal with Abigail just yet, though. I needed more time to think.

chapter 32

We didn't go far. The building where Kenny hid was only a block from a light industrial area. My sense of direction told me we were on the northern edge of the Barrows, close to the Earth Mother's magical prison walls. The ruins remained, only the area between buildings spread out into parking lots and other wide expanses of asphalt and bare ground. How odd. I would have thought Aiakós would prefer his little army closer to keep an eye on them. I said so to Étienne.

"Oh, he does. But I've refused. My men work for me. I don't want Aiakós to meddle with that. Best to keep my distance."

"And Clark?"

"Clark, I'm forced to accept. He is Aiakós's spy. His job is to watch me." He grinned. "He's not very good at it, either."

"Is Aiakós mad about me cutting on him?"

"I guess not. He laughed when Clark complained."

I shuddered.

"You fear Aiakós. You should. Why don't you fear Michael? You climb into his bed."

"Not without body armor and a stunner."

Étienne laughed, spontaneous and genuine. I had to wonder, though, had he followed me last night, too? The Barrows was a relatively small place with lots of eyes on the streets. Étienne with his security force probably owned some of the observers.

I didn't tell him that Michael had given me everything he was, freely and honestly. We'd sealed our connection with sex powerful enough to bind us beyond escape. What would it take to bring it to love? I still didn't know.

Étienne drove to one building where two men in gray fatigues stood by a single door. Like those around it, the building was a tall warehouse with a small boxy office tacked on to the front.

"Do your men know about the Drows in the ruins?" I asked.

"Drows?"

"Yeah. Like Spot. And the thing that tried to kill Michael."

"Drows. That's a good name. Yes, they know."

"Do they kill them?"

"Not on my orders. Most of those are farther south anyway. I encourage the men to stay away from that area."

"Could Spot come in with me?" I cupped a hand around the little lizard. "I hate to leave him out here in the sun, and if he flies, someone might be tempted to use him for target practice."

Étienne lifted an eyebrow and stared at me and the little Drow on my lap. He laughed. "Will he behave?"

"Sure." I glared at Spot, who had the grace to act humble.

"Okay. I don't let these guys play with guns much anyway. Some of them are . . . volatile."

"Volatile?"

"Ex-cons, most-wanted by some agency. But a few mercenaries, too. They're better."

"You don't hire smart ones?"

"Of course. A few intelligent men are necessary. The rest are men who will take orders. Smart ones might try to take over. Like I did with Clark."

Somehow, I couldn't see Étienne ever taking orders. He'd had complete control when he called his men to him the other day. He'd also, for some reason, wanted me to know that he had assembled a formidable fighting force in the Barrows.

When I climbed out of the SUV, I sat Spot on my shoulder. He made an easy fit with his wings folded and his tail draped loosely around my neck. Not comfortable, but not awkward either. It would slow me down if I had to fight, but I didn't expect that.

The two men in gray fatigues stood up straight when Étienne approached. The office rooms appeared barely used, but when he opened the door to the main warehouse, that didn't appear to be the case there.

A bleacher had been set up on one side of the building, and not far away I saw something familiar. A practice mat. Some men sat on the bleacher and others crowded around the mat, where two combatants struggled with each other. The men watching laughed and hooted, cheering the opponents on.

Étienne led me toward the bleachers, where the men quickly moved aside for us. I quickly counted twenty-six. All wore gray fatigue pants and T-shirts.

Étienne leaned back, relaxed, with his elbows on the bleacher seat above him. I sat beside him, not relaxed at all. Spot, perched on my shoulder, talked softly in my ear. I wished I understood his chirps and clicks. I'm sure his observations would be interesting. The men stared at me, some with interest and others with the blank faces of men who guarded their emotions well. Some appeared patently stupid while many had eyes that said they were far more intelligent than they wanted to announce to the world. All were well muscled and physically fit. Not surprising, since an area across the floor had more workout equipment than the Archangel.

The struggle on the mat was going nowhere, with the two opponents locked in each other's arms, neither able to move. Neither could gain the advantage.

A man approached Étienne. He was older, dark-skinned, and had gray sprinkled in his close-cropped hair. He had a powerful, stocky body and intelligent eyes set in a smooth face. His right hand was twisted though, with the knots and crooks of severe arthritis, something I'd seen many times when I'd volunteered at nursing homes as a teenager.

"Darrow." Étienne acknowledged him.

Darrow nodded. They exchanged a look, one that said more than words. There was camaraderie there, a closeness I had heard in my father's voice when he spoke of his old army buddies. Once a year, he closed his restaurant and they all came to party and talk about the old days. Mother and I were forbidden to attend.

Darrow stared at the men on the mat and shook his head.

"Bad, huh?" Étienne said.

"Worse." Darrow sighed. "All right, you incompetent assholes," he shouted at the men on the mat. "Cut loose and let someone else try."

The two men obeyed promptly. As they broke, another lumbered onto the mat. This one had a great hulking body balanced on tree-trunk legs and surprisingly small feet. His unnaturally flat nose suggested that someone had seriously objected to his face at one time. His bald head had a few dents, too. He scanned those watching him with contempt—and challenge. His gaze slid over me, stopped for a moment, probably on Spot. I doubt a mere woman would be considered a threat. I would've loved to sic Eunice on him.

"All right," Darrow said. "Somebody with brains want to take Hogg down?"

"Hogg?" I glanced at Étienne. "You're kidding."

He grinned. "Looks can fool. Hogg has two things going for him. Size and the fact that he actually reached the fourth grade in school."

"A genius, huh?"

"Of course, he's wanted in Kansas for the murders of his girlfriend and her mother, in Texas for robbery with injuries, and in Tennessee for vehicular homicide."

I stared at him, more than a little appalled. "Why do you—"

"Don't ask. A little advice. Some of these men are better than others, but there are no innocents here."

"Not even yourself?"

He simply shook his head.

I did wonder why he had offered such information, unless it was a warning.

Étienne chuckled and slid an arm around my shoulder. I didn't know if he meant it as an intimate gesture or a warning to the men not to mess with me. I let it be.

A man stepped onto the mat, a lean man with quickness to him that I admired. He and Hogg circled, looking for the advantage. Hogg made short sideways steps on those small feet. He lifted each foot completely off the ground with each step. Every time he lifted one, he became vulnerable. If his opponent watched those steps, caught him at just the right moment. But he didn't. He lashed out and caught Hogg in his massive chest with a foot, but Hogg had both feet on the ground at impact. All he had to do was lean forward and grab. He used his weight, barreled forward, and fell on his unbalanced opponent. It was over then. The same scenario played out with the next one, and it was easy to see that in hand-to-hand, Hogg had only one move: use the solid mass of his body to overcome his opponents.

"May I try? Please?" I asked Étienne.

He frowned. "What? No. If you get hurt, I'll have to kill Hogg. And Michael will kill me."

"I'll be okay." I stood and made a great show of setting Spot on the bleacher seat, stripping off my jacket, and removing my weapons.

Etienne, in spite of his protest, didn't try to stop me.

I stepped onto the mat.

Hogg stared in surprise. Then he laughed.

"Étienne!" Hogg shouted. "You gonna send your little girlfriend in? I hurt her and you shoot me, right? You come fight, bastard." He shook his fist at Étienne.

Étienne shrugged. His face remained calm.

"Come on, Hogg." I smiled at him. "You're not scared of a girl, are you?" I wanted to get him pissed. He'd make mistakes. "I promise not to hurt you too much."

Hogg sneered. "I don't like women."

"Oh, you like boys, then? Wouldn't have thought that, but whatever gets it up . . . right?"

The men around us snickered.

Hogg didn't wait. He charged. I wasn't there when he arrived. Twice, he tried the same move. Twice, I dodged him. Rage had him huffing and blowing like a sounding whale.

"You gonna run, whore?" He'd stopped charging and gone to his weight-shifting mode, exaggerating like a sumo wrestler, actually lifting his feet off the mat. My legs were longer than his.

Timing and speed. Nothing more. As he began to lift his right foot, I kicked him in the face. He went down with a grunt, ass first, then on his back. He struggled to rise, but couldn't. He lay there, arms and legs pumping, choking on blood. I guess I'd flattened his nose a little too much.

I planted my hands on my hips. "I guess someone needs to roll him over. Wouldn't want him to suffocate." I glanced around at the surprised faces. "Would we? Want him to suffocate?"

No one moved. Finally, Darrow walked over to Hogg, grabbed him with his good hand, and jerked him onto his side. Blood ran out of Hogg's mouth, but he breathed again.

Darrow came to me. "Now, tell them how you did that." He nodded at the men, all staring avidly at me.

I explained about watching the movements of your opponent, how Hogg did his little step-step, and how I hit him at the right time.

"I saw that part." He shook his head. "You're too fast. No . . . no human is that fast. You gonna come to work here?" Darrow asked.

"Nope. I have a job."

"She works for the Golden Boy." Étienne approached. He threw an arm around me and hugged me to him. "Apparently he has better fringe benefits. Not that she's ever tried any of mine. I guess I'm not pretty enough."

That got him a laugh from the boys.

I didn't reply. I escaped from his encircling arm, slipped on my gun, and strapped on the knives. Spot climbed up to ride on my shoulder. Étienne watched me, smiling.

"Where can I take you?" he asked.

"Harry's." His comment had pissed me off. Was I feeling protective of my relationship with Michael?

We were walking away when I heard the stomp of feet behind me. I turned to see Hogg racing toward me, knife in hand. Before I could move, Spot lifted off. He landed on Hogg's head.

Hogg screamed and flailed his arms as Eunice had, trying to catch Spot.

Spot flew away to land on the bleachers. Something was locked in his teeth.

Hogg had dropped the knife and clutched his head, still screaming and choking. He turned in a circle as if desperate to ward off an attacker who had already gone.

I hurried to Spot. An ear dangled from his teeth.

I shook my finger at him. "Spit that thing out! It might poison you."

Spot dropped the ear.

Behind me, I could hear Étienne laughing. He came and slid an arm in mine. "Let's go. I've had all the entertainment I can stand for the day."

Spot flew to my shoulder.

Étienne didn't speak much on the way back to River Street, but he smiled occasionally.

I didn't talk either. My mind turned to Kenny. He obviously knew something. I wanted to talk to him again, preferably without Étienne around. Even after our little bonding session at the warehouse, I didn't fully trust him.

Étienne stopped in front of Harry's.

"Thank you for taking me to him," I said.

"You're welcome. Madeline, please be careful. Not everything here is as it seems . . ."

"I know."

He nodded. I climbed out and he drove away.

I went upstairs to check on Grace. Spot went briefly to her but then headed out the window. I peered out to the street and saw Hildy, Eunice, and Lillian standing outside.

I had to face them sooner or later. I headed downstairs and crossed the street to the Armory—and walked into an argument.

"Go back to Justice," Hildy shouted at Eunice and Lillian. "You're messing things up here. There's a balance here—" She stopped when she saw me.

All three of them turned their attention to me and glared, but I ignored it. "What balance, Hildy?"

Hildy grunted. "You can't go around playing cops in the Barrows. You start a war down here, people start to pay attention. Sooner or later . . ."

Étienne *had* said that Eunice and Lillian had been killing pimps and Bastinados.

"Your so-called balance is weighed in favor of evil," Eunice said.

Lillian nodded in agreement. "Evil is using the Mother's cloak of forgetfulness to thrive. It is hiding people and terrible deeds. We will right that balance. There will be no war. If the Earth Mother denies these good people the benefit of the law just because they live in the Barrows, we will provide it."

I sighed in relief. At least this wasn't about me. I wouldn't interfere. The faint odor of Spot's earlier deposit still circulated in the air, along with the cloying sweetness of air fresheners. It was past time to randomly search for the Portal. If it was not used on the solstice, I would have more time to look. If it was used, it would be in the Zombie Zone tomorrow at midnight, the beginning of the solstice. I quietly left and walked to the Archangel, where Michael waited for me.

Tomorrow would bring disaster or victory, and would probably change us all.

chapter 33

June 25—Dark Moon Solstice

The morning dawned bright and warm, approaching the summer yet to come. I left Michael to his business close to noon and walked to the Armory. For the first time in my life, I understood the meaning of the word *sated*. Michael and I had made love last night until I fell exhausted into a deep, dreamless sleep. It was ever surprising to be lost in pleasure rather than violence and vengeance.

"Tonight begins the solstice," Hildy snarled at me as I walked through the door. "The dark moon is rising. You don't have the Portal."

"I know."

"No, you haven't searched for it." Hildy smacked her hand down on the counter. "You've been too busy fucking that demon."

"Hildy!" Lillian came from the back room. "Leave her alone."

Eunice followed Lillian, but said nothing.

I ignored Hildy and her opinion. I couldn't tell her

everything. I didn't have time. I had something I needed to do. "Lillian, will you drive me to Abigail's house? I need to have a serious discussion with the witch."

"Yes," Lillian said. "But Eunice and I are going with you."

Oh, this would be good.

Abigail sighed when she saw the Sisters, but she allowed us to enter. She invited us to sit and brewed tea. The kitchen was big and warm and the table we sat at was covered with a sky-blue cloth. The air was filled with the scent of dried flowers hanging from a rack by the windows hung with pure white lace curtains.

While the tea brewed, Eunice moped and stared at the wall and Lillian sat, hands gracefully folded in her lap, quiet as a nun.

"What brings you here?" Abigail asked as she sat with her own tea.

I decided to be completely honest. We had no time for anything else. "I found my third killer yesterday."

They said nothing. All watched me with interest.

"I didn't kill him." To my surprise, I'd yet to have regrets about that action.

"Of course you didn't kill him," Lillian said. She lifted the teacup and smiled.

"We found him two days ago." Eunice stretched out her legs. "Pitiful bastard."

"You didn't tell me!" I sat up straight and almost spilled my tea.

"No. It's your mission, not ours." Eunice picked up her own cup. It seemed delicate in her thick fingers, but she handled it easily.

"Bullshit! You and Lillian interfere when you get damned good and ready."

Lillian fiddled with her cup, an edgy gesture unsuited to the Sister I had known. "Madeline, when Mother Evelyn sat in the Judgment Room and gave you permission to kill, I don't think I could have been more surprised and furious."

"I don't understand."

Lillian shook her head. "Killing in vengeance is wrong, no matter what the circumstances. Your need for it is an aberration, set on you by magic. It was our goal at Justice to break you of it. Then Evelyn gave you the freedom to negate all of our years of hard work."

"Why did you spare him?" Eunice asked.

"The man who killed my parents no longer exists. Something has burned his mind away. I decided it wasn't worth it."

Lillian grabbed me and hugged me. Tears glimmered in her eyes. She was a deadly cold Sister of Justice, but not unfeeling, apparently. Eunice snatched me away from her. She hugged me so tight I gasped for breath.

"Eunice, I need my rib cage unbroken, if you don't mind."

She released me but still held on. "Good. You'll make it."

"Make what?"

Lillian grasped my hand. "We are killers. Cold as winter on the tallest mountain. We go where we are told. We kill when we are told. We hate it. If we didn't hate it, we would not have been permitted to take our vows. We did not want Sisterhood for you." She released my hand and smoothed the tablecloth by her cup. "Now, let us return to your mission. Perhaps Abigail can advise us."

That sounded good to me. "Oh, yes. And would it be too much to ask for everyone to tell the truth?" I leaned forward and spoke directly to Abigail. "I'm looking for a stone called the Portal. Do you know what it is?"

The calm on Abigail's face disappeared in a flash. Her eyes narrowed and I got the uneasy feeling that she might be preparing to blast something—or someone.

"Yes. I know of the Portal. Why do you ask?" Abigail had one hand on the table clenched into a fist. Her magic shifted and stirred around her like a fog creeping into the woods.

"The Portal is in the Barrows."

Abigail nodded. "The Portal is a powerful talisman from another world. No one knows how it came here. It has some unique properties. The Barrows is the worst place it could be."

She hesitated as if determining if she should continue. "The Portal draws power from that other world, its home world. Not earth magic."

"Witches can use it?" I shifted in my chair uncomfortably.

"Yes. But the Portal is incredibly difficult to use," Abigail said. "Not many witches have the ability, and it takes years to learn. The witch who originally found it a thousand years ago kept it long enough to create chaos. She opened multiple doors to other worlds, let all manner of creatures come in. Once it was retrieved from her, the Mother gave it to different witches to protect, no longer than a year each, to hide it and keep it safe. By allowing it to remain with one of us for only a short period, the world was kept safe from harm."

The puzzle pieces now moved in my mind. Curves and lines came together into a whole, a complete picture. "And all those witches gave it up when the time came?"

"Yes." Abigail relaxed a little. "Except for one, about twenty years ago, who fell under its curse. She decided it was hers and she would not return it." She glanced at Eunice and Evelyn. "The Sisters sent a Triad to retrieve it. The Triad failed. The witch used the Portal against them."

Eunice's jaw tightened and Lillian bowed her head.

Abigail continued. "Two Triads were sent the second time, armed with the Morié and Solaire. The witch escaped, but she had to leave the Portal behind. To my knowledge, that witch has not been found. She won't be, unless she uses earth magic, and as far as I know, she has not. The Mother keeps track of us through our use of earth magic. If a witch doesn't use earth magic, she can hide—for a while.

"Once the Portal was retrieved, we continued to pass it on between different witches, but more secretly. Few knew who had it at any given time."

"Moving it so the witch who wanted to keep it couldn't find it," I whispered.

Some things that seemed obvious could not possibly be. Alien magic. A witch who seemed to be in hiding.

My mind raced. The disguised paintings at the River Street Café. The waiters who trembled in fear. A body aging and warped by the misuse of magic.

Oonagh.

Her so-called feeble attempts to live. Kenny's babbling and hatred of witches. It all pointed to her. Could the witch who orchestrated my parents' deaths be here in the Barrows?

Abigail watched me with sad eyes. I realized she knew far more than I thought. "When a witch has the Portal on her person, the Earth Mother not only can't see it—she can't see the witch. The magic in the Portal blinds her. And because of the other-world magic in the Portal, the witch carrying it cannot touch or use earth magic."

A tight knot formed in my stomach. I knew what had happened to my mother.

"Madeline?" Lillian laid a hand on my arm.

Eunice leaned forward. "You're as white as those curtains on the window, girl."

"My mother died because she was wearing the Portal as jewelry. When they came in, they kept her from taking it off. She couldn't call on the earth magic to save herself." The realization stunned me. All these years, I had blamed the Earth Mother for not coming to my mother's aid.

Abigail nodded. "Oh, my dear. Yes, that is a possibility." Sympathy rolled off her in great waves.

Kenny had told me the truth. He had been instructed to prevent my mother from removing the Portal. When he finished with her, he stole it from her body. He'd run to escape the witch who had sent him to kill her. I didn't know why he'd kept it, and I doubt he could tell me. Had he seen the value in it? Had the Portal so mesmerized him? Pieces of the puzzle were missing. Deep agony filled me, but I forced it down.

Abigail cleared her throat, and I realized she was close to tears. My mother and father died because of my mother's vanity. I loved her still, but oh, how much tragedy came from that one deadly sin. She could've hidden the Portal. She didn't have to wear it.

"There is another reason a witch may keep the Portal for only a year," Abigail said. "If a human carries it for a time, they go insane. The same is true for a witch. It takes longer for a witch, but madness will strike her eventually, too. Holding the Portal also takes a physical toll on its keeper."

This final piece of information clinched my suspicions.

"Your missing witch is called Oonagh," I said. "She's here in the Barrows. She has the Portal. She's dying and can't access earth magic to cure herself without announcing her presence and setting a small army of Sisters after her. She sent those men to kill my mother and steal the Portal."

"And the one who had it didn't take it back to her. He kept it," Lillian said. "He ran away and hid. Why did he come here, though? How did she get it from him?"

Abigail frowned. A slight V formed over her eyes. "I am not an expert on talismans of that sort, but it is possible that once its magic began to affect his mind, the Portal began to influence him. The Portal would gravitate to a place where it could return to where it belonged."

"That would be the Zombie Zone."

"Yes," Abigail said. "It would be."

So, Kenny was driven insane and the Portal led him to the Barrows, where Oonagh found him, took the Portal from him, and left him to wander the streets lost in madness, helpless and alone.

"Well." Eunice straightened. She flexed those powerful muscles. A tone of excitement filled her voice. "Let's go find this witch. Madeline has the Morié and the Solaire. She can take point."

"It won't be just the witch. She has bodyguards," I said.

Abigail shook her head. "I doubt you can find her now. She is most likely hidden, preparing for the solstice. She's going to use the Portal on a dark moon solstice. That is when it would be the most powerful. What does she want?"

I had a good guess. "I don't think it's what she wants, but what she needs. She's dying. She can't use earth magic to cure herself. I'll bet she's trying to get enough power from the Portal to cure herself. Every time she uses it, the walls between the worlds thin a bit more. She brought the Drows here."

"And how do you know that?" Lillian locked her attention on me.

"A Drow told me." I held my hand up. "Don't ask right now. This is my mission."

Eunice muttered under her breath, "Exactly what does this Portal do?"

Abigail sighed. "I'm not completely sure. It never came to me to hold. I know it amplifies the will of the witch—if she can control it. Control is the key. I doubt that even I am strong enough to do that." She straightened. "I need to go and talk to the Mother. She rarely intervenes, but maybe she will tell me what we can do."

Lillian smiled. "Sisters of Justice never count on the Earth Mother. We may take her orders, but we know how unreliable she is. You witches would do well to remember that."

chapter 34

Abigail walked out into her garden and we sat in silence, each forming our own thoughts, making our own plans. When my phone rang, I didn't know what it was at first. I pulled it out of my pocket.

"Madeline!" Riggs shouted. I jerked the phone away from my ear.

"What's wrong?" I asked, cautiously bringing the phone back to my face.

"Michael's been kidnapped. I saw it. There were twenty men. He took out almost half of them, but they threw something on him and he went down. They put him in a car and drove away. I couldn't do anything."

A bitter taste formed in my mouth. No, he couldn't have done anything. Even I'd be put off by those odds. "Where did it happen?"

"Behind the Den."

"Which way did they take him?"

"Into the Barrows."

"I'll find him." I tried to speak with calm determination while I suppressed the urge to scream.

I ended the call. "Michael's been kidnapped."

"You cannot go searching for him!" Eunice was adamant. "Tonight is the solstice. You have to find the Portal!"

"Madeline, I'm afraid I agree." Lillian sounded sympathetic.

"No. You're wrong." I stood and checked my weapons. "Michael is a part of this. He always has been, I think."

The most obvious kidnapper would be Oonagh. Her kind of adoration would demand kidnapping, to keep him from thwarting her. Make him a prisoner until after the solstice, then do with him as she wished. The creepy men at her place the day we went to lunch might be only a handful of the muscle she had at her disposal—another reason not to go at her head-on.

"You gonna walk?" Eunice demanded. She gave me a furious scowl and held up her keys. "I won't drive you."

"I will get there however I can." I headed out the door.

Lillian followed me. Eunice did not.

"Madeline, please be reasonable." Lillian kept pace with me. She tried to take my arm, but I pulled away.

I didn't say anything. I was reasonable. Michael was mine. He had been from that first moment, even if it had taken me a while to recognize it. I stopped on the sidewalk, hands clenched into fists in frustration. I had no way of expressing the urgency of the moment other than going back in and wrestling those car keys from Eunice.

That's when I saw the bus heading toward me. The

sign on the front said OUT OF SERVICE. It slowed as it approached. Jim opened the door. "Hey, lady. Need a ride?"

"I don't believe this," Lillian said. She had a genuine look of shock on her face. I'd never seen that. Other than the occasional smile, she had the stoicism of a nun.

I grinned, but Jim's appearance was too coincidental. I knew it must be the Earth Mother's doing. Perhaps she did intervene directly when needed. Eunice was still inside and I had no time to go back, get her, and argue with her. She might try to physically stop me, too.

Lillian followed me as I climbed on the bus. "Jim, I need to get to the Den as fast as you can go without getting a ticket."

"You got it." He grinned, cheerful as a kid at his birthday party.

Before we could take a seat, the diesel engine roared and belched out a cloud of black smoke behind us. I laughed and grabbed a seat behind Jim. Lillian sat beside me. She didn't look happy at all. "Did you just happen to be driving by?" she asked Jim.

"Nope." He held up his cell phone. "My grandmother called. She told me to drive down this street and get my ass here fast. Only she didn't say ass."

Lillian shook her head, like she still didn't believe it. I accepted the blessing in silence. I would've bet anything his granny was a witch, but now wasn't the time to get into it.

"You look like the world is falling apart," I said to Lillian.

"Madeline, my world has been falling apart since you arrived at Justice." She ran a hand through her short cropped hair, hair that now had some gray. "Eunice and I are not novices. We are the elite. Before you arrived, we had been working in the field, serving the Earth Mother. When Evelyn called us to Justice to train you, we thought it was a waste of our time and talents. But then we met you. We saw your pain, your anger. And your strength and potential. We knew we needed to mold you into a woman of power to erase your destructive tendencies. We knew you were important to the balance of our world. And that is why we invested a good portion of our lives in you. When you were able to forsake your vengeance . . . we were so proud."

I slid my hand into hers. She'd humbled me. She and Eunice had given a part of their lives to me. But she was wrong. I hadn't forsaken revenge. I'd merely chosen not to kill a witch's mindless tool. The witch who'd given the orders had to die.

In minutes, we rolled through the invisible barrier that the Earth Mother would not cross lest her presence shatter it and allow Aiakós his freedom. From that point on, she would observe, but not interfere.

Jim maintained the bus at a steady speed down River Street. He ignored the people who stood near the street edge, ignoring the OUT OF SERVICE sign and flapping their arms like chickens trying to fly.

"Are you sure you want to do this?" Lillian asked.

"I don't have a choice. I need to go after Michael." I looked at her hard. "I think it's imperative. Apparently the Mother thinks it is, too. She sent me the ride."

Jim pulled up in front of the Den. I hugged him as we climbed off the bus.

"Want me to wait?" he asked.

"No. Leave the Barrows." I had no idea what was going to happen, and the next few hours might not be safe for anyone on these streets. "Call your granny and tell her I said thanks."

The western sun had dipped below the orange-streaked horizon, and soon the malevolent dark moon night would begin. I ran around the Den and into the alley, and Lillian followed. I had no clue where to look, but I knew whom to call. I slowed to a fast walk.

"Termas!" I called for my great scaly friend. "Anyone!"

"Who are you calling?" Lillian asked.

"Backup."

I'd gone two blocks in the quickly fading light when young Termins ran out of the building. His clawed feet scrabbled along the asphalt and his scales gleamed in the last vestiges of twilight. The much larger Termas was right behind him, growling in what sounded like reprimand. He snatched Termins just before the young one plowed into and over me. I heard Lillian gasp. I twisted to face her, to stand between her and the giant Termas and his young.

Lillian had drawn a gun. Of course, all she saw was a Drow.

"Lillian!" I held out a hand. "They won't hurt you. Put the gun away. Trust me. Please."

She stared for long moments. Termas stood still and made no menacing moves. She holstered the weapon.

She didn't comment, but she kept her eyes on the massive scale-armored Drow.

I turned back to Termas. "Please, take me to Kyros."

Termas nodded and went back into the building, carrying a struggling Termins under his arm. We followed him. Once inside, he picked up a small lantern— I'd bet for our benefit. We trekked through the semi-darkness of several other buildings where holes had been cut in walls to facilitate travel without going outside. The stink of dry rot was thick here and our feet stirred up dust. I drew the neck of my shirt over my nose and mouth to keep a fit of sneezing at bay. Lillian made no comment; nor did she ask questions. Finally, we entered what I recognized as the dimly lit room I'd been in only a few nights before.

Kyros stepped out of the darkness. I turned to Lillian. Her hands were at her sides, clenched into fists, but she didn't draw gun or knife. At least Eunice had stayed behind. I doubt I would have been able to control her.

"Thank you for trusting me, Sister," I said to her. I laid a hand on her arm to reassure her.

"You seem to be very generous with trust, Madeline." Her voice was full of dismay. She shook her head. "I have seen more Drows than you ever will. Most are mindless animals. Intelligence makes these more dangerous."

Kyros stepped closer to Lillian. She tensed, but didn't reach for a weapon. He lowered his head to her. "I wish I could find a way to convince you that we want nothing but to leave this place in peace."

She met his gaze, then gave a slight nod that might have meant anything.

"You are looking for Michael," Kyros said to me. "The Tektos saw what happened and told me. I'll take you to him."

I almost hugged him, but he looked too much like Aiakós. I still had no proof that I could trust this creature. Intuition alone was carrying me through this night. "Can someone else take me? You need to gather your people. Tonight is the dark moon solstice. I'm betting that the talisman will arrive in the plaza close to midnight, when it actually begins. The witch won't want to lose a minute. All we have to do is take it away from her; then you and your kind can return home." I hoped that Lillian would not connect the word *talisman* with the Portal. I didn't need her knowing that the Drows needed it to travel home.

Kyros smiled. "Is that all?" I didn't know his expressions, but I think this one conveyed sarcasm. "Madeline, anyone who is able to command the stone, even incompetently, is dangerous."

"And that includes you?"

"Indeed."

"We'll have to take things on faith. As soon as I obtain it, I'll give you the talisman so you can return home."

"You're supposed to return it to the Sisters, Madeline." Lillian spoke quietly. My euphemism hadn't fooled her after all.

"Why? So another witch can use it to destroy something? It doesn't belong here."

Now I had to wonder if I could trust Lillian. Would I have to battle her and Eunice to get the Portal out of this world? That would truly break my heart. I said a silent prayer that I would not have to do that, though I don't know to whom I prayed.

Kyros spoke to Termas in a garble of words, almost like Chinese.

I stepped closer to Lillian. "I'll explain later."

"It ought to be interesting," she grumbled.

Termins, the little Beheras, bumped his thick scaled shoulder against her leg. She staggered. He turned a fearsome but innocent face up to her. She drew a deep breath and knelt beside him.

"Watch the claws," I said. "He's an herbivore, but he's still a kid. And a bit clumsy."

Termins lifted his hand. Lillian grasped it carefully to keep the claws from her. They remained like that, each engrossed in the other. Lillian, the Sister of Justice, had just bonded with a Drow. What next?

"Termas and another will take you," Kyros said. "They will carry you. It's dark now. It will be faster."

"Okay." I raised an eyebrow. "Lillian?"

Lillian rose, silent.

"You can go back if you like," I told her. "They'll lead you to the street."

She crossed her arms. "And let you have all the fun? Certainly not. You are the leader of this quest. I'll follow you."

A great wave of love welled up in me for this woman. Now all I had to do was find the strength, the resolve, to do what might need to be done this evening.

"Madeline?" Kyros laid a hand on my shoulder. "Please be careful. It's only been a short while, but we are all quite fond of you."

"Yeah, I like you, too. Wish we could have met at a better time."

Termas lifted me and the other Beheras picked up Lillian. The trip wasn't comfortable, but it was fast as the Drows ran through the now pitch-black night.

chapter 35

I knew I'd be covered with bruises from banging against Termas's armored skin when we came to a stop in an alley, but we'd gotten there in record time. I had no plan, no agenda, only the deepest need to find Michael.

I could see lights ahead, enough for me to pinpoint our location.

"Damn," I whispered. "This can't be right."

This was the light industrial area where Étienne had brought me to watch his men wrestle and train. Dark dread filled me. All my suspicions about Étienne coalesced into one atrocious ball. The large building that housed his troops sat across a wide street and parking lot. The windows were covered, but I could see men moving around in the light spilling from an occasional open door. Farther down was the training facility where I'd trounced good old Hogg.

Something cold and full of dismay wiggled in my gut. Étienne. What was he up to? I did not want him as an enemy because I liked him—and he would make a formidable adversary.

Termas lifted his great arm and pointed at a building fifty yards down the street. It, too, was a warehouse, though not a large one. And it was guarded. Étienne's troops again. Two men carrying large rifles stood in front of a door.

A vehicle came our way. Termas grabbed me and dashed into an alley. Lillian and the other Drow followed, but not before I got a good look at the door guards as the headlights flashed on them. They wore military-issue night-vision goggles. Sneaking up on them would be near impossible. We'd have to find another way in.

We made our way around to the back of the guarded building. Everything appeared sealed tight, but there were no guards. I smiled as I remembered Sister Tara's lessons on B&E. *Nothing is impenetrable.* Our target building's back wall towered over us, substantial steel doors barring our way through, but I could see light coming from above in places where the roof met the walls. That light illuminated little, but obviously our Drow friends could see quite well in the dark. Not far away, perhaps inside, I could hear the grumble of generators providing electricity.

"Let's see if we can find a hole," I said. Termas and his companion searched with us, carefully feeling our way across the building wall. All doors seemed secure and entrance impossible. It was Lillian who found a way in. At the bottom of a ramped loading dock was a large grate, probably a drain, big enough that Lillian and I could get through. The Beheras could not.

Trash covered most of it, but we quickly cleared that away. I grabbed the grate and jerked. It didn't budge. Was it bolted down? Termas put his big hands on my shoulders and moved me aside. The grate made a popping sound when he jerked it off, but it sounded loud in the night. It revealed a three-foot square.

"Termas, go back and help Kyros get ready to go."

Termas didn't move.

"Please."

He drew me close for a moment, murmured words, sounds I could not understand. Not that it mattered. The gesture was universal, a moment of caring in an uncaring world. All my years at Justice I'd lived without such comfort. I'd grown stronger, but now I questioned the cost. He released me, and he and the other faded into the night.

Lillian followed me as I crawled in. My hands and knees protested as they landed on small, hard objects, pieces of debris small enough to make it through the grate. They wouldn't do any permanent damage or lacerate the skin, but they did hurt.

I hadn't even thought of a flashlight, nor had I had time to obtain one. The floor sloped steadily down.

I'm not normally claustrophobic, but I felt as if the dimensions of the hole closed in on me, tight as a glove, as I forced myself along. My elbows scraped against the walls and I battered my head more than once.

I came to another grate, this one in the floor. I couldn't see, of course, but the tunnel went on, past the grate and into, I hoped, the building. It made sense, sort of. When it rained, the water drained from the confines of the loading dock into the tunnel, then into the floor grate and not into the building. So what was the rest of it for? We continued to crawl until we hit a chute. I skidded down like a skier on a slope straight to hell and crash landed on my ass in a pile of trash, which, thankfully, contained no sharp objects. It made a lot of noise. I scrambled to my feet. There was light here, a single bulb on the ceiling, and I could see the purpose of the chute. I'd landed in a basement, and an ancient coal-fired furnace sat across the room. Long dead, it had once warmed the floors above us and the tunnel and chute had brought it fuel. Lillian followed me, but landed far more gracefully. She stood and brushed the dust off her clothing.

Lillian removed her jacket and tossed it aside. "Get that coat off," she whispered to me. "You need quick access to your weapons. You think your enemy is going to give you time to kill him?"

I stripped the jacket off, stuffed the extra ammo in my pockets, and we made our way to the door. I nodded silently.

"You have the strangest friends." Her voice was soft and low. "In fifty years of fighting Drows . . ."

"I can't think of them as Drows, Lillian. Aiakós, yes. He's a Drow."

Lillian nodded. It made me wonder if she had actually seen him. She and Eunice had obviously been exploring if they had found Kenny.

There were steps leading up to what I hoped was

our destination. I found a switch on the wall at the top of the stairs and turned the light off behind us. No one challenged us as we went into an empty storeroom. From there, we were able to peek out a door to the main warehouse floor.

"Shit," I whispered.

Lillian, who stood at my elbow, pinched my arm for speaking at all. Even a whisper at the right moment could announce our presence. The pinch hurt and reminded me that though she had ceded leadership of the mission to me, I was still a novice.

The warehouse was a hollow open room, about seventy feet square, with good lighting. Overhead lights were bright enough to show Michael standing in a large cage made of steel bars. Most of the rest of the warehouse was empty. I knew Michael's strength, and the bars looked like they couldn't hold him—then I noticed the wires running across them to an electrical panel. Michael stood perfectly still. He must've believed he couldn't break through it, at least not without serious injury. He appeared unhurt, but fury emanated from every inch of his taut body.

Two armed guards stood inside the front door, the only reasonable escape route. One of those guards was Clark. The bandage stood stark white across his face where my knife had marked him.

The distance across the room was too far for stealth. While I was deciding how to proceed, the guards perked up and stared at the front of the building.

Étienne entered. Dismay welled up inside of me at

proof of this betrayal. With all his secrets, I knew we'd been heading toward this moment, or one like it. I had wanted to believe that we wouldn't find him here. I had genuinely liked the man.

Oonagh followed Étienne into the room.

chapter 36

Étienne dismissed the front door guards. Clark looked like he would argue for a second, but then he went on.

Oonagh approached Michael's cage. She didn't seem to be bothering with the illusion of health right then. It probably sucked up a lot of her energy. She wore dark slacks and a fleece jacket she drew around her as if she were cold in spite of the warm summer evening. Her gait was steady enough, though.

Étienne's handsome face was pinched in a frown, and he stared around as if he expected an attack. At that moment, if I'd had reinforcements, a couple of Drows and Eunice, I'd have given it to him. Such an action would be very satisfying but completely stupid.

Michael kept a straight face as Oonagh came closer to him. When he spoke, his voice carried a tone of gentle censure. "Oonagh, I had thought better of you. I thought you brave and—"

"Brave? Because I was dying? I prefer to live." Oonagh held out a hand, but it shook. She quickly clenched a fist and pulled it back. "After tonight, I'll be healthy again. I'll be immortal. Then we'll bargain, you and I."

Michael moved closer to the bars. "Why? You have nothing I want, Oonagh."

"Don't be too sure about that." She reached into her jacket and drew out something small. I couldn't see at this distance, but it had to be the Portal. "This will give me everything."

I bit my lip. Everything? That covered a lot of territory, and since her incompetent experiments brought the Drows here, she really was stretching it. Her illness seemed to be precluding much in the way of logical thought, a definite advantage for me. I shuddered to think of what we didn't know about the Portal. Even Abigail was uncertain of its exact powers.

Oonagh continued her speech. "I can give you riches, Michael. Fabulous wealth. Surely there is something you desire." She smiled and pleaded with him as she held the Portal out. When she spoke again, it was as if she were not speaking to him, but to herself. "It came from another world. The witches thought they could keep it from me." She giggled like a little girl. She caressed the stone and held it to her cheek. "Oh, I'll slaughter them; destroy them all."

Destroy who? The witches? Would she, in her madness, try to take on the Earth Mother herself?

Michael held out a hand. "I don't know what that is, Oonagh, but I know enough to say it's dangerous." I heard the surge of charismatic power in his voice from where I hid with Lillian, the voice that so charmed patrons of the Archangel and the Den. Even now, I was in awe of Michael. "We can talk this out, Oonagh. You don't have to take chances. I know a witch who can heal—"

"I am a witch!" Oonagh spit the words out. "Do not speak to me of witches and their damned Earth Mother. They abandoned me long ago. They let me hold this magnificent talisman and then thought to snatch it away." She clutched the Portal to her chest and stuffed it back into her clothing.

Magic suddenly rose and filled the room. Not earth magic, but the other strange power to which she clung. Earth magic always felt clean to me, like chimes in a slight breeze. This felt like a deep drumming, like a creeping migraine where the slightest touch sent agony shooting to the brain like lightning, cracking and burning.

Lillian gasped. The effects of the alien magic gave me the shakes and vibrated through my skull. It didn't incapacitate me. It was different from earth magic, but it obviously affected her. It might kill her without any protection.

I forced the Morié into Lillian's hands, then removed the Solaire from my neck and dropped it over her head and around hers. They were designed to protect against earth magic; would the blade and amulet protect against the Portal? I soon received my answer as Lillian immediately breathed easier. The Portal's magic affected me but I could still function. I glanced back into the big room.

Michael was on his knees, arms wrapped around his head. Étienne rolled on the floor.

Oonagh giggled again. Like a cancer, the madness of the Portal was consuming her as it had Kenny.

It made my choice easier. The Portal could not be

given to the Sisters, who would, as instructed, give it to the witches. Eventually, this would happen again. Worse, it could end up in Aiakós's hands and unleash hell—literally. He could hide from the Earth Mother and wreak havoc upon the Barrows or maybe even the world. The only alternative was to take a chance on Kyros. What price would I pay for that, though? Go to prison? Face a Triad of Sisters hell-bent on killing me? Maybe. The deed still had to be done, and I wasn't completely sure I could pull it off. Odds were good I'd get killed trying.

"Now, that's what I like," Oonagh crowed. "Men on their knees. Oh, I have plans for both of you. Get up, Étienne. We need to prepare." She marched out of the room—or tried to march. Halfway to the door, she wobbled and had to slow her pace.

Étienne rose slowly, like an old man with arthritis. He fought to stand. As he did, he stared in my direction for a brief second. Did he know I was there? He left, and the warehouse was silent except for the distant hum of the generators.

"Let's go," I said as the door closed behind them. "No telling when the guards will be back." I briefly wondered if we should barricade the door, but that would take too much time. Michael turned at the sound of my voice as I rushed toward the cage. "Madeline! Don't touch anything!" A note of panic rose in his voice. "It's all wired. You need a special key to the panel to deactivate it."

"Can I short it out without frying you?"

"Don't worry about me. Get to Aiakós and tell him

what's happening. He is probably the only one with the strength to stop her. Whatever she's planning to do."

Oh, no. I might be stupid to trust Kyros, but no way would I involve Aiakós until I had to. I glanced at the electrical panel. The wires ran up to the ceiling and across the room. There had to be a second panel that controlled it. "If I cut the electricity off, can you break out?"

He nodded.

I started toward the side of the room, my eyes turned up to follow the wires. I'd gone ten feet when someone laughed. I whirled.

Clark, that rapist of children, had silently returned. He was pointing a pistol straight at me. "Oh, I have been waiting for this."

He wore the bandage over his missing eye, and the diagonal cut across his face was still raw and criss-crossed with stitches, like someone had sewn it up with shoelaces. His single eye was a narrow slit, filled with rage.

Lillian eased closer to him, to a good knife-throwing distance.

I laughed at him. I needed to get his attention, keep him talking. "Clark. You still hanging around? I thought they would've gotten rid of your useless ass."

Clark grunted. He glanced at Lillian. "You get your hands up, too. I knew something was up right now. Étienne said to leave this building unguarded. He ain't that stupid."

"Clark!" We both whirled toward the voice. It was Étienne. He strode across the room. When had he come back? Where was Oonagh?

Time slowed to a crawl.

Clark glanced at Étienne, then back at me. My gun was still in the holster. In spite of the fact that he held a gun of his own, his single eye hampered him. He had to turn his head back and forth to see both of us since we were so far apart. He turned the gun to me.

"Pay attention to me, Clark." Étienne snapped the words.

Clark ignored him. He pulled the trigger. The sharp bark of gunfire echoed in the almost empty steel building.

Lillian threw her body in front of me. The impact of the bullet drove her back and into me, knocking me to the floor. She gave a sharp cry and collapsed on top of me.

Another shot, this time from Étienne.

Clark danced and turned at the impact of the bullet in his back. Body armor. Étienne's next bullet hit him in his ravaged face. He crumpled and fell, gun clattering on the concrete as his dead fingers released it.

Lillian was still on me so I gathered her up and cradled her in my arms. Blood covered the front of her body. So warm, it spread like a fever, covering my hands and soaking through my clothes. She wasn't dead, but she couldn't live and I knew it.

"No. Lillian . . . don't . . . ," I sobbed. Guilt and shame poured through me, along with the knowledge that someone I loved would die in my place.

"Madeline." Blood ran from Lillian's mouth as she called my name.

Étienne knelt beside us.

Lillian's eyes fluttered open. "Love you."

She relaxed as her last breath escaped.

"Lillian. No!" A scream of loss and agony formed in me. A silent scream that I did not have a strong enough voice to release. Its power racked my body in great shudders. All that remained was the memory of her—and her love. These were her final gifts to me. Like precious gems, I would carry them always. I would also carry the burden of guilt, the knowledge of the sacrifice she had made for me. Guilt and knowledge were stones that would weigh on my soul forever.

Étienne had left me and was at the door shouting at someone to get ready. The guards had probably heard the shots and he wasn't letting them in. Oonagh must have gone. She would not be ordered back so easily.

"Listen to me." Étienne returned. He caught my jaw in his hand. "I'm sorry I didn't get back in time. I knew you'd come. I saw Clark go in, but I was with her and I couldn't rush it." He released me. "You don't have time to mourn, Madeline. I will be in the Zombie at midnight with sixty armed men. Men I trained. There will be four armored cars. We will be escorting her. You can't stop it. I want you to leave. Leave the Barrows. If you try to fight her, she'll destroy you."

I released Lillian carefully. I stuttered and tried twice to speak. "No. Not without Michael. Lillian died helping me get to him."

Étienne shook his head. He grabbed my arms and dragged me to my feet. "If I let him go, will you leave the Barrows?"

"No." The word came out in a shout. I shoved him away. He didn't try to hold me. "I'll fight. You should want me to fight. Étienne, that stone she's using is called the Portal. It has power, power that's driven her mad. You saw that. It opens doors between worlds. The Mother knows what else it will do. If Oonagh can't control it, it could destroy this world. She brought the Drows here by using it, by playing with it." I held out my hands. "Why are you helping her?" My last words came out like a scream.

Etienne lowered his head. "I don't have time to tell you everything. Just know that she owns me. I was very sick once. I wanted to live and I made a devil's bargain with her. She healed me. I didn't know the cost. Just know that I'm paying now."

I didn't know if I believed him, but the look in his eyes, the hurt in his voice, felt genuine. It didn't change the fact that we were enemies, though.

He shook his head. I could see desperation on his face. "I'll release Michael. You go with him to Aiakós and prepare to fight. But I won't give you my men to kill. I trained them. I'll fight with them." He relaxed and his face softened. His fingers brushed my scar. "Ten minutes after I leave, the electricity will go off in here. I'm taking all the guard with me. The cage isn't locked." He nodded at Michael. "I'm not stupid enough to let him out while I'm still in the room."

"Aiakós thinks you trained these men for him. Not to fight against him." I had little sympathy for Aiakós, but the idea of that kind of betrayal offended me.

"Madeline, Aiakós is no better than Oonagh. He'll

destroy worlds to get anything he wants." He glanced at Michael. "Wouldn't he, Michael?"

"Yes," Michael said. His voice carried no inflection at all.

Étienne slid his arms around me and held me tight. "Remember, I'm going to fight for her. I am your enemy." He kissed me hard on the mouth. He released me, then smiled. "Maybe in another life. You and me." He turned and headed for the front door.

"Étienne?"

He turned back to me.

"Is there anything I can do to help you?"

His expression was stark and cold. "Kill the witch, Madeline, and I'll be free."

chapter 37

I gently laid Lillian on the floor and went to Michael. His face was a mask of deliberate calm. Only the tightness around his mouth betrayed his fury. I wondered if this was the first time in his adult life someone had dared to restrain him. "Don't get too close." He held up a hand to warn me.

"Is there another way to shut the electricity off?"

"Another panel in the back of the room. Wait. Don't try that until the ten minutes is up. He may be telling the truth this time." He drew a deep breath. "Madeline, I . . . your friend . . . I am so sorry."

A few tears leaked from my eyes. I fought the pain, but it kept nagging me to give in and scream my sorrow to the world. "She wouldn't let me come alone."

Warriors, assassins, magnificent bitches. Sisters of Justice. May the Earth Mother save you if they hate you. Or if they love you. They can break you. Body and heart.

Michael stirred as if he could make time pass faster. "I knew Oonagh was dangerous. But I didn't think she had the power to control Étienne, his men . . ." His voice softened. "I didn't pay enough attention. You paid a great price for my ignorance. And, yes, my arrogance."

"I hate that she has Étienne."

"He means it when he says he'll fight you."

"I know. But if he doesn't get in my way I'll kill the witch for him. I'll kill her for Lillian, for my mother and my father." I stared into his eyes as I stood across from him, just out of reach.

I lifted my hands. Lillian's blood had dried to brown stains. Now we would see what Michael's pronouncements of love for me were worth. This was the moment when trust became absolute.

"Michael, please don't tell Aiakós about the stone Oonagh has. I have to get it away from her. I have to get it out of the Barrows. Oonagh might tear worlds apart out of madness; Aiakós would intentionally tear worlds apart without conscience. I think you know that. Will you trust me?" I held out my hands to plead with him.

"You didn't trust me enough to tell me about it." His voice was rough and filled with accusation.

I heard coldness there that broke my heart. "No. I barely knew you and when we . . . accepted each other, we didn't talk about such things."

Michael didn't speak again. He simply stood. The electricity went off and the building darkened, leaving only low emergency lights. It was enough to see.

"Don't touch it yet," I said. "I'll find something to test the—"

Michael thrust the cage door open and stepped out. I should've known he wouldn't be good with directions. "Where are we? I was unconscious when they brought me here."

"In the Barrows, where Étienne trains his men. About a mile and a half from the Armory. We need to go there first." I went to Lillian, but he beat me. He scooped her body up and held her close.

"Thank you," I said.

"You wouldn't leave without her."

I'd never heard his voice so cold, so full of fury, even when the thieves attacked at the Archangel. This Michael frightened me, but he had enough compassion to know that I would want to bring Lillian home. I fought the urge to cry then, but Lillian would have berated me for any emotion at all until the job here was done. Control emotion, no matter how traumatic. A Sister of Justice was in control.

We went out a back door cautiously. There was no sign of guards.

I had the phone and tried to call the Armory and Riggs, desperate to get someone to pick us up, but the service kept cutting out. We were still too deep in the ruins.

We kept close to the buildings and alleys to hide from the occasional vehicle. Far more traffic invaded this place than deeper in the ruins. I suspected Étienne's force created some of it. When a line of headlights moved toward us and we had no alley to hide in, Michael kicked open a door to an abandoned building.

And came face-to-face with a group of Bastinados huddled around a couple of battery lanterns.

Shit.

The stunned Bastinados stood for a few brief seconds before they drew their guns—useless guns. Michael laid Lillian gently on the floor, then, in one lightning move, caught a Bastinado by the arm. He twisted and tore the arm off at the socket. How could he? It wasn't possible. *That's horror movie stuff*, I thought. The Bastinado shrieked and fell to the floor as blood pumped out of the hole where he'd once had an arm. He flopped along and continued to cry out. The lanterns were the next casualty and the room plunged into darkness.

Gunshots, the flash of fire from a muzzle, and I dropped to the floor. There was nothing to hide behind.

Shouts and screams continued, giving voice to an orgy of violence and terror. Michael roared, full of pure animal fury, as if each blow, every tear of flesh brought a release of dammed-up rage. And it went on and on until I wanted to scream myself. The smell, the coppery stink of blood. I felt a fine spray of liquid land across my body. Waves of nausea rose up to claim me.

Finally, silence filled the room—except for the deep, ragged breaths of the last killer standing.

We'd left the door open, and lights from a passing car gave me a vision I instantly prayed I'd never see again. Michael stood straight and tall and covered in crimson. It dripped from his fingers. Bodies and assorted limbs lay around him, the predator supreme. His fingers curled and ended in claws, and his face was pure Aiakós. Michael was indeed his father's son. The light faded.

I dared not move. I'd seen some aspect of this when he'd defended against the thieves, but nothing so savage. I had seen nothing of it when we'd made love.

"Madeline?" His voice sounded deep, far deeper than usual. "I won't hurt you. I am in control."

I swallowed hard. Was I bound to this dark creature for the rest of my life?

"You tore them apart."

"They would have killed without remorse. We would be toys to them. The Earth Mother keeps the law from this place, blinding them with her spell. She hides it from those who could provide order, not chaos. Therefore, we who are born of chaos must make our own law. I have tried many years to be what I am not. Human. I'm not fighting it today. Can you live with this?" he asked.

"I'm probably the only one on this earth who could." True. The strangeness of witches and the savagery of the Sisters had taught me well. Perhaps I was the perfect mate for him. I felt him come and pick up Lillian again. He did not touch me.

By the time we stepped outside, he had returned to the magnificent visage he usually presented to the world—only covered with blood. We had to cross River Street through a break in traffic, but no one seemed to notice a blood-covered man carrying a body and a woman with a gun. Just another night in the Barrows.

I had Michael go to the alley by the Armory. I needed to prepare them. Eunice and Hildy waited for me when I walked in.

"Where's Lillian?" Eunice stood, feet planted, fists curled, as dangerous as she'd ever been since I'd known her.

"Lillian's dead, Eunice. She jumped between me and a bullet. But we have to mourn later. Destruction is about to rain down on our heads at midnight if we don't stop it." I swallowed. "Michael is outside with Lillian's body. He'll bring her in, but I don't want you to attack him. It wasn't his fault."

Eunice stood for a moment, staring into nothingness. That did not mean she felt nothing; nor did it mean she would not erupt into violence. When she spoke, her voice was soft and deadly. "Who killed her?"

"A man named Clark. He's dead."

Hildy said nothing. I think the moment had robbed her of all words.

I had Michael bring Lillian in. Eunice and Hildy stared at him.

"Whose blood?" Hildy croaked, her cigarette-scarred voice failing her.

"Bastinado," I told her. "There was an incident on the way here."

Eunice said nothing

Abigail opened the door and walked in. For a moment I saw hope in Eunice's eyes that the witch might be able to heal our fallen Sister, but she knew better.

Abigail went straight to Lillian and laid a gentle hand on her forehead for a moment. "Rest, Sister of Justice. I pray the Earth Mother grants you a new life, one full of wonder and peace." She turned to us. "I've been instructed to help you. I can assure you my magic works quite well here in the Barrows. I will not kill, but I will aid in any way I can. I will save lives."

Eunice silently lifted Lillian from Michael's arms and carried her to the back of the building. Before she left the room, she stared at me long and hard. I couldn't meet that stare and turned away.

"I'm going to Aiakós," Michael said.

I laid a hand on his chest. "Please, give me a minute. I want to go with you."

"You think I'll tell?"

"No. I don't think he'll believe you about how bad things are about to become. His arrogance won't let him."

He said nothing, but went to Hildy's phone to make a call.

Hildy growled low in her throat. "The time will come when the Sisters will fight. Debts will be paid." Hildy stared at me when she spoke, but nothing in her demeanor said she threatened me.

Once we are shown the path, we still have free will. We obey or disobey at our own risk. In the Barrows we make our own choices. Hildy was the wild card in all of this. What choice would she make?

"Hildy?"

"What?" She wouldn't meet my eyes.

"Are you with me? Or not?"

"I'm with you." She sounded defeated. She pretended to cough. Careful ears could tell it was a sob.

"So am I," Eunice said as she returned. "Don't forget

these." She held up the Morié and Solaire. She'd taken them from Lillian's body.

"You wear them for now."

"But you need to kill the witch." Eunice proffered them again.

Abigail cleared her throat. "I know you are immune to earth magic, Madeline, but the Portal's magic is different."

"I've already been tested. That's why I gave Lillian the Morié and Solaire."

"What! You're immune to . . . Why didn't you tell us?" Eunice held the objects close to her heart now.

"Because I had to keep one thing of my own at Justice." I stared into her eyes. "You bitches tore everything out of me, almost broke me, but that secret, you couldn't steal."

Eunice dropped her arms to her sides. She started laughing, but it broke into a sob. The inestimable Sister Eunice had given in to emotion. "Lillian was right. She said . . ." She straightened. "No wonder she was so proud of you. You are our leader, Sister Madeline. Tell us what you want."

I rubbed my hands over my face. Leader? Me? Hildy and Eunice were going to do what I told them to do? Michael certainly wouldn't. What a disaster.

I told them what was about to happen. "The witch that has the Portal will be in the Zombie Zone near midnight. She's dying and thinks it will heal her and give her immortality. She will bring men with guns to cut a path. A lot of men and guns. You and Eunice get armed and go there now. Carefully. Keep to the shadows. Find a building close to the Zombie plaza, go inside, and wait for me. Don't attack any Drows. They won't hurt you—"

"The hell they won't." Hildy stepped back.

"They won't. If you can't leave them alone, Hildy, stay here. If you attack them, you will destroy any chance we have of succeeding tonight." I moved closer to reinforce the command. "You ceded control to me. Do you now withdraw it?"

Hildy shook her head, but she radiated her reluctance. She went to the counter and dug around behind it, probably looking for cigarettes. She found a pack and shook it at me. "This is going to be one hell of a fuck-up."

"Most likely, yes," Eunice said. She turned to me. "We'll be there. Shall we take the witch?" She nodded at Abigail.

"I doubt she'll let you leave her behind."

"And that one?" Eunice nodded at Michael, who had stood aside and watched all of this drama without comment. "Wearing blood like a suit?"

"Bastinado blood," I reminded her. Though difficult, I managed an indifferent shrug. I really didn't want to think about the incident.

Michael's eyes were on me as he spoke. "I stand with Madeline. Where she goes, so will I." He grasped my hand and brought it to his lips. "And her secrets are mine."

With his strength, his love, his loyalty, how could I lose? The fact that I faced overwhelming odds seemed far away at that moment.

A sedan rolled to a stop in front of the store. Michael had been in his Jag when they kidnapped him, so his staff at the Archangel brought what they had. Now all we had to do was enter the demon's den and persuade him to help us fight.

chapter 38

Michael left his driver to walk back to the Archangel while he drove us to the Zombie. He also called Riggs to tell him he was okay and to order him to take the Jag back to the exercise studio—and stay out of the Barrows until morning.

After those calls, Michael didn't speak and neither did I. I don't know what he was thinking. I tried not to think at all. He parked the car on a side street and we walked the last two blocks through the ruins to the Zombie. A good move, really. If there was a pitch battle in the plaza, it would be in a position for a fast getaway.

A odd kind of power swirled around me as we entered the Zombie plaza on foot. It felt like magic, but not. It did not bode well for the rest of the evening. My mother had told me that there were places in the world where powers of different kinds met—and tore apart. When I was ten, we went to Mexico to the site of an ancient temple. I felt the powers swirling around me, shifting, dancing like ghosts—and there were ghosts. One latched on to me and terrified me until we left the next day. I tried to explain it to my mother, but she didn't understand. She saw no ghosts.

We walked into the building and up the stairs to Aiakós. "Madeline?" Michael stopped midway up the stairs.

I studied my angel. My dark angel. He stood there covered with blood, stinking of blood, but still beautiful. Still desirable. This night had been a nightmare, one filled with fear and loss. Everything this man had done since I met him had been for me. "I'm still yours, Michael. If we survive tonight, we'll work things out."

He smiled and started to reach for me, but I backed up, a risky maneuver on the stairs.

"Not when you're covered with blood. Please."

"Blood." He spoke softly. "I will never be free of blood." Then he turned and moved on.

We entered the elegant red and gold room where I'd first met Aiakós. The red of the drapes matched Michael's clothes.

Aiakós frowned at Michael. "Are you injured?"

"No."

"You seem to have had an interesting evening."

"It will get worse." Michael sounded fatalistic, but steady as stone.

"Of course it will." Aiakós moved closer to Michael, as if he didn't want to take his word on injuries. "You are covered in human blood. I take note of the moon and the movements of this world just as the witches do. Dark moon, solstice, the so-called Zombie . . . Someone or something will die." He nodded at a door. "There are clothes and a place to wash in there, if you like."

Michael turned to me. "You tell him."

While he walked out, Aiakós watched me with those gold, inhuman eyes. Ancient eyes that had seen things I could not even imagine. I told him everything about Oonagh, whom he did not know. How her incompetence and desperation to live had brought the Drows here. About Étienne's betrayal. I did not tell him about the Portal.

"We need to keep her from getting to the plaza. If Oonagh starts working magic and can't control it she could destroy the Barrows." Very tired, I went to the table and sat in one of the chairs. "Tell me why you let Étienne build his little army." Whether it was rational or not, I wanted to throw some blame at Aiakós for what we'd be up against.

"To protect me against strays. Creatures that come through that hole in the world. I do guard it, you know. I wanted my men here, closer, but he insisted they be at a distance. I see why now."

"He did you a favor, though probably not on purpose. If they were here, all she'd have to do is walk in. Now they will have to fight to claim this territory."

"How many men does Étienne have?" Aiakós asked.

"Sixty. He said."

"Do you believe him?"

"No. I have backup, though. I've made friends. Some of the larger Drows will fight for me. The big armored ones are herbivores, but they can fight. I have two Sisters of Justice and Abigail."

Aiakós drew up, suddenly alert. "Abigail. Innana's most powerful witch? Against a rogue witch? The

Earth Mother's witches are battling each other? I don't think this has ever happened before. For what purpose?"

"To keep Oonagh from disrupting the balance more than she already has. Abigail will try to counter any spells Oonagh conjures." I waited, tried to keep calm, to keep balanced. Had I explained enough?

Aiakós smiled. He appraised me quietly for a moment. "You surprise me. You've been busy, haven't you?" His eyes narrowed a bit. Was he suspicious? I wanted off the subject of the Drows. He didn't need to know how I had learned about them.

"Very well." Aiakós stood. "We have about four hours. It should be a good fight." Like the Sisters, he actually seemed pleased at the prospect of a fight.

"Aiakós?"

"Yes, Madeline."

"I am not a witch, but I am sensitive to magic. When I came into the plaza a little while ago, I felt something. Some power, not earth magic. Do you know what it is? Will it affect what we do tonight?"

Aiakós studied me, his golden eyes bright. "In the center of the plaza is a . . . soft spot in the universe. The power you felt is a slender thread of the greater universe, part of the weaving of different worlds as they work their way into our world."

"Is this because of the dark moon and the solstice?"

"Possibly. But it comes and goes at different times. I have traveled between worlds, and I know virtually nothing except that earth magic is only one part of a whole. The whole is vast and beyond the ability of small creatures to understand, and in that scheme, even I am a small creature. What will happen tonight? It depends on how much blood is spilled, too. Earth magic, and many other magical forms, respond to the blood of sacrifice. If those who fight here do so out of great belief, great self-sacrifice, it will release much power. Here, when earth magic mixes with other things, it creates an echo that brings all manner of things to pass."

In the realm of the Sisters, the practical—the fist and blade—reigned. In the realm of earth magic, the unusual, the chaotic would certainly be a moving force. And somehow they all had to come together. Tonight would change many things. I knew that our schemes were narrowly conceived when we played games with demi-gods. To speculate on whether we controlled our own destiny was useless. We could not deny the events. And we couldn't understand them.

Michael returned. Clean and perfect, as usual. He drew me into his arms and led me to the side of the room. He ran his hand over my cropped white hair and held me tight. We didn't talk. We simply stood there and held on.

It seemed hard to believe that it had been only five days since I came to the Barrows. Five days filled with sacrifice, agony, and loss, all because a witch feared dying beyond all things. But there had been love and joy, at least for me. I believed that the Mother would protect the earth if we failed here, even if it meant abandoning us to whatever disaster befell us.

The door opened and Abigail walked in. Aiakós went to her, and to my eternal surprise, bowed to her.

"Steward of the earth. You honor us. Though we have never met, your mistress praises you above all her other daughters. She told me you were the finest of her children."

Abigail laughed softly. "Really? She told me you were a liar and a rogue."

Aiakós laughed out loud. "And so I am. But be welcome in my home, such as it is." He offered her his hand and she accepted it. She didn't hesitate as I had.

He led her to a seat at the table.

Abigail spoke first. "As I told Madeline, I will do what I can to help. I won't kill, but I will defend."

Then Aiakós asked the question I'd avoided. He hadn't been satisfied with my answer. "Why is she coming here? What does she wish to accomplish? And tell me why I should involve myself in this battle of witches. What will I gain? Or lose?"

Abigail shrugged, quite artfully, I thought. "Oonagh is apparently ill. She has not accepted the Mother's order of life, death, and rebirth. She wants immortality. There is much power in this place on this particular night. I believe she will try to find something to heal herself. What will you gain, Aiakós? Nothing. It is what you will keep that you should look to. You are susceptible to earth magic, and you are a guest here in this place by the grace of the Mother. The magic the witch plans to call upon tonight could easily take your life." She stared straight at him. For a brief instant, I saw pure rage in her face. Abigail hated him. She didn't miss a beat though. "Specifically, I am here to defend *you*, Aiakós."

Aiakós pounded his fist on the table in front of him. It cracked—the sound bounced around the room—but did not break. "I am a prisoner here because Innana fears me. I am not a guest."

I jumped. Abigail sat, graceful and relaxed. He did not intimidate her.

Aiakós leaned back in his chair and glared at her, but said nothing.

Abigail turned to me. "Now, is there anything I can do to help you? I have my assignment, but I can do other things."

For a moment, I couldn't speak. Then I said, "At some point, we could use some light. Étienne's men are equipped with night-vision goggles. I saw them. Removing that advantage might help."

"I can provide excellent light. It can be selective, too. I simply need a place where I can observe."

"I have to go," I said to Michael. "I'm going to try to stop them from getting here. If they do, it will be up to you, Aiakós and Abigail."

"I can go with you," he said. He drew me into his arms. Oh, how warm, how safe.

I leaned back and smiled at him. "No, my love. You stay here and keep an eye on him."

My words didn't escape him. "Am I your love? You've never said it."

I didn't hesitate now. "I think you were that from the first moment I saw you."

He released me, but I could feel the reluctance.

"Thank you." I hugged him again. "For letting me go."

"Against my will and all instinct that says to keep you close and protect you."

I kissed him, then walked back down into the plaza. Eunice stepped out of one of the abandoned buildings on the side. She stood in the doorway and stared out at the darkened streets. We went inside the building. She closed the door and turned on a small battery lamp. Hildy stood to the side.

"She stepped in front of you?" Eunice asked. Her mind had returned to Lillian. I didn't know if she was speaking to me or herself. She eyed me again.

An ache filled me. "Yes. Lillian died for me, Eunice. You better not do the same tonight."

"You damn well better believe I won't." I knew what she meant. She would survive. I believed her.

"Oh, puke." Hildy said as she stepped out of the shadows. She was a sight. She wore a bronze helmet and carried a shield and a sword so long it was a miracle she could lift it.

"Hildy, will that outfit stop bullets?"

She tapped the sword against the shield. "Kevlar. Got a vest, too. Justice needs to come into the new age."

"Hildy?" I just realized something. "You're not coughing. Or wheezing."

Hildy muttered a short string of curses.

Eunice chuckled. "The witch healed her. She wouldn't have made it out the door carrying all that weight. The witch fixed it so Sister Hildegard will get deathly ill if she lights up again, though. Fucking witch doesn't do anything for free."

"Indeed." I jumped at the voice. Kyros stepped out of the darkness.

Eunice had her gun out and aimed at Kyros's face, and Hildy had the sword up and ready in seconds.

I jumped in front of him. "Stop! This is Kyros. He's the leader of the Drows who want to go home. They're going to fight for us. We can't do it without them. They're our army."

Eunice and Hildy didn't say anything.

I turned to Kyros but kept my body between him and the Sisters.

"Just before Étienne and his men enter the plaza, Abigail is going to provide light. Lots of light. The men will be wearing night-vision goggles. I don't know if the light will temporarily blind them, but I hope so. They're coming with some armored vehicles. Or so he said."

"I will disable the vehicles," Kyros said over my shoulder. "They will come from the north. They have been clearing the way for some time. We will fix the street so they cannot get vehicles past. They must then come on foot. If they arrive right at midnight, they will not have time to go around. There will be other surprises, too. The buildings are relatively tall here. Some of us can fly and drop heavy objects."

"Kyros, I'm afraid you might lose some of your people."

"I know." I could hear the sadness in his voice. He wasn't human, but like the others from his home, he was capable of some humanlike emotions. "We are willing to make the sacrifice. If we stay here, we will all perish. This way, some of us will go home."

I did like his courage. "Will you promise me you will personally stay out of the fight? If you go down, the others have no hope. I know bullets won't hurt you, but . . ."

"I will stay back. At least until failure seems certain. I am not a warrior. If Aiakós sees me, he will forget the fight. He will tear me apart. That will most certainly be painful."

"Okay, maybe Spot and his buddies could drop some stink bombs on them."

"Stink bombs?"

"You know. They could . . . ah . . . shit . . . ah . . . defecate on them. It has a really potent smell."

He chuckled as he backed away into the darkness. I had to admit, the image was pretty entertaining.

I turned back to the Sisters. "Any questions?"

Eunice holstered her gun. "This Aiakós . . ."

"Looks like Kyros, only bigger and badder. Think house cat compared to tiger."

"Are they all like him?" Hildy asked. "The Drows?"

"No. He's the only one like that." I described the Drows to them and what they needed to watch for, especially the Custos and their poisonous saliva. They accepted it in silence. When I finished, they stared at each other.

Eunice grunted at me. "Fucking iguana of yours. I puked for three hours."

"I'm sorry. Spot thought you hurt me."

Eunice turned off the light and opened the door again. We needed to hear them coming.

Darkness had long settled over the silent ruins. Only

a few lights showed in Aiakós's building, and there was no evidence of activity.

I tensed as I heard the distant sound of engines. They stopped, maybe two blocks away. Shouts came, followed by a bit of gunfire. Then more silence. Kyros, true to his word, had managed to stop them. It wouldn't have been hard. The Beheras could probably have dug some holes or piled concrete in the way. There was no time to drive around.

Time is a malleable thing. You can slice it into seconds, but it doesn't make a bit of difference. There's always too much of it but somehow not enough. The only thing you know for sure is that you can't outrun it. Standing there in the night, it seemed to stretch forever.

Footsteps came toward us—the shuffling footsteps of many silent, well-trained men. But there were no armored cars. Then they stopped, cut off by a loud, deep grunt. Then another and another until the night was filled with the sound of giant bullfroglike noises.

Painful screams filled the air. Shots rang out. Men shouted. More screams split the air. The battle for the Zombie had begun.

Light and magic filled the night like a new dawn. Abigail had given us the ability to see our enemy half a block away. The Custos flew over them and I knew they'd been dropping venom on the oncoming army. I shivered.

Armed men staggered on to the edge of the plaza. Some more impaired than others. It looked like there were fewer than sixty. The witch Oonagh would be in the middle of the pack, well protected.

The giant scaled Beheras surged out of the buildings, claws out, using their great arms to club anything they could hit. Men went down, tripping over one another.

Chaos reigned. Shouts, gunshots . . . shrieks of pain.

Hildy charged into the battle, shield up.

I went right behind her.

Where were Aiakós and Michael? They should have been there.

One of the Beheras stepped in front of me and pushed on, clearing a path. The bullets didn't seem to affect them. I used my gun selectively. Any unprotected body part—an arm, a knee, a throat—was subject to injury. Screams and gunfire hammered my ears.

I saw a Custos down, dying, but still crawling along, biting any unarmored flesh it could find. A head, complete with helmet, bounced in front of me, then a leg. Hildy, with her ancient weapons, was showing her skills on the battleground.

Then came a roar that filled the plaza with animal rage—a sound that echoed through the empty buildings and streets. It filled the air with terror. Aiakós had arrived. Michael was probably with him.

Where was the damned witch? Étienne's troops were in disarray. I had to get to her before someone got a lucky shot.

I felt her before I saw her. Her strange, alien magic shimmered in circles that radiated outward. I knew she'd come here with the intention of healing herself, but she had misjudged again. All of her will was now bent on protection. In the middle of this power center, she was hunched over, debilitated, her illness corroding her body. Her skin rippled as if it would peel off at any second.

She saw me. "Where's your Triad, Sister?" I heard her shrill voice over the pandemonium of battle, amplified by magic.

Her eyes widened as I stepped through her inner circle of power. It buzzed and turned my stomach, but with one gasp, I made it through.

"My Triad is here, but I wanted you for myself. You killed my mother. You killed my father. All for that trinket you're wearing." A murderous rage filled me as I spat the words. "You're a coward, so afraid of death that you sold your soul and the lives of others around you."

"Your mother was a useless rag of a woman who dared call herself a witch." Oonagh held the Portal tight in her fist and clutched it to her breast over her heart. "She had no right to this."

I had a knife and I had a gun. But neither would suit me. I wanted to do this with my hands. Before I could reach her, she hit me with a spell of such magnitude I staggered. The alien magic did affect me after all. It burned for an instant before it faded away. I kept moving. Another burning spell knocked me to my knees.

I forced myself up and lunged toward her.

Drawing deep breaths, I had to tell her. "You have no power over me, witch."

I knocked her over backward.

I straddled her and locked my hands around her throat. She'd lost her ability to hold her circle of power.

She beat at me with her fists, but they were no more than taps against my skin. I squeezed. She choked. The muscles under my hands knotted as she struggled to breathe. Her eyes bulged.

"How does it feel?" I taunted her. I suddenly realized she couldn't hear me. She was desperate for her own life's breath. For one brief second, I saw my mother's face. What was I doing? I had refrained from killing Kenny out of pity. I had no pity for Oonagh. But I would not kill again. Let others have the vengeance they would. Except for one thing, I was done here.

I released her and tore the Portal from her hands.

"No! Give it back! I'll die without it." She rasped out the words and clawed at me.

"Yes. The Earth Mother will judge you, Oonagh." I rose and left her there. "Vengeance is hers. I'm done with it."

I quickly stuffed the Portal in my jeans pocket. The battle still raged, but men along the fringes were running. I did a quick glance around for Étienne. He lay in the gutter in a pool of blood. After binding himself to Oonagh so he could live, he had lost his life to protect her. I started to go to him when something else caught my attention. Eunice. She lay facedown in the street.

"Eunice." I raced over, stepping around several severed heads scattered on the pavement. I fell to my knees beside her. I could not lose her. Her chest rose and fell. She was alive. If I could get her to Abigail . . .

I searched around for Termas. He was the only one who could carry her. All of the Drows chased the fleeing men. Eunice groaned.

"Eunice? Can you get up?"

She made it into a sitting position, then lumbered to her feet. I held her steady. We maneuvered among the bodies, her arm slung around my shoulder, until we stood by a building. I could see no obvious wounds. She leaned back against the wall and slid down to sit on the sidewalk.

"I'm not hurt bad," she said before she lost consciousness. I had to get her help.

But I didn't have time.

"There you are." Aiakós's deep voice rumbled behind me. "Give it to me."

I stood to face the blood-covered savage beast. Nothing of the urbane and sophisticated creature I'd met earlier remained. His scarlet mane stood like a crest over his head, and his eyes glowed. He'd gotten bigger—and taller. His claws were two inches long, curved, and deadly sharp.

"Where's Michael?" I demanded, trying to distract him. "Is he hurt?"

"Michael can't help you, little witch. Give it to me," he snarled. He grabbed my arm. The claws bit deep.

"Give you what?" I tried to sound innocent, but the pain came through. I wanted to jerk away. I didn't. It might tear my arm off.

"Whatever the witches are fighting over. I don't know what it is, but I'm sure I'll find a use for it."

He swung me around and threw me to the pavement. I rolled away and drew my gun.

Aiakós slowly approached, heedless of my weapon.

As I watched him stalk toward me, clarity dawned. I saw the selfish hunger in his eyes. Though I'd been defending Aiakós as Michael's father, I knew he wasn't like the others I'd met here. There was no ambiguity about him. He was evil.

Now was the time to be a Sister of Justice. Not to avenge my mother and father or the life I could've had. I needed to deliver justice for the Drows he had slaughtered like animals. This was for the Barrows, the good people who lived with evil because the Earth Mother, for her own selfish reasons, held this rogue prisoner here. This was for Michael, who would never be free from his father. Unless . . .

I focused on him, his eyes and teeth of a lion, aimed my gun straight at his heart, and pulled the trigger.

One.

Two.

Three.

Four.

He jerked with each hit, which all landed square in the chest. He didn't stop.

Five.

Six.

The gun clicked. Out of ammo, and no time to reload. I drew my small bronze knife, which Lillian had given me. *A special knife, forged in the shadow of Mount Ararat before Christ's birth.*

He bent over me. His claws sank into my shoulder. I screamed, but I stabbed him in the leg. The only place I could reach.

He howled. Where the bullets had been ineffective, the knife cut deep into flesh and scraped bone. He released me and danced back.

I rolled away. It was a hopeless struggle, but I had to get out of his reach. I stumbled to my feet, made a single step to run. Aiakós grabbed my leg. His claws punched through my jeans and into my thigh and I went down. Not as bad as the Custos's bite, but it hurt enough that I shrieked anyway.

I tried to stab him again. He had my wrist.

Termas and one of the Custos rushed out from a building.

"No!" I tried to shout, but it came out in a strangled sob.

Aiakós released me and rose to his feet. I lay on the ground by him, sobbing in agony.

Aiakós's deep voice rumbled in a language I couldn't understand—but I heard the emotion. A threat disguised in soothing tones. I thought of Michael.

Termas spoke in a series of clicks and grunts.

Aiakós stared down at me. "Well, it seems you have charmed these beasts."

I was shaking, cold and hot at the same time.

He crouched beside me. "I will kill them. You know that, don't you?"

I spat in his face. He slapped me back down to the ground, my head bouncing against the pavement. "Where is it?" He caught my shirt and ripped it open.

I laughed through the pain. "I threw it away."

He sank his claws in again. The same leg, only

deeper this time. Monstrous pain soared through me. I screamed again and it seemed as if I would never stop.

Termas roared and charged.

Aiakós jumped up and met him head on. No contest. Aiakós lifted him bodily and tossed him across the plaza. Termas landed on the sidewalk, rolled, and lay still. Aiakós didn't wait for the Custos. In a flash, he was on the smaller Drow. His fist smashed into the Custos's head and it collapsed.

Aiakós, the great beast, the father of my life's true love, returned to me. I curled into a ball. He crouched again, looming over me like a vulture. My wounded leg jerked with involuntary spasms.

"Now. Let us talk without interruption."

"Shove it up your ass, demon." Hildy approached, sword in hand. Eunice, still unsteady, was beside her.

"No!" I cried. "He'll kill you!"

Then Abigail stood beside them. The witch who could use the earth magic that Aiakós called his weakness. Her eyes were dark with exhaustion, though, and I doubted her ability to do anything.

Aiakós stared at them. "I can kill her before you touch me." His voice rumbled with the threat. "Even you, witch."

"Then we'll all die, demon." Hildy grinned. "Come play with me."

"No." Michael stalked toward us. "There's another way."

chapter 39

Through the haze of pain, I could see the street was littered with bodies, the dead outnumbering the living. It was relatively quiet. My ragged breathing sounded loud in my ears.

"Let me give you something that's worth more." Michael knelt by me and brushed his hand over my forehead.

"Michael, don't." I gasped out the words. "Please don't. Let me die." I didn't know what he would offer, but it was too much.

Michael shook his head. "I will do as you wish, Father. I will build your kingdom here in the Barrows. You know I can do it. You've seen what I did before you came here. If I had been in charge, this thing with Étienne would not have happened. Give me her life, and you can have mine."

I sobbed in despair. "Don't. No."

Aiakós stared at him for a very long time. All I could do was lie there and watch. Would he give up some unknown thing for Michael's loyalty? How much did he value his son? Then he smiled, showing those jagged teeth. "I accept your offer, my son." He stood and stalked away. I did notice his leg still oozed blood where the bronze knife had cut so deep.

I cried out long and loud, but then Michael had me in his arms.

Abigail was there. "Let me . . ." She paused to catch her breath. "No, I don't think I can do it. I'm too weak. I might kill her. Get her to a hospital."

I cried when Michael lifted me.

"Michael, if you love me, please do as I say," I begged.

"I need to get you to a hospital." His face was a grim mask, but tears leaked from his eyes nonetheless.

"No. No. Take me to that building on the left. Take me inside. Please."

"You have to get help." He pleaded. "Not go running around the Barrows."

"Do as she says, pretty Drow." Eunice stood close. "She's earned it."

"There isn't much time. Please," I begged again.

He started toward the building. Every step was agony for me, but I kept my teeth clamped shut. The instant we entered the room, my Drows surrounded me.

And Kyros came.

Michael's eyes widened, his mouth open in surprise.

"Greetings, nephew," Kyros said to Michael.

Kyros turned to me. "Forgive me, I only just arrived. I had to gather a few of my people. If I'd come earlier . . ."

"He'd have killed you," I cut in. "Set me on my feet, Michael."

Michael, apparently still surprised by Kyros, did as I asked. I moaned, but hung on to him. It required both hands. "Kyros, the stone. In my pocket. Get it."

"Now, wait a minute," Eunice grumbled.

"As long as it is here, witches will be tempted, Eunice. He can take it to another place."

"What place?" Michael demanded. He tried to pull me back, but one of the Beheras stood behind him and would not budge.

"Your family home, young prince." Kyros deftly retrieved the Portal. "I am sorry. We must go. There are only minutes."

Kyros kissed me on the forehead. He smiled at Michael. "Forgive me. I see now I should have contacted you before. I wish we'd had more time to talk, but perhaps someday I can return."

He hurried to the door, and the others followed him. The comparatively diminutive Tektos clung to the Beheras's scaled shoulders.

Termas came to me with Spot. I was overwhelmed with happiness to see that Termas had recovered from his encounter with Aiakós.

For a few moments I was able to force the pain down and say my good-byes.

"Spot." I reached out my hand to touch him. He barked and licked my fingers. I turned to Termas. "Take care of that little one of yours." I think he smiled, but it was hard to tell.

"Stand back from us," Kyros said. He marched out the door, taking his people in a great cluster behind him.

Michael lifted me in his arms again and carried me out to where I could see. He remained strangely silent.

A golden glow filled the plaza in a warm circle of light. Out of the corner of my eye, I saw Aiakós approach the plaza again. He hadn't gone far. He stopped short of the glowing circle's edge, then quickly stepped back as if it presented a danger.

Kyros laughed at him. Then he spoke in a language I didn't understand, but I heard, or perhaps I imagined, pity in his voice.

The circle grew brighter.

Kyros turned to us. "You have a family, Michael. Make him tell you about us."

With that, the light grew incredibly brilliant and covered Kyros and the surviving Drows, consuming them. It vanished, leaving only darkness and silence—until Aiakós's scream of pure rage filled the night.

"Uh, I think we should go now." Eunice, woman of few words, had stated the obvious.

We went back into the building and made our way out to the other side, where the cars were parked. We'd survived the dark moon solstice—and I was going into shock.

I was shivering and sweating at the same time. My mind went to black and then drifted back. The conscious world moved in and out as it had that night the Custos bit me.

As we left the Barrows and crossed that magical ward, she arrived.

The world fell silent. Pain faded away.

"Daughter, you have exceeded my hopes for you. You did

a great thing, giving the stone to Kyros. You assessed that he was no threat and aided him. That was wise."

"Yeah, wise. Sure. Am I dead?"

"No. Your immunity to earth magic remains. I may not heal you, but I will sustain you until you receive aid. You will live."

"Why are you doing this?"

"It amuses me. And will irritate Aiakós immensely."

"Sure. Right before he kills me."

"He will not. He values Michael and what he has offered. This game is not over, but you need battle no more. Sleep now."

I did sleep. Five days later, I woke up.

chapter 40

June 30

The pain eased in a fog of drugs. Eunice, Michael, and Hildy appeared as I went in and out of consciousness. I opened my eyes once in those five days to find Mother Evelyn at my bedside. The word *shock* didn't begin to cover my surprise.

"I am proud of you, darling," Mother Evelyn said. "You cannot know how much it hurt me to send you out as I did. Your mother was my only child. I've longed to tell you all these years, but the Earth Mother forbade it until your training and mission were over."

"You're my grandmother? I thought Sisters of Justice didn't have kids."

She smiled. "For the most part, we don't. But we aren't celibate, and your grandfather was a most compelling man. I wish I could have told you before. If the Earth Mother grants my wish, I'll see you again." She bent over and kissed me, and her cool hand smoothed my forehead.

I must have fallen back to sleep, because she was

gone when I opened my eyes. Sunlight filtered through a window, illuminating the spare hospital room in which I lay. Eunice was there. "Where did Mother Evelyn go? She was just here. Who brought her?"

Eunice stared at me for a long time. Then she said, "Mother Evelyn died five nights ago. On the solstice, while we were in battle. Old age. Went in her sleep. A rare thing for a Sister of Justice."

"No, she was here. She kissed me and . . ." I trailed off. If she had died, then I had been touched after her death. I decided to let it go. I was glad she'd come, even if I'd never know how and why. Sisters of Justice were all about secrets anyway.

Eunice came to stand over me.

"What did you tell the doctors about my injuries?" I asked.

"You went camping and were attacked by a mountain lion."

"And they believed it? Are there mountain lions in Missouri?"

"I don't know, but they didn't have any other answers." Her mouth twisted. "We have a problem."

"Of course we do."

She grunted. "While I was unconscious, someone stole the Morié and the Solaire off me."

I moved—and regretted it. "Maybe Michael can help us find it."

"He'd better. If his royal nastiness gets hold of them, he just might be immune to earth magic, too."

I rubbed my hands over my face. "I'll work on it when I get out."

"There's another thing." Eunice grinned. "Your scar is gone. It went away when the Portal did. I saw it. It faded." Her tone was matter-of-fact. "Your eyes are dark, not blue. And if you want to keep white hair, you'd better get your roots done."

I insisted on a mirror then. I had no idea what had happened. I'd have to talk to Abigail. Maybe she would know something.

"Did you take Lillian back to Justice?" I asked.

"No, the witch buried her in her garden. It seemed a nice enough place."

Michael came later that evening. He kissed me, long and sweet, and drew a chair close to the bed. "How are you?"

I reached out and patted his beautiful cheek. "Still here. What's been happening? Was there anything in the news about the fight?"

"No. There's never anything in the news about the Barrows." He kissed my hand. "I've been cleaning up. There was extensive damage. And I was soothing the savage beast. He raged for a while, but he's calmed down now."

I remained silent. Aiakós was the last thing I wanted to deal with.

He rubbed my hand against his cheek. "I love you."

"Even now? I think I look a little different." I ran a finger across my smooth cheek.

"Even more. I love your eyes, so deep and dark."

He kissed me again, and only pain stopped me from crawling out of that bed and into his arms.

Two days later, I was permitted to go home. My legs were still in bandages. The puncture wounds from Aiakós's claws were not healing quickly. I'd need a lot of physical therapy to walk properly again.

Michael came for me, but he couldn't shake Hildy and Eunice.

"I want to go to Abigail's house first," I said to him as he placed me in the Jag.

Abigail greeted me joyfully as Michael carried me into her kitchen. She welcomed Eunice and Hildy with enthusiasm, too. I guess her attitude about the Sisters of Justice had changed a bit. Michael, Eunice, and Hildy were a bit put out when I asked to talk to Abigail alone, but they did go outside.

I sipped the tea she placed in front of me. Not healing, but it tasted good. I told Abigail the complete story of the scar and how it appeared on my face.

She listened carefully, then said, "You say your mother was wearing the Portal when she died?"

I nodded.

"This is conjecture, but I think your mother, in fear and anger, unintentionally cast that spell, crying for vengeance through the Portal. When you touched her body, the spell was released. The Portal left this world, and I feel certain that the spell dissipated with it."

For the first time since the battle, my heart soared with hope. "It's done. I'm done. With vengeance, anyway."

"That is something you are well rid of, Madeline. I wish you love and peace."

Something about the way she said it sounded a little off. "What's wrong?"

Abigail hesitated a moment before continuing. "I'm concerned. At the point you staged your surprising little coup and the Portal left this world, something else came in. I felt its emergence into our world. I spoke to the Mother, but I've heard nothing yet."

I remembered Eunice's words about the missing Morié and Solaire. "I suppose there will always be trouble in the Barrows."

She smiled. "Perhaps you can help to curb it. Will it be your home?"

I leaned forward, trying to stretch my back without causing major pain. "I'm committed to Michael and he's committed to Aiakós, so I guess it will be."

I remembered then what Eunice told me in the hospital. "Abigail, will you show me Lillian's grave?"

She took my hand. "Of course."

Abigail had buried Lillian in the woods behind her home. It was a pretty spot. Eunice, Hildy, Michael, and I mourned. As we stood there, I remembered Sister Sarah, an old warrior who told me wild tales of Drow battles around the world. She had died in her sleep. Apparently an amazing event, since most Sisters died fighting. Or so I was told. The Sisters of Justice were rarely burdened with humility.

Rules at Justice had forbidden me to go into the administration building without express permission, but I could visit other places on the grounds—as long as I didn't cross that invisible line that marked my prison walls.

One such place was the cemetery. A small path led to it from the gardens. I'd been there several times as I explored the confines of my prison. The Sisters' graves were all marked by a single granite stone carved with a single name and date—the date of death. No family members ever came to visit from the outside. Sister Lillian once said that the Sisters of Justice were the ultimate orphans. Having grown up in a loving family, it made me sad to think that those few Sisters I did like had only their fellow assassins to mourn them.

They always held the funerals at sunrise. I had watched, and when I saw them leave with Sarah's body, I had followed at a distance. The cool predawn mist had swirled across the ground and the air had a hint of fall.

A younger Sister had carried Sarah. She'd shrunken in her last days and was no burden. They'd wrapped her in a white shroud. No coffin, for she would go to the earth to become a part of its history, not the history of men. I had stood back, certain I'd be punished, but wanting to see, to know. Sister Eunice turned and beckoned me to stand by her. Of course, she'd known I was there.

They had lowered Sister Sarah gently into the grave. I didn't know what to expect. They shocked me. They consigned her to the Mother with a prayer that when she returned, it would *not* be as a Sister.

Then each had spoken in a solemn voice and given a personal memory of Sister Sarah. The mist had seemed to dampen those voices and bring them low to the earth. I had strained to hear them. After Eunice spoke, she had pushed me slightly forward.

"Speak."

I had memories, too. "Thank you, Sister Sarah, for your tales of great adventures and exciting places. I will remember them, and you, always."

Eunice had laid a hand on my shoulder. "Our lives are not our own. We are servants of the Earth Mother, and her commands are grievous and incomprehensible at times. Death is our freedom."

"Hush, Eunice." Sister Lillian had joined us.

Eunice had walked away. I didn't know why, but that event fundamentally changed how I looked at the Sisters—and for some reason, how they looked at me.

Then they had handed me a shovel and told me to cover the grave. For the next two hours, as I always had, I paid in sweat and toil for the lessons I received at Justice.

I did not have the strength to speak the words to thank her for her lessons and her ultimate sacrifice for me, so I silently prayed that Lillian would not return as a Sister of Justice.

After that, Michael lifted me again. He seemed to enjoy it, and of course, with his super strength, I wasn't a burden.

"I'll start physical therapy soon," I said. "Then I can walk on my own."

"Oh, good." He carried me toward the car. "In that case, I have plans for those legs."

*   *   *

Three weeks after the eventful dark moon solstice, I had one of Michael's employees drive me to the Armory. Michael had hired a private physical therapist at the Archangel for me to work on walking again. I was doing so, but not well and not far.

To my surprise, the word *pawn* had been removed from the front of the store. So what was it now? Just the Armory? First thing I noticed when I hobbled in was the fresh smell. Pine, I thought. The glass counter was gone, replaced by a couple of desks. Eunice sat at one and Hildy at the other. As usual, they glared at each other.

"So, what's argument of the day, ladies?"

Eunice muttered under her breath, but she immediately stood and brought me her chair. "We're going to start this school. Self-defense for women—and girls. Might pick a few girls off the streets and send them to Justice. But Hildy's stupid idea . . ." She threw up her hands. "No one is going to want to learn sword fighting."

Hildy bared her teeth. "What do you think, Madeline?"

"Oh . . ." Now, how did I answer that? I couldn't run. "Self-defense is good. Sword fighting isn't practical for everyday purposes, but maybe good for the curious. It's exercise, at least." I wanted to change the subject. "So, you're going to stay here, Eunice?"

She stood behind me and laid her hands on my shoulders.

"Yeah. I'll stay. Good place for a fight. Me and Hildy

are getting too old to do some things, but there's plenty of action here."

I was pleased that Eunice was staying, though the *plenty of action here* concerned me.

The next day, I ventured into the Barrows again with Michael so he could talk to Aiakós. I wasn't ready to confront the creature that had crippled me and bound my lover to him. I casually searched the plaza. It wasn't likely that Eunice would have lost the Solaire and Morié. She's a large woman and getting them off would've been difficult.

An SUV pulled up and Étienne stepped out. He gave me that same go-to-hell smile I knew so well. He'd lost weight, his face had thinned, but other than that, he seemed the same.

"What are you doing here?" I said. "I thought you were dead."

"It takes more than that to kill me. I was injured, and playing dead seemed like a good idea at the time." He grinned. "I'm working for Aiakós again." He slipped an arm around me and hugged me close. "He doesn't trust me, of course, but he saw the job I did with my men. Impressed him."

Etienne was a survivor, one of those people who managed to come out of a deadly situation on top.

He reached out and brushed his fingers through my dark hair. "I love your hair now."

"Do I look much different? Without the scar?"

"Beautiful. But you were always that."

Michael approached us, and Étienne made a quick departure. I had a feeling it would take more than

Aiakós's favor to make Michael forgive Étienne for kidnapping him and locking him up.

Michael ran his hand through his hair. "Have you ever tried to convince someone from another world that you can't have everything you see on television?"

I laughed. "He's the only thing from another world I know. What does he want?"

Michael snarled. "A casino and a luxury hotel."

"Illegal. Right?"

"It is here."

"What do you propose?" I asked.

"Commercial and residential, starting at River Street and moving east. It's too slow for him."

"Has he mentioned Kyros?"

"No. And he won't talk about it if I ask. I wish I could have talked to Kyros." Michael sounded wistful.

"He said he might come back."

"Now, wouldn't that be interesting."

Michael slid his arms around me. And gave me a wonderful kiss that promised more to come.

"You're all the family I need. We just have to make it official."

I paused. "What does that mean?"

A devilish grin lit up his face. "Madeline, I love you. Will you marry me and be my wife?"

I was overwhelmed. "I love you, too," I whispered in his ear. Until now, the words hadn't come so easily. I laid my head against his chest. "And, yes, Michael, I will marry you."

He encircled me with his strong arms, planting kisses across my lips, my face, my hair before pulling back. "You know that means you get Aiakós for a father-in-law, right?"

I laughed. "That's one reason why they put *for better or worse* in the vows."

With that, we walked away from the plaza toward the car that would take us home.

Read on for a look at the first novel in the
Earth Witches series,

VIPER MOON

Available now from Signet Eclipse.

The Barrows
July 21—Full Moon

Mama wanted me to be a veterinarian. She'd probably have settled for a nurse, teacher, or grocery store clerk. She never came right out and said, "Cassandra, you disappointed me" or "Cassandra, you have so much potential," but I knew I'd let her down.

The idea of me running down a slimy storm sewer in the desolate, abandoned ruins of the Barrows section of Duivel, Missouri, probably never crossed her mind. The unconscious five-year-old boy strapped to my back and the angry monster with fangs and claws snapping at my heels were just part of my job. Maybe Mama was right—I'd made the wrong career choice.

I'm in good shape, but I'd run, crawled, and slogged through the sewer for over an hour. My chest heaved in the moldy, moisture-laden air by the time I finally reached my escape hatch. The glow from phosphorescent lichen gave me enough light to see the manhole shaft leading out of this little section of hell. Claws clattered right behind me and the tunnel echoed with slobbering grunts. This particular monster was an apelike brute with porcupine quills running down its spine and glowing green eyes.

Up into the manhole cylinder, two rungs, three . . . Roars bounced off the tight walls . . . Almost there—a claw snagged my slime-covered boot.

I jerked away and heaved myself out onto the deserted street.

Not good.

Clouds covered the full moon's silver face, so my vile pursuer might actually take a chance and follow me. The Earth Mother has no power here in the Barrows, save her daughter's light in the midnight sky. Maiden, mother, and crone, signifying the progression of life from cradle to grave, that ancient pagan female entity had called me to her service years ago. Now, in her name, I ran for my life. In her name, I carried this innocent child away from evil.

I'd managed to get off two shots and my bronze bullets hurt the ugly sucker, but a kill required a hit in a critical area like an eye. I could stop and aim or run like hell. I ran.

Its claws gouged out the asphalt as it dragged itself after me.

Under usual circumstances, I wouldn't have gone below the street. I'm good at kick the door down, grab the kid, and run. This time a bit of stealth was required since the door guards carried significant firepower. I was definitely outgunned.

Most things living in the storm sewers were prey.

The small creatures ran from me. This time I'd crossed paths with a larger predator determined to make me a midnight snack.

I'd parked my car on the next block, so I sprinted toward a dark, shadowed alley that cut between the three-story brick buildings. Derelict vehicles and broken furniture made my path an obstacle course as I threaded my way through the debris toward the pitiful yellow light of a rare streetlamp at the alley's far end.

A coughlike snarl came from behind. The creature would leap over things I had to go around. I wouldn't make it, and if I did, those claws would tear the metal off my little car like I would peel an orange. I'd have to turn and fight soon. I hoped I could take the thing down before it overwhelmed me.

Halfway down the alley, a door suddenly opened in the building to my left. A Bastinado in full gang regalia, including weapons, stepped out. Though technically human, Bastinados are filthy, sadistic bastards whose myriad hobbies include rape, robbery, and murder.

I had nothing to lose as terror nipped at my heels and gave me momentum. I rammed the Bastinado with my shoulder, knocked him down, and rushed inside. Drug paraphernalia and naked gang members lay scattered around the room. I'd crashed their party and brought a monster as my date. The Bastinado at the door certainly hadn't stopped it.

The creature roared louder than the boom box thumping the walls with teeth-rattling bass. The Bastinados grabbed their weapons. They barely glanced at me as I crossed the room at a dead run. Two guards stood at the front door, but they had their eyes on the monster, too. I shoved my way past the guards. Screams and gunshots filled the night. Throw the door bolt and I emerged onto the sidewalk.

I raced down the street. I hadn't gone far when the ground suddenly heaved and shuddered under my feet. The whole block thundered with a massive explosion. A vast wind howled, furious and red, and surged down the street in battering waves.

Tornados of brilliant orange fire blasted out the windows of the building I'd escaped, and washed over the street like an outrageous, misguided sunrise. A hot hand of air picked me up and slammed me to the broken concrete. I twisted and landed face-first to protect the boy strapped to my back, then rolled to my side with my body between him and the inferno. I covered my face with my arms. More explosions followed and the doomed building's front facade crumbled into the street while burning debris rained from the sky.

What in the Earth Mother's name had been in there?

When the fury abated a bit, I forced myself to my feet and headed for the car. Was the pavement moving or was it me staggering?

The sound of the explosion still hammered my eardrums. I opened the back door, peeled away the straps and protective covering holding the boy secure against my body. I laid him across the backseat. He didn't seem injured, and he still slept from the sedative I'd given him to keep him calm.

It wasn't until I climbed in the driver's seat and fumbled for my key that I noticed the blood—my blood—

too much blood. Slick wet crimson streaked down the side of my face and soaked half my shirt. Shards of glass protruded like rough diamonds from my forearm's blistered skin. It didn't hurt—yet. Pain would come soon enough.

I turned the key in the ignition. Nothing happened.

Another deeper blast rumbled under the street, shaking the car.

Sirens sounded in the distance, police, fire trucks, ambulances, rushing to the scene. They rarely entered the Barrows, but the magnitude of the blast I'd lived through couldn't be ignored.

I turned the key again. And again.

Last month I'd had to make a choice. Fix the car's starter or buy special hand-loaded bronze bullets. I'd chosen bullets.

The fourth time I twisted the key, the engine jerked to life. It sputtered twice, then smoothed. I popped it into gear and rolled forward, away from the fiery beast still raging behind.

Symptoms of shock crept in and pain found me. It rose by increments, increasing in intensity with every passing moment. My heart raced at a frantic pace and my arms shook so I could barely hold the wheel. Sweat formed an icy second skin as my body temperature took a nosedive. Sweet Mother, it hurt. The street blurred and shifted in my vision. Worse, though, was the feeling of pursuit. My little car chased through the deserted streets by some invisible, unimaginable horror. With considerable will, I kept my foot from mashing down the gas pedal.

Clouds drifted away from the cold, exquisite full moon.

"Follow," a soft voice whispered and urged me on. The white orb in the sky suddenly filled the windshield, rising to a brilliant mass of pure, clear light. I drove toward the radiance, navigating well-known streets as if dreaming of driving. North, keep moving north. A stop sign? Okay. Don't run that red light. If a cop stopped me, they'd call an ambulance, take me to the hospital, and I'd die. I was already beyond the skill of modern medicine's healing.

The child in the backseat moaned, as if in a nightmare. I had to stay conscious long enough to get him to safety. I wouldn't go down for nothing.

The guiding brilliance faded as I reached my destination. Control of the automobile eluded me, however, and the mailbox loomed. Before I could hit the brakes, I'd rolled over the box and the small sign that marked the home and business of Madam Abigail. The sign offered psychic readings, but gave not a hint of the true power and grace of the woman who dwelled and worked there.

I plowed through the flowered yard. Abby was going to be seriously pissed at me. Two feet from the front porch, the car jerked to a halt. Abby would find me. Abby would care for me as she always had. Luminous moonlight filled the night again, then faded, leaving only sweet-smelling flowers that lured me into painless darkness.

ALSO AVAILABLE

Lee Roland

Viper Moon
An Earth Witches Novel

Cassandra Archer is the Huntress. She has faithfully served the Earth Mother for years, rescuing kidnapped children from monsters—both human and supernatural—dwelling in the ruins of the Barrows District in Duivel, Missouri. But when two children are kidnapped under similar circumstances, all clues point to a cataclysmic event on the next dark moon. Now Cass must race against the clock and prevent a sacrifice that could destroy the entire town...

Available wherever books are sold or at penguin.com

"Like" us at facebook.com/ProjectParanormalBooks

TOUCH THE DARK

by Karen Chance

Cassandra Palmer can see the future and communicate with spirits—talents that make her attractive to the dead and the undead. The ghosts of the dead aren't usually dangerous; they just like to talk…a lot.

Like any sensible girl, Cassie tries to avoid vampires. But when the bloodsucking mafioso she escaped three years ago finds Cassie again with vengeance on his mind, she's forced to turn to the vampire Senate for protection—and the price they demand may be more than she's willing to pay.

<u>Also Available</u>
Claimed by Shadow
Embrace the Night
Curse the Dawn
Hunt The Moon

Available wherever books are sold or at
penguin.com

JESSICA ANDERSEN

NIGHTKEEPERS

"Raw passion, dark romance, and
seat-of-your-pants suspense, all set in
an astounding paranormal world."
—#1 *New York Times* bestselling author J. R. Ward

In the first century A.D., the Mayans predicted the world
would end on December 21, 2012. In these final years
before the End Times, demons from the Mayan
underworld have come to earth to trigger the apocalypse.
But the modern descendants of the Mayan
warrior-priests have decided to fight back.

<u>Also Available</u>
Dawnkeepers
Skykeepers
Demonkeepers
Blood Spells
Storm Kissed
Magic Unchained

Available wherever books are sold or at
penguin.com

S0014